Andrew has a PhD in environmental and marine science, Grad. Cert. in strategic studies and a Grad. Dip. Ed. He has published in peer-reviewed science journals and co-founded the New Zealand Aquaculture Magazine. Andrew has served as a watchkeeping officer in the navy. He has lectured and taught statistics, and marine and maritime studies at a technical institute. During this period, he consulted with the fisheries and aquaculture industry. Subsequently, Andrew contracted to the offshore oil and gas industry in environmental management. He then taught secondary school science and mathematics and is a future school's STEM industry focus advocate.

To the mother of my children, Belinda, I dedicate this story. Through all the ups and downs, bonds are formed and a lifetime of memories is made. Adversity brings strength and the courage and discipline to carry on.

A.D. Morgan

SKIMMER – HARVEST

AUSTIN MACAULEY PUBLISHERS™
LONDON * CAMBRIDGE * NEW YORK * SHARJAH

Copyright © A.D. Morgan 2023

The right of A.D. Morgan to be identified as author of this work has been asserted by the author in accordance with sections 77 and 78 of the Copyright, Designs and Patents Act 1988.

All rights reserved. No part of this publication may be reproduced, stored in a retrieval system, or transmitted in any form or by any means, electronic, mechanical, photocopying, recording, or otherwise, without the prior permission of the publishers.

Any person who commits any unauthorised act in relation to this publication may be liable to criminal prosecution and civil claims for damages.

This is a work of fiction. Names, characters, businesses, places, events, locales, and incidents are either the products of the author's imagination or used in a fictitious manner. Any resemblance to actual persons, living or dead, or actual events is purely coincidental.

A CIP catalogue record for this title is available from the British Library.

ISBN 9781398446281 (Paperback)
ISBN 9781398446298 (Hardback)
ISBN 9781398446403 (ePub e-book)

www.austinmacauley.com

First Published 2023
Austin Macauley Publishers Ltd®
1 Canada Square
Canary Wharf
London
E14 5AA

No people, in particular, have contributed to the telling of this story. However, I would like to acknowledge life's circumstances and all those that have passed through my life. In doing so, the experiences and insight gained over many years have brought this story into existence.

Table of Contents

Hook	11
Mini Synopsis	12
Chapter 1	13
Chapter 2	23
Chapter 3	31
Chapter 4	42
Chapter 5	50
Chapter 6	57
Chapter 7	65
Chapter 8	73
Chapter 9	83
Chapter 10	93
Chapter 11	101
Chapter 12	108
Chapter 13	116
Chapter 14	127
Chapter 15	134
Chapter 16	141
Chapter 17	151
Chapter 18	157

Chapter 19	166
Chapter 20	178
Chapter 21	185
Chapter 22	195
Chapter 23	202
Chapter 24	211

Hook

On board the Chinese-owned GlobeCorpMining deep-sea mineral harvester a technology is being developed that has the potential to undermine the Skimmers. A crewmember, a youth from China is convinced his sister who works on the Harvester is in danger. As Brother and Sister struggle with family history, it becomes apparent that there is more to the Skimmers than the crew is led to believe.

Mini Synopsis

Skimmer – Harvest is the second book in a series set in 2040 about youth and their ability to adapt and cope with an on and off-planet mining economy. The crew of Ngarra's deep sea mining Skimmer are at Xed Ocean Academy under the watchful eye of officials. Previously, they had been pursued at sea for a technology one of the crew developed. A technology that enabled Xtract mining drones to learn autonomous group behaviour. Connor, one of the crew has developed the technology further. But Jonah and Rick are at odds about the future of the Skimmer program. Rick wants to separate the Skimmer program and protect the technology. Jonah wants to maintain the relationship with the major funder of the crew program, the Chinese owned GlobeCorpMining. She has a close relationship with Chang's father the Chief Operating Officer. Chang is a crewmember of the Skimmer. He resents his father for what happened to his mother. Chang's sister however works on the Giant mineral Harvester and is used against him. She is threatened if he doesn't get a copy the technology. The Sea Hunters become embroiled in the manipulation and deception. They must maintain order at Sea in "the Area" while also dealing with a request to become involved in securing this technology. One of the senior officers on the Harvester has other ideas though. She coverts the project that Chang's sister is working on and wants to bring both technologies together to accelerate their own program. She has other ideas for its use. Chang becomes a pawn that is played by all sides, culminating in a face off at the Harvester. Meanwhile, Rick wants to advance the Skimmer overdrive trials and bring forward his people's agenda for them.

Chapter 1

It had been a close call for Ngarra's crew. They had been chased around the ocean in their sub surface mining skiff or Skimmer by the Sea Hunters. They had managed to avoid being disabled by a sub-surface interceptor drone's Acoustic Remote Cavitation or ARC array. Using a breaching pod deployed from an interceptor drone, the Sea Hunters would have boarded them. A security and inspection team would have detained them and handed them over to State sponsor authorities. Contravening regulations and Skimmer contractor protocols for carrying out mining operations in "the Area" was serious.

Crews on Skimmers monitored an artificial intelligence called SAI. It ran the Skimmer and controlled the Xtract mining drones. A laser signal communication streamer was deployed to the seabed four thousand metres below through which the Xtracts were controlled. The Xtracts ascended and descended, scooping up and sieving out manganese nodules. These were loaded into trays along each side of the Skimmer, opposite a recess within which the Xtract drones docked. It was essential to have a crew on board a skimmer as the Xtracts often malfunctioned.

It had been over six months since the incident at sea had occurred. Ngarra's Skimmer had been delivering a load of manganese nodules to the giant Chinese-owned GlobeCorpMining Harvester ship positioned well South of the Cook Islands in international waters. Another Skimmer and its Xtract mining drones had disappeared. It had been taken off the communication grid in "the Area" by its crew and no one seemed to know why. "The grid" as it was called, was installed in "the Area" to allow underwater laser signal communication with Skimmers using surface buoys and sub-surface Eel drones. Being off the grid was a violation of regulations and contractor Skimmer protocols. Ngarra's crew happened to be in the right place at the right time and their Skimmer had been tasked to track down the rogue crew.

At Xed Ocean Academy crew training and monitoring centre, Jonah and Rick were trying to determine why a skimmer crew had gone rogue. The governing council was concerned about the implications it would have for funding of the crew program into the future. The council consisted of representatives of industry that funded Xed and the Ocean Academy. Concern was also growing over the Chinese owned GlobeCorpMining being a major funder of the Skimmer crew training program and their involvement in the development and ongoing maintenance of the Skimmers and their Xtracts.

Jonah as a founding member of Xed and the Ocean Academy also had a personable relationship with the chief operations officer who also happened to be Chang's father. Concern was growing about this relationship. Furthermore, Chang was a crewmember on Ngarra's Skimmer. His relationship with his father was strained due to family circumstances. His sister was an AI research scientist working on the Harvester and had a close relationship with their father.

Jonah had reached out to Chang's father who offered to help distract the Sea Hunters from their pursuit of the off-grid Skimmer. This had given Ngarra's Skimmer time to find and recover the crew first. However, it quickly became apparent that something was afoot. Everyone seemed to want to get hold of an AI technology Connor, an autistic youth had developed on board Ngarra's Skimmer.

Contractors leased or owned Skimmers and Xed Ocean Academy provided crews. The contractor that had leased the Skimmer that had gone off-grid wanted to recover its property and prosecute the offenders. At the time, emergency administration orders had been issued by the International Seabed Authority, "the Authority". Under the International Maritime Organisation and the United Nations Convention on Law of the Sea, the Sea hunters had a mandate to track down, disable the Skimmer and detain the crew. The Sea Hunters were funded through levies to carry out monitoring, compliance and enforcement operations in "the Area" under "the Authority" regulations.

Little did Jonah know that Rick, who was key in helping set up the Skimmer crewing program, was working with the Sea Hunters to try and secure this AI technology that Connor had developed. He was concerned about the future of the Ocean Academy Skimmer crewing program, given its close ties with the Chinese owned GlobeCorpMining. For him, the pursuit of the off-grid Skimmer and its rogue crew had become a means to an end; securing the technology. Rick had even coerced Chang into trying to steal the technology. In return, Chang had thought he would have the opportunity to work with his sister on the giant Harvester ship. Chang was sure his father had something to do with him getting into Xed Academy. Chang despised his father and blamed him for his mother's situation. He longed to see his sister.

Ricks military background meant he was well connected when it came to national security arrangements. His people were suspicious of the close relationship between GlobeCorpMining and the Xed Academy Skimmer crewing program. In turn, Jonah had become suspicious of Ricks motives, but she couldn't prove anything. For Jonah, Xed and the Academy was her life. Through funding the crew program Chang's father had been a big supporter and advocate of its growth. Despite the mounting concern, she had always kept the relationship professional, but Rick didn't like it. He was advocating for the council to consider separating the crew program from both Xed and the Ocean Academy. It was a security breach on campus that had led to the rogue crew being threatened and coerced also into using their Skimmer to create an opportunity to secure the technology Connor had developed.

***

Since the incident at sea, for over six months Ngarra's crew had been posted ashore at Xed Ocean Academy.

Ngarra was with Chang on duty at the Academy crew monitoring and communications centre. Ngarra meant 'together with you' in one of the dialects of indigenous Australians. Being tall and slim and with olive coloured skin and piercing brown eyes, he had a commanding presence and demeanour.

Connor was tucked away in his research lab working on the technology he had developed. Connor with his strawberry blonde hair, straight and hanging just below his ears that often dropped across one side of his face was tucked away in his research lab working on the technology he had developed.

Jonny, the Skimmer pilot and Stella were helping at the simulation centre with training new crews. His imposing appearance was at times intimidating. Being Tongan-Maori, he was solid and at over six foot with dark hair cut very short and brown eyes with deeply tanned skin. Standing next to Stella it was quite a contrast. Her shorter stature with blue-grey eyes, long brunette hair tied back, and chiselled features complimented her bubbly personality.

Jesse the Skimmer communications and security officer was overseeing students in the adjacent learning hub. Her dark hair, green eyes and lightly coloured skin and slim build matched her gothic appearance and quiet and calm demander.

It was early morning and in his lab Connor's ocean bubble hologram of simulated Xtract mining operations was running. As usual he was thinking out loud. For key words SAI, the artificial intelligence, was using natural language processing to look up libraries of source code script and information on patterning and group behaviour in nature. Connor was looking for that elusive clue to making the group of simulated Xtracts in the ocean bubble hologram learn autonomous group behaviour without human input. He knew it had something to do with the layered decision-making algorithms for deep learning that he had got SAI to construct and the holographic representation of the mesh within which the Xtracts now operated. Although the Xtracts now had collective memory, they still were not capable of learning by themselves. The mining simulations kept falling apart.

Jonah and Rick arrived to talk with Connor. He was absorbed in his own thoughts and barely acknowledged them. He carried on talking to himself.

'Good morning, Connor,' said Jonah as they walked in.

'Every time an Xtract is grabbed by a simulated giant squid the response starts off correctly,' said Connor. 'Other nearby Xtracts gather around and move in on it. They don't resume mining until the giant squid let's go. But if the squid does something different the simulation falls apart. We're missing something.'

Connor looked right through Jonah and Rick as if they were not there. Connor was on the autism spectrum; a genius some thought but emotionally a little backward. Connor found it hard to connect behaviour and body language, or even feelings with emotion. Not to say he wasn't emotional, and the crew certainly knew that.

'Can't help you with that one,' said Rick startling Connor out of his thoughts. 'Surely it is just a matter of time before you have a breakthrough. I mean this mesh that you have developed is on the verge of learning by itself and taking control of the Xtracts. It has a memory; you just have to connect it with independent learning.'

'A mesh for collective memory,' said Connor. 'Yes, the Xtracts are surrounded by a mesh. Hmmm, maybe it's the wrong way around.'

Connor walked off talking quickly. Jonah smiled and looked at Rick. Around them were displays filled with projections of data analytics, algorithms and coding scripts.

Jonah and Rick decided to leave him to it and walked off. They would catch up with him later.

'He is close to cracking it and moving to the next level,' said Rick. 'I would like to get them all back on a skimmer doing mining runs so he can run some tests on all this. Maybe that will help overcome this hurdle he has come up against.'

'This is big,' said Jonah. 'A lot of people are now aware we have something. How are we going to test all this out there and protect our people and the technology?'

As they discussed what to do, they walked across campus towards the Skimmer Simulation training centre, the sim centre as it was called, and crew monitoring complex.

The campus was busy as usual. Students were coming and going from the learning hub at the front of the sim centre.

'It's a risk we have to take,' said Rick as they entered the sim centre.

They walked through the entrance and learning hub greeting staff and students along the way. They both waved at Jesse as they walked through to the simulator.

Jonny and Stella were in the instructor area between the two submerged Skimmers, one on each side. Through the huge cut out section along one side of each Skimmer crews could be seen training. A mining simulation was underway where something had gone wrong with an Xtract.

'Looks like you two are onto it,' said Rick as they passed through.

'Well one of us is,' said Jonny as he smiled at Stella.

'Jonny's a bit slow,' said Stella as she smirked at him.

Jonah smiled at their antics. As usual Jonny made a warrior face typical of his Maori Tongan heritage at Stella. Stella gave him a playful punch in the shoulder.

'We'll leave you both to it then,' said Rick as they moved on.

Jonah and Rick carried on past the submerged Skimmer's and walked to the rear of the sim centre. They passed through security and into the crew monitoring and communications complex. Walking out onto the mezzanine they looked out through the surrounding soundproof glass at the monitoring stations below and crew status displays on the main wall at the front. From the floor below Ngarra and Chang looked up, saw them and waved.

Rick and Jonah walked down the wide stairs and over to where they were standing. Ngarra had just briefed the duty officers who returned to their stations. The main screen on the front wall above them was showing where all current Skimmer crews were deployed in the Penrhyn Basin within "the Area".

'How is it going with the crews?' said Jonah.

'Fine,' said Ngarra. 'Load schedules are on track; a few boarding's and inspections by the Sea Hunters, but no hold ups. Crew vitals look good and no assets are non-operational at present.'

'I thought being on a skimmer was boring,' said Chang sarcastically. 'But this tops it all.' He stretched his arms and yawned.

Rick managed a smile and looked at Jonah. Chang was such a grump.

'Actually,' said Rick as he smiled at Chang. 'We came over to discuss putting your crew back on a skimmer. Connor is at a crucial stage with the technology. If we can run some tests out there, he might overcome the roadblock he has right now. He is stuck.'

'Not that again,' said Chang trying not to care. 'Seriously, look how much trouble it caused us last time.'

'Sounds great me,' said Ngarra as he mouthed at Chang to back off. 'When do we go?'

'Soon,' said Jonah. 'I am worried about others that are now aware of this technology and what they might do next. We need to work out how to get these sea trials done without attracting too much attention.'

Rick was quietly thinking. His people had another agenda and things were in play. He had to ensure the advanced propulsion system tests using the retrofitted overdrive installed on Skimmers continued. Issues still needed to be addressed. It still at times compromised the stability of the rim driven blade drives when used. Operators were not following protocol and aligning the power train correctly when using the overdrive. It resulted in overspeed on the rim drives, taking them offline. Then there was also project Cygnus, or Cygnus 121 as his people called it. He had to be patient, waiting for an opportune time to continue to pursue his people's broader agenda.

As they talked Chang was quietly thinking about getting back out to "the Area" on rotation. Despite his stance on carrying out more trials, it was an opportunity to get back to the Harvester and see his sister. Last time they were out there both he and his sister's life were threatened unless he got hold of Connor's work. He still thought she was in danger.

'Well. Standby anyway,' said Rick. 'Let's go Jonah. We need to organise these tests of Connor's tech to tie in with the upcoming crew change at the Harvester.'

'Yes,' said Jonah. 'Let's get going then.'

They walked across the floor and back up the stairs leaving Ngarra and Chang to think about going back out to sea on Skimmer mining runs.

'Time for a break anyway,' said Ngarra to Chang as they watched them leave. 'Let's catch up with the others over something to eat.'

Ngarra handed over to one of the duty officers and said to contact him if anything came up.

They left and followed Rick and Jonah, walking back through the sim centre and exiting the learning hub through the main entrance. They walked to the rec centre to get some food. On the way, Ngarra messaged the others from his smart watch to meet for some food and catch up.

***

Ngarra's crew had gathered around a table with their food and were chatting away about the last six months on campus. The sense of routine and relative calm had been good.

'Well,' said Ngarra as he looked around at everyone smiling. 'It looks like we are going back to our Skimmer.'

Instance silence followed his comment. Everyone paused in the middle of eating. They all looked at him and at each other and then erupted in conversation about it.

'Where's Connor?' said Stella managing a somewhat nervous laugh about Ngarra's announcement. That was her way of dealing with intense situations; always the comedian.

'Funny you should say that,' said Jesse. 'That is what this is all about I am guessing. Going back on rotation I mean; given what Jonah and Rick have said.'

Over the last six months she had ongoing discussions with Jonah about what Connor was up to, the technology and where it was heading, and the safety of the crew.

'The A team is back!' said Jonny as he gave a little fist pump.

'Did you want to apply?' said Stella laughing. 'We are taking applications now.'

The others managed to laugh as well.

'Depends on what's on the menu,' said Jonny patting his tummy.

The others laughed again at his antics. The mood around the table lightened.

Typical Jonny and Stella thought Jesse. Always the clowns but both could be counted on when needed. They were good for crew morale.

'Anyway,' said Ngarra as he waited for them all to quieten down again and listen. 'Jonah and Rick said to be ready. Once they organise the next crew swap at the Harvester we will be on our way. We are going to test some of Connor's technology again while on a mining run.'

'Sure, we are,' said Chang with a hint of frustration. 'Look how much trouble that got us into last time.' He pointed his fork at them as he tried to talk with a mouth full of food. 'What about my sister, no one has said anything about her.'

'It's a full rotation,' said Jesse. 'Between mining runs we will be at the Harvester. It shouldn't be a problem to arrange a visit and check she is okay. Besides, won't your father look out for her. After all, he is the Chief Operating Officer of GlobeCorpMining.'

'I guess so,' said Chang looking a little angry and distressed. 'He may not care much for me or my mother's situation, but he certainly looks out for my sister. But it's not him that worries me. He has little time for me, never has. It's the people that the run the Harvester. I don't trust them when it comes to my sister at all.'

'Either way,' said Aamir you will have to be careful. 'Allah willing, if your sister is not safe, you might be able to do something about it.'

Rumour was that he would be reassigned and not come with them. No one was quite sure what his posting was going to be though.

'If Chang's father is aware of the technology Connor has developed and its potential, then it is in his best interest to look out for us,' said Jesse.

'True,' said Ngarra. 'Perhaps for us, hiding in plain sight is the best thing to do.'

'Agree,' said Jonny with a mouth full of food dropping onto his plate.

'Bit hard for you to do, isn't it?' said Stella. 'I mean hide in plain sight,' she said looking him up and down and laughing.

Jonny was about to reply but choked on another mouthful and spat food out everywhere. Everyone erupted into laughter as Stella got a spray.

'Gross,' she said jumping out of her chair and punching him in the arm.

Jonny coughed a few times, laughed with the others and then cleaned up his mess.

They all sat down again. Everyone relaxed and talked about other things. The conversation continued for a while before they got up and returned to their workstations.

***

The day was getting on and Jonah's secretary had arranged a council meeting to discuss the crew change and the trials of Connor's technology. In her office, they both prepared for the meeting. Rick walked in and together they all waited.

As usual images of each council member would appear in a circle in the meeting room. These were representatives of industry that had a vested interest in Xed and the Academy.

'It's time,' said her secretary.

'Right, let's go then,' said Jonah.

They moved through to the meeting room.

An image of each member nation's industry representative appeared. They all greeted each other and waited for Jonah to say something.

'Normally there would be no need to call a meeting about a crew change,' she said. 'But we are going to run further tests on the technology during mining operations.'

'I think there is growing concern amongst the council about keeping this technology secure,' said the industry representative from Australia.

'Yes,' said Rick. 'But we can leverage that. GlobeCorpMining's interested in it and the relationship Chang's father has with Jonah is important. It's in his best interest to protect the technology as well. He certainly wouldn't want others getting hold of it either. Even if GlobeCorpMining can't access it themselves. That gives us some cover at sea.'

'What about the people that run the Harvester research program itself?' said the member for the UAE. 'The Peoples Liberation Army; The PLA Navy has an advanced research program that could benefit significantly from all this. Chang's sister is leading the civilian team looking into it. We know that now. How much influence does his father really have?'

'He reports directly to the CCP sub-committee that runs the Harvester program,' said Rick. 'But yes, the PLA Navy is ambitious and an ongoing concern. He may not have complete oversight or control.'

The others on the council erupted into a discussion about corporate security and what other agenda's might be afloat.

Jonah had to step in and quieten everyone down. She didn't want paranoia setting in. Although, at times with some of the things Rick said that he seemed to encourage such paranoia.

'Right,' she repeated until they quieted down. 'All good points, I am sure. Either way, we need to test the technology. Connor needs to run the trials to try and figure out how to overcome a hurdle he has come across.'

'It's dangerous though,' said Rick.

Jonah frowned at him and wondered what he was going to say now. 'Maybe we could get the Sea Hunters to watch over Ngarra's Skimmer,' he said.

'No,' said Jonah emphatically. She wished she knew what his connection with the Sea Hunters really was. 'Last time they tried to disable and board Ngarra's Skimmer to apprehend the rogue crew. Who knows if they were just using that as an excuse to get at the technology? Let's just run the trials during normal mining operations and keep it as inconspicuous as possible.'

'Okay,' said Rick reluctantly agreeing. 'And if anything does go wrong, they return to the Harvester and with Chang's father's help we get them off it and back to Xed Academy.'

Everyone agreed and nodded in support. Jonah and Rick looked at each other. Jonah signalled it was time to end the meeting.

'Right, that's it then,' she said. 'We will give you an update once the trials are underway.'

'Don't muck this up,' said the member for Australia as all their images disappeared.

Jonah and Rick had a brief conversation about getting ready for the crew change and how to keep Connor's technology secure on a skimmer. Each then went off to finish their work for the day and head home. It had been a long day.

As Jonah stood at her desk and checked her schedule she kept wondering where it was all heading. She could sense change, upheaval, and an urgency to secure this technology of Connor's.

Chapter 2

On the same day, Jonah and Rick were talking about sending Ngarra's crew back to "the Area", Lee and Sue were standing on the drone deck of the Harvester. Lee, being of Chinese descent and just like Chang had spent much of his life outside of China. He had of course like Sue adopted an English first name, which was not uncommon.

They were on the observation level of the hex, the control tower that could be raised and lowered from the drone bay below. The drone deck stretched off into the distance around them.

The mineral Harvester ship was huge, ten times the size of the Shell Prelude anchored off Western Australia. A feat of Chinese engineering that followed on from the Island building they had carried out in previous decades. A support base run by the PLA Navy was based in the Cook Islands.

The Chinese, through partnerships with industry, had developed a monopoly on mining tenements within "the Area". Contractors leased or purchased Skimmers to mine the manganese nodules. Using the Xtract drones they extracted the nodules from the seabed four thousand metres below and loaded the Skimmer trays. Contractor Skimmers then delivered these manganese nodules to the Harvester.

'Nice day again,' said Lee as he looked out at the distant horizon. 'No supercells of weather baring down on us.'

'It is not quite the season for it yet is it,' said Sue. 'Although, it's more unpredictable now given rapid climate change. Weather patterns have certainly changed. Our meteorological centre in operations is monitoring the situation.'

'Those super cells coming out of the convergence zone wreak havoc on all the small Island nations to the north of us,' said Lee. 'Along with changes in sea level there is not much left of some of them now. The low-lying ones I mean. Some have been abandoned.'

'Doesn't stop the pirates though,' said Sue. 'And we now have a booming yellow fin tuna industry.'

'The PLA Navy protects and manages that fleet of vessels from piracy using its vessels,' said Lee. 'The industry and government partnerships the Chinese now have with Island nations have really benefitted the region.'

'And that's despite all the population displacement from climate change,' said Sue. 'Anyway, our Chief Operating Officer for GlobeCorpMining will be here soon.'

'We were meant to get those Xtract mining drones to swarm,' said Lee. 'The mimic drone program; no Skimmer crew required on board. But that's not possible unless the drones can be made to pass on or infest each other with this tech Ying Yue has developed.'

'They will still need the laser communication signal streamer for now,' said Sue. 'His daughter Ying Yue, Chang's sister is doing the best she can developing the technology. It takes time.'

'Speaking of Chang,' said Lee as he checked in with a duty officer on the arrival time of Chang's father and looked to the horizon. 'That incident six months ago was to our advantage. We know Xed Ocean Academy is up to something with those mining drones.'

'What we need is a way to access what they are doing,' said Sue. 'That information hub officer Connor seems to know something. It would be ideal to get Connor and Chang's sister together to develop our Xtract technology further.'

'Let's see what Chang's father has to say about it all,' said Lee. 'We haven't seen that Skimmer crew on here delivering nodules for a while. I assume they have been posted ashore for now.'

'Besides,' said Sue. 'If we can't get hold of Connor or the technology, then we need to focus on protecting our asset, Chang's sister. If security is compromised, I have been ordered to follow protocol irrespective of what Chang's father thinks.'

'He would be devastated if that happened,' said Lee. 'Maybe that is why he is coming out to the Harvester. He seemed worried about his daughter's safety the last time he spoke with us.'

'I am sure the need will not arise to follow protocol with respect to his daughter,' said Sue smiling. 'How would security be compromised anyway?'

'We are operating in "the Area" under International Seabed Authority regulations and the International Maritime Organisation,' said Lee. 'The agreement means that in terms of contractor Skimmers, the Sea Hunters can board us and detain individuals in breach of regulations and international conventions. We would not be able to prevent it. If we tried, it would cause an international incident on board.'

'That's why we operate independently of contractor Skimmers that come and go from the moon pools. We may not be able to touch them but as a state flagship, we have right to follow our own protocol for Chinese nationals that compromise security on board,' said Sue. 'If it's one of our own, we can deal with it.'

The duty officer came out onto the observation deck of the hex and interrupted them with an announcement. 'Transport drone inbound,' he said. 'Ten minutes out.'

Lee and Sue looked down and out across the drone deck. A couple of patrol drones took off. A few drone hoists were raised from the bay below. Docking clamps were positioned for landing. A drone deck crew on duty checked that everything was in place. After several minutes, it was quiet again. A low humming could be heard, and in the distance, a black metallic object could be seen approaching.

Lee was humming his song again. 'This is the end, the only end my friend.'

'You and that song,' said Sue. 'Who did you say it was, Jim Morrison.'

'That's right,' said Lee. 'The Doors. Can't help it. It is stuck in my head every time we are up here.'

They looked out to sea as the transport drone approach.

Some of the Harvester crew were swapping out. They would be taken to the Naval support base in the Cook Islands, which now had all the amenities needed for meeting Harvester security and crew requirements.

As usual it flew in low over the ocean, came up on an angle and hovered off to the side. Looking like a flattened chinook helicopter, they had four encased horizontal rotor blades. The back two were closer to the fuselage and set a bit higher with a stern ramp beneath and in between. The front two were set lower and wider, mounted on small wings.

It moved across the deck and approached a docking clamp. It levelled out in a hover directly above it. The docking clamp secured it. Once secured it was lowered onto the cradle. The transport drone powered down.

Chang's father exited the drone first. His aide and a security officer followed him. The crew joining the Harvester followed behind. Quickly they grabbed their belongings, walked to the side of the deck and disappeared down a short set of stairs to a lift.

Standing at the base of the hex the crew that had finished their rotation were waiting patiently to board the transport drone and head off. Chang's father and his entourage passed through them. He greeted some of them, chatted briefly and walked up the stairs to where Lee and Sue were waiting. They all shook hands.

'It's been a while since I was last out here,' he said looking around and out towards the horizon. 'The Harvester is huge isn't it. The monolith as we like to call it.'

They watched on as the crew swapping out boarded the transport drone and the ramp closed. It powered up and after a short time the docking clamp raised and released the drone. It hovered briefly, then tilting slightly forward took off across the deck and over the side.

'Welcome aboard,' said Lee as they turned to enter the hex. He bowed his head forward as was their custom. Sue did the same thing.

'We have some refreshments waiting for you, sir,' said Sue. 'I am sure after a long flight you would like to freshen up and have something to eat.'

'That would be good,' he said. 'Then we shall meet and discuss the lack of progress on this project. I have a sub-committee that is getting frustrated. A frustrated communist party subcommittee is one that will start looking for other solutions out here to move this all forward. The PLA Navy is growing impatient as well. They are also overly ambitious about all this. It concerns me.'

They went inside and the hex lowered itself to the drone bay below. Waiting in the foyer they stepped out and walked across to the adjacent lift. Drone hoists spread out into the distance. Technicians were working on a few transport drones. Patrol drones were in rows not far from where they were standing. A few bay doors were open to the sides. He watched as a patrol drone took off. The docking clamp released it. It hovered briefly, tilted and moved out through the bay door.

'I will see you shortly for a meal,' he said as they all entered the lift. 'We can meet over a meal and discuss a solution. Then I want to go to the lab complex and speak with my daughter. Dinner tonight will be with her. I have to leave tomorrow and get back to the support base at the naval facility.'

'Yes, sir,' said Lee. They both nodded and bowed forward slightly.

The lift took them all below and one of the stewards on duty escorted him, his aide and his security officer to their accommodation.

Chang's father was a well-respected and powerful man. He had a lot of communist party support for his success with the Harvester program and the long and enduring relationships he had built up around it.

***

A short time later they were seated at a table, enjoying a variety of dishes of Asian cuisine. His aide and the security officer sat to one side and kept to themselves.

'Why is it that we still can't fully automate the Skimmers and go crewless?' said Chang's father. 'The trial of our prototype during that incident six months ago was successful.'

'True, the crew monitored it remotely from the Xed Academy sim centre,' said Lee. 'They were able to synch with its SAI. But we must remember that it is all about the drones. No way exists to get the drones to the seabed and back without controlling them individually through the communication streamer. Those Xtract drones are only semi-autonomous. It still takes a crew to oversee their operation.'

Hmmm, he thought. 'So how do we move forward. According to Jonah at Xed Academy they are working on something. What I need to know is how to convince the communist party subcommittee that we are still working towards a solution.'

'I would suggest that we need access to the work of this youth called Connor,' said Sue smiling. 'Both him and your daughter would make a formidable team.'

'What about the mimic drone project?' he said.

'Good point,' said Lee. 'We can use that to keep the sub-committee happy. The prototype works for individual drones but that is as far as we have got.'

'It can be transferred between individual mining drones then,' he said.

'Yes,' said Lee, 'but the ability to infest and spread is limited.'

'Are we still saying it is to mimic behaviours and patterns observed around them,' he said.

'It seems a good cover,' said Sue.

'That will do for now,' he said. 'I think the world has had enough of infections and viruses given the last few decades. Let's keep that quiet.'

He thought briefly about his wife. Her biotech work had been fundamental in developing the mimic drone program. He regretted what happened though. It had made Chang so angry, growing up and finding out what happened at that lab.

They carried on eating and talking about life on the Harvester. Chang's father updated them on news from the Peoples Republic of China. The conversation was subdued and for the most part everyone was content to sit quietly and finish their meals.

'Right,' said Chang's father as he pushed his plates away. 'Let's make our way to the lab and catch up with my daughter.'

'Yes, sir,' said Lee. They all got up and moved off. His aide and security officer got up and followed them closely.

The group moved through Harvester operations to the lab complex. Along the way they passed duty officers. Recognising Chang's father, they stopped, and nodded and bowed their heads forward slightly in recognition. He gave them a brief smile and praised them for their commitment to the Harvester program.

'My daughter!' he said walking into the large lab complex and seeing the Skimmer suspended above a moon pool some distance below. 'So wonderful to see you.'

She turned. Hearing his voice, she knew exactly who it was. They embraced briefly and she smiled.

'It has been so long,' she said.

'Not that long really,' her father said. 'I have heard great things about your work.'

His daughter smiled at the praise she was given.

'The mimic drone project is progressing, and the remote operated Skimmer program is as well. We haven't looked at how it will impact on any interface with use of the retrofitted overdrive installed on them yet though. We don't have access to that, even during maintenance on board. But it's the Xtract mining drones I am struggling with. The communication streamer is still essential so SAI can control and direct each one. We still have not got each drone to infect all the others.'

'So, I hear,' he said as they walked over to the large observation platform high above the moonpool below. Suspended across from them was the prototype autonomous Skimmer.

'I am being pushed by the sub-committee to leverage my relationship with Jonah at Xed Academy and gain access to this youth Connor and the technology he has developed. Some sort of partnership in technology development. They want you and Connor to work together.'

'How is that going to occur?' said Lee politely. 'National security concerns mean Xed and the Academy are unlikely to buy into that.'

'They did it for the Skimmers,' he said. 'And that included an arrangement to install and trial these overdrives on some and their integration with the rim driven power train.'

'Yes,' said Lee. 'But that was us funding them to use their future submarine and advanced propulsion technology and adapt it for the Skimmer design. In retrofitting some of them the agreement was we would not have access to that tech. We just needed to establish a more efficient supply to the Harvester into the future and saw an opportunity. This is different.'

'True,' he said. 'But in terms of Connor's Xtract tech there must be a way around having no access given we funded the Skimmer crew training program at Xed Academy. I will get in touch with Jonah and discuss the situation. In the meantime, make it your priority with this mimic drone program to remove the need to use a communication streamer to control these mining drones individually.'

A brief conversation ensued about how they would go about doing it before the group headed off.

'Father,' his daughter said as the group turned to leave. 'Are we having a meal together tonight?'

'Oh, yes! Definitely,' he said. 'I am looking forward to catching up and not talking about work. See you them.'

She smiled and gave him a brief hug. Looking a little embarrassed he turned and walked out, and the others followed.

***

Later that evening at dinner they sat alone. His daughter did not get to see him often. He was always so busy. The Cook Islands and China were a long way from the Harvester located far out in the South Pacific Ocean.

The conversation turned from work to their family.

'How is our mother,' she said looking a little sad.

'Not well at all,' he said. 'After so many years, she remains weak. I wish I hadn't encouraged her to take on that biotech drone integration project all those years ago.'

'You weren't to know there was going to be an accident and she would be exposed,' she said. 'But Chang hates you for it.'

'Yes, that he does,' he said. 'But I have no idea what to do about it. I got him into Xed and the Academy and away from everything. But he is so angry now.'

'Have you tried talking to him,' she said.

'No, I wouldn't know what to say. He won't even talk to his mother about it all. He blames me for everything that has happened to our family. And now he just blames the world for it all. At least, he is doing well on those Skimmers though. But that incident and being coerced by using his family as leverage shook him up. At least, that is what Jonah told me. It still concerns me.'

'I would like to see him,' she said. 'Maybe I can talk to him.'

'I have told Lee and Sue that next time Chang is on a skimmer offloading nodules at the Harvester that they are to give him every opportunity to see you.'

She smiled at the thought. She really loved her father. Despite the rough times, she liked the thought that he was around even if she could not see him that often. He had been there a lot when she was little, and they had a deep bound. As she and Chang got older life got in the way but that was okay, she thought smiling to herself. She was proud of her father's accomplishments.

They carried on eating and enjoying the opportunity to catch up. They stayed up late and talked. Finally, with a simultaneous yawn they both smiled and thought it time to head off and get some sleep. It had been a long day. His daughter said good night and with a smile went to her accommodation. At least, she could easily talk over message board with him whenever she wanted.

Chapter 3

At Xed Academy the next morning, Rick was in Jonah's office discussing Connor's work. They were going over details concerning sending Ngarra's crew back out to their Skimmer on the next crew change. With a coffee in hand, they were both looking out over the campus.

It was a clear morning. They could also see out over the ocean to the distant horizon. Below, students were arriving and heading to the sim centre at the Ocean Academy, or the adjacent buildings at Xed. Above them they could see small taxi drones coming and going. The taxi drone port on the roof of the admin block they were in was busy.

Rick was keen to get some more testing of Connor's tech done. He wanted to see if Connor could find a way to overcome the issues, he had encountered with the Xtract mining simulations in the mesh for the ocean bubble hologram.

Although Connor had got the Xtracts to behave as a group autonomously, he had not been able to get them to retain and implement independent unsupervised group learning. Even over multiple variations and iterations, without Connor's input the simulations still fell apart. Apparently, he had come across a possible solution, again from his obsession with patterns in nature.

'We are almost organised with the Skimmer crew change,' said Rick. 'The Harvester transport drones are booked. I want Ngarra's crew on that trip.'

'Great,' said Jonah turning towards him. 'The plan is to get them to run the tests on their first mining run. Once Connor has loaded and synched his ocean bubble hologram mesh with their SAI, they deploy the Xtracts. The communication streamer will still be deployed during testing. For now, we need it to monitor them. The idea is to remove the need for SAI and the crew to control them through it, that's the whole point.'

'Exactly,' said Rick. 'Given that we know the simulation still breaks down, if the Xtracts are not synced we would lose them without the streamer. Then the

Skimmer contractor would bill us for an operation to locate them and recover them.'

'That would be an expensive recovery operation,' said Jonah. 'The contractor would have to get the Sea Hunters to locate the infra-sound signal from the locator beacons on the Xtracts.'

'Yes,' said Rick. 'Since we would have breached contractor protocols for crewing the Skimmers and deploying the Xtracts it would be us paying for it. If Connor makes some progress on this memory and learning thing, he is having problems with, it could change everything. He hasn't been able to get SAI to develop the algorithm stack for the mesh to work.'

'He seems close though,' said Jonah. 'He seems to have come across something that occurs in nature that may work. Connor was talking about each Xtract being able to control every other Xtract simultaneously. It was to do with the mesh he created for the ocean bubble hologram. Currently, it doesn't link collective memory with learning. He seems to think it has something to do with the ocean bubble hologram itself. Even so, with SAI's assistance and using natural language processing he has come a long way.'

'The change of scene may help his thought process,' said Rick.

'I hope so,' said Jonah. 'A lot is riding on this, and we know others are after the technology as well now.'

'Speaking of that,' said Jonah. 'We still have a security breach here, and GlobeCorpMining is still trying to find out exactly what we are up to. After what happened last time, we had a lot of explaining to do to State sponsor authorities.'

'I have briefed the Sea Hunters that we are running some Xtract drone trials,' said Rick. 'They will be in the general area during Ngarra's mining run and keeping a watchful eye on things.'

'I still think someone else is across all this, including the Sea Hunters and they will use whatever means they can to get hold of our technology and even Connor,' said Jonah. 'Besides, what about Chang and his sister. She works on the Harvester. What a family nightmare. I think they are all tied up in this somehow, and in danger.'

'Danger from what?' said Rick with raised eyebrows and trying to act surprised.

'Bringing Connor and Chang's sister together would be the logical thing to do. But whoever has both these researchers together in one place is going to win out on all this.'

'I see,' said Rick. He looked out over the campus again. 'The problem is getting Ngarra's crew and their Skimmer to and from those moon pools without incident.'

'Surely Chang's father will look out for us,' said Jonah. 'I have a good relationship with him, and his son is on our Skimmer. His daughter is on the Harvester. That's a good thing, right?'

'It is indeed,' said Rick. 'However, the Peoples Liberation Army Navy has become powerful. They have people on that Harvester. Ambition is a dangerous thing and some people in the PLA Navy are single minded in their pursuit of it. The CCP sub-committee that Chang's father reports to may not be aware of or able to provide oversight or even control such ambition.'

'Well at least there is little interest in compromising their ability to operate in "the Area",' said Jonah. 'We know no one would ever allow that to happen.'

The conversation continued for a while longer. Both eventually headed off to catch up with the day's work before the crew change briefing.

***

Later that day everyone had gathered for the briefing that had been organised. Crews would be heading out to the Harvester to swap out with crews currently on the Skimmers.

It was like any other crew change briefing. They had all gathered in the auditorium adjacent to the sim centre to hear the details that some had heard many times before. For graduates new to the crewing program, there was apprehension and excitement. Some were being placed as individuals on Skimmer's to consolidate their training. Others were being sent out to swap with and replace entire crews.

From the equivalent of year ten or about fifteen years old, they were selected from school and entered Xed. Jonah had been one of the people around the world that had taken an education system that was failing industry and revolutionised it. They didn't teach by age and year, but by ability or level only. Some progressed quickly, others slowly but it worked well. Students got over their age differences and built up the resilience that had been lost to youth in previous decades.

With industry support, students either moved into roles in robotics, drones and automation in industry when graduating from Xed or entered the Ocean

Academy and the Skimmer crewing program. From ages eighteen to twenty-four, roles and responsibilities varied according to aptitude and progress through the program.

Ngarra's crew were sitting together near the front. They were one of the most experienced of the young crews. They looked up and behind them at the other crews, some they knew, others not so much. A few greetings were exchanged and waving of hands. Jonny and Stella had been chatting and joking around with a few others sitting up behind them when Rick and Jonah walked in with other instructors and admin staff. They quickly raced back down to the front and sat down.

Jonah looked over at them and smiled. While everyone was quietening down, she walked over.

'We need to see you after this briefing to go over what you lot are going to do for those Xtract tech trials. See you afterwards.'

She walked back over to the centre of the floor space at the front of the auditorium and stood with the others.

'Right,' said Rick. 'Quiet and listen up.' He paused and waited for silence. 'Another crew change is about to take place for which you have all been given the details of. Make sure you are on time and by that, I mean arrive early at the Harvester transport drone port for uplift. Last time, the operators had to wait for late comers. Like I said before, if you aren't adult enough to stick to a schedule then you will be grounded until you can.'

Some chatter erupted as others pointed fingers at and hassled a few of them that had been in this situation before. For some, lessons learnt took time, but the Academy was patient and consistent in its expectations, instilling discipline and issuing consequences for non-compliance. Together with teaching to ability and level and not year and age, they had overcome the failures of the education system in previous decades.

'Alright, quieten down,' said Rick as he paused again. 'Next, some feedback from the Harvester. On your downtime, a few of you have not been abiding by Harvester protocols. I have names and have spoken to these individuals so if you can't check yourself, you will be sent back here.'

More laughter followed as some crew members joked about some of the things that had happened staying overnight on the Harvester. Despite the laughter, it was serious. Those people that had received their written warning had no more chances.

'Okay, okay everyone this isn't a circus,' said Rick trying not to smile at his own comment as he paused yet again. 'Next, the Sea Hunters have a job to do. Again, I have had reports of a lack of respect being shown if you get boarded for an inspection.'

There was a roar of laughter and someone yelled, 'yeah Ngarra,' from up the back. Ngarra stood up, turned and gave a bow and sat down again. Laughter and jeering followed.

'Okay children shut it and listen up,' said Rick again. He was getting a bit grumpy with the antics. 'You are obligated to comply with any instruction they give you. Lastly, these are contractor Skimmers so it is your job to look after them as best you can. Any damage is paid for by us. A few of you have let us down in this regard. Especially when using the advanced propulsion system; the overdrive for the trials. Some crews have been complacent and not compensating for alignment of the overdrive with the rim driven power train. It costs us money and time when the rim drive is offline. If that continues, you will be removed from the program.'

Silence followed Ricks comment. It was serious and no one wanted to be removed from the program. Being part of it was a steppingstone to a resource industry that was now focussed just as much on being off planet as it was in the ocean. In fact, much of how things had developed in the ocean using the Skimmers had been replicated for preparing for and operating off planet. The retrofitted overdrive propulsion system and ongoing trials were a part of that process.

Rick looked around at everyone. 'We have the names of those crews and individuals as well,' he said. 'Anyway. Enough from me, I will see you at the transport drone port.'

Jonah stepped forward next and addressed the crews. She had been listening intently. It was nothing unusual. They always had a few issues to deal with. The crews were young and sometimes needed follow-up on their behaviour. At Xed and the Academy, Jonah had got rid of teaching and instructing by age and year. They focussed on levels of ability and competency or readiness to learn. They spent a lot of time on developing emotional intelligence and resilience in these youth. So, crews were often of mixed age ranging from eighteen to their mid-twenties.

'Thanks Rick,' she said stepping forward to the edge of the front row to speak to the crews. 'You are all doing well out there. However, we still have the standard issues going on when monitoring SAI's control of the Xtracts during mining operations.'

A mutter went through the crews about drones malfunctioning and always having to repair them. The chatter got a little louder as others discussed how unproductive it was having to monitor SAI as it controlled each individual drone through the deployed laser signal communication streamer.

'All right, all right quieten down,' said Jonah as she paused and waited. Everyone quietened down and she continued.

'The whole point of crews is to do exactly what you are all moaning about. Sure, there are ways to improve Xtract mining operations and we are working on that. But for now, this is what you have to work with.'

The briefing carried on for a little longer. Mundane issues were bought up about housekeeping and meeting contractor quotas. Once the briefing was finished everyone got up and left. As the last of the crews wandered out of the auditorium, Ngarra's crew walked over to where Jonah and Rick were standing.

'Back on the horse boys and girls,' said Jonny as he pretended to be riding one.

'Yeah,' said Stella. 'One great big horse for you and your pantry jockey boy.'

As a typical Tongan Maori, he was of solid stature, loved his food and was an imposing person. He was a gentle giant, but the crew had seen him angry. He was very protective of his fellow crewmembers. He particularly hated bullies, having been bullied himself in his youth.

The others laughed.

Jonny certainly liked is food and he was a big boy. Jonny made a warrior face and jumped at the others.

He liked doing it to Chang in particular. They still had a bit of a dislike for each other over what happened last time they were on a skimmer. Jonny had punched him over bullying Connor.

'All right you lot,' said Rick. 'Cut the tom foolery out and listen up.'

Jesse glared at Jonny and Stella and motioned for them to shut it. Ngarra looked around intensely at his crew and they all went quiet. He wasn't one for humour at the best of times. The crew often had bets on getting him to smile or laugh. Ngarra had strong cultural ties to his indigenous Australian heritage. He was proud of what he had accomplished for his people and the opportunities it had created for them.

'Once you get to the Harvester and swap with a skimmer crew,' said Rick, 'I want you to get going as soon as possible. You will be using the Skimmer from last time, the same one.'

'Will we run overdrive trials again?' questioned Jonny. 'Overdrive protocol HG4S6S2,' said Jonny. 'HG462, a secretive woman or so we have been told. How does it work anyway?'

Jesse frowned at Jonny and motioned for him to zip it.

'Not now,' said Rick ignoring his question. 'Ask Jesse about it later. We need to get Connor's Ocean bubble hologram up and running on that Skimmer and synced with SAI and the Xtracts as soon as possible.'

'Rick said the Sea Hunters will be in your general area during the trials and will keep an eye on things,' said Jonah.

'Really,' moaned Ngarra. 'Is that needed. I mean it has been quiet since the incident last time. Besides, I thought you didn't trust them. I mean, didn't you say they had been compromised. What about the security breach here?'

'What about my work?' said Connor. He had been lost in his own thoughts and snapped out of it when he heard them talking about the security breach.

'Last time everyone wanted it,' he said. 'We will get it to work this time. It could change everything. It will be so cool. I'm stuck on this problem you see, it's like this.'

Connor was about to launch into one of his long explanations on the development of learning autonomous group behaviour in Xtracts. Being autistic, he often had difficulty linking social situations with body language and emotion. He had at least some awareness of this though.

'Connor,' said Chang snapping at him. 'Leave it for another time. Listen up and stop waffling on.'

Chang was envious of Connor's work as it made him think of his sister and her work on the Harvester. He wanted to see her again. His thoughts turned to his father. It made him angry.

'Who pushed your button,' said Jonny as he made a sudden move towards Chang and smiled.

Chang jumped back and waved him off. He was generally grumpy about most things and Jonny loved winding him up about it.

'Cut it out you lot,' said Jesse.

'Enough,' said Jonah sternly. 'Now, the Sea Hunters are just keeping an eye on things and nothing else. We still have the risk of piracy to deal with out there as well.'

'That's right,' said Rick. 'Connor, once the Skimmer is in position for its mining run you are to carry out those Xtract trials for the tech. Make sure the streamer is deployed so if something goes wrong, you can resume mining operations and recover the Xtracts.'

Connor nodded enthusiastically.

'We will keep in touch anyway,' said Jonah. 'The location within "the Area" that you are going to is close to a grid buoy and the eel drones. The laser communication signal will easily enable a live video feed on the message board, rather than just a video recording or audio link.'

'On that note,' said Rick. 'See you at the transport drone port. The day is getting on and we still have another short council meeting to attend.'

Jonah and Rick walked out of the auditorium and left the others chatting about what lay ahead.

***

Back in Jonah's office they waited. Of the twelve members the usual four to six members would be present. They represented the interests of the others. They had to again go over what precautions were being put in place to protect the technology. The security breach that occurred during the previous incident had not been solved. Concern existed about how this might impact on carrying out the Xtract trials during a mining run. They wanted to reassure the council.

'It's time,' said Jonah's secretary looking at her smartwatch.

They walked into the meeting room.

Images of the council members appeared around them.

They all greeted each other.

The usual representatives of those that funded Xed and the Academy were present. They waited patiently for Jonah to start the meeting.

'Once again,' said Jonah, 'here we are at a crew change briefing and mining operations update. It's a standard crew change. You have all been sent the updates on Xed, the Academy and the Skimmer crew program. However, we need to go over the trials of the technology that will occur.'

'Last time,' said one of the council members, 'it took some convincing of State sponsor authorities and a skimmer contractor not to press charges over what happened. We want reassurance the crews are not going to run around the ocean on some wild adventure again.'

Rick jumped in before Jonah could speak.

'Rest assured,' he said. 'This is a trial being conducted during an in-situ mining operation. The Sea Hunters will be in the general area keeping an eye on things.'

'What about the security breach?' said another council member. As per our recent meeting, that has not been solved. There is concern that the Sea Hunters were somehow involved. How are we going to mitigate the risk that the technology will not be compromised out there?'

'In addition to the Sea Hunters,' said Jonah, 'Chang's father is very supportive. I mean, his son is on the Skimmer and his daughter is working on the Harvester. I have his assurance that GlobeCorpMining is not interested in accessing Connor's work. They don't want to cause an international incident in "the Area" any more than we do.'

'Doing this in plain sight or hiding in plain sight is why it will work,' said Rick. 'No one wants to be seen doing the wrong thing and compromise participation in this great mining economy in the deep ocean or off-planet for that matter.'

Rick's military background and experience meant he was used to dealing with these sorts of situations. He had another agenda though and his people were becoming more insistent that he follow it through. He understood Jonah suspected he was up to something.

'We will take your word for it,' said another council member.

'I will update you once the crew change has taken place and Ngarra's crew and Skimmer are on location,' said Jonah.

With that the council members nodded, and their images disappeared. Jonah and Rick were left standing along in the meeting room.

'Right,' said Rick. 'The day is nearly gone, and I still have some stuff to do in the sim centre. I will catch up with you tomorrow.'

'Of the twelve,' said Jonah, 'it's always the same ones we deal with. I've always wondered why we rarely see the others.'

'We don't need the twelve disciples of technology and change all present,' said Rick with a chuckle. 'We would never make any decisions. Not quickly anyway. Besides they are an advisory panel. I guess they have other things to do.'

'You're right with that one your majesty,' said Jonah smiling and having a chuckle at her comment and the thought.

Jonah was about to ask him about the Sea Hunters and her concern over the unsolved security breach.

However, Rick quickly took off.

'Got to go,' he said waving as he took off.

Rick walked down the corridor and took the lift to the ground floor. He exited, walked across the internal space that stretched from floor to ceiling. As he hurried on past a few of the staff they greeted him. He walked out of the huge foyer and main entrance and across campus to the sim centre.

With having two council meetings in quick succession, Rick needed to get in touch with his contact on the Sea Hunter unit and brief them about what was going on. He was concerned about the amount of confidence Jonah was placing in Chang's father that everything would be okay. He knew his people were not so sure about that. He also knew Jonah suspected that it was him that was involved in the previous security breach. He had to be careful. He had still not been able to convince the council that what he was trying to do was the way forward. Even with the support of his people and their connection with the council it was proving difficult. There were many levels of relationships to consider and account for.

His people were worried about what was coming. It was very much a family affair, Chang's father, his sister and Chang himself were all tied up in it in one way or another. And then there was Connor. What a mess and it all centred around Connor and his work. They didn't want the overdrive propulsion system trials compromised either or project Cygnus for that matter.

Rick walked into the sim centre, greeting a few students and staff along the way. He passed by the student learning silos and walked through the instructor area between the two large, submerged Skimmers in the sim centre. Students were being guided through some training scenarios.

Moving through security he entered the crew monitoring and communication complex. Duty officers greeted him as he walked down the steps from the glass-enclosed mezzanine above. Rick was in a hurry. He walked to the rear, passed through security again and entered "the room".

'The room,' as it was called was where the entre sim centre AI was housed. Rick went to a workstation and using his smart watch entered an encrypted code that gave him access to his contact with the Sea Hunter unit.

A pause followed and then he heard Max's voice.

'Rick what can I do for you,' he said.

'I'll be quick,' said Rick. 'Your team will be keeping an eye on this Skimmer crew while it runs these Xtract trials during a mining operation. I also want you to be prepared for a situation that might arise on the Harvester. I don't trust GlobeCorpMining and neither do my people. The situation between Chang, his father and his sister concerns me. I still think something else is going on and they are all at risk out there, as is Connor. I must go and will be in touch later. Be careful out there.'

With that, Rick logged off and got out of the room as quickly as he could. He went back to the crew monitoring and communication complex to finish off some work for the day. He gathered his thoughts and prepared for the crew change that was going to happen.

Chapter 4

On the same morning, Rick and Jonah had briefed Ngarra's crew at Xed Academy about the Xtract trials, Chang's father and his sister were up early on the Harvester.

They were in the lab complex.

Her father was not one for using the names of his children and often just referred to them as daughter or son. Today was different. Ever proud of her accomplishments he made sure to say her name in front of the others. Ying Yue was her name which meant 'reflection of the moon'. A name that had a deep meaning for him. Watching over his family he often felt hollow. Hollow about not being able to make them see through each other's differences.

'Good morning, everyone,' he said as they prepared to launch the prototype fully automated and crewless Skimmer for further trials. 'Ying Yue will be overseeing this whole operation. I am here to observe and report back to the sub-committee.'

Everyone on the team acknowledged his presence. Ying Yue moved off to the control room overlooking the large hanger. The Skimmer was suspended high above the moonpool below.

The modified Skimmer had been trialled once before. A crew at Xed in the sim centre had connected with it remotely. They had been able to sync with the SAI and monitor it.

The trial today was important and a little different than the previous one. The Skimmer was given a set of coordinates in "the Area" not far from the Harvester. It would go to that location and carry out a mining operation with its Xtracts. It would do it without any human intervention.

'System checks complete,' said one of the technicians.

Automated systems had been tested and confirmed as nominal by SAI.

'System checks meet autonomous control criteria,' said Ying Yue. She looked at the displays in the control room that monitored SAI. She hoped nothing would go wrong.

Her father watched on.

'Launch status nominal,' said another technician. 'Skimmer is watertight, SAI has control.'

'Confirmed,' said Ying Yue. 'Watertight and launch ready. SAI has control.'

All the technicians moved away from the Skimmer to safe zones. Ying Yue watched and waited for them to get into position.

'Initiate launch sequence,' she said.

A technician in the control room did a final check and then initiated the launch sequence. Once the Skimmer was lowered into the moonpool below and the suspension clamps released SAI would take the Skimmer out.

The Skimmer slowly descended from the hanger bay into the moonpool below. As it entered the water a gentle wave slopped back and forwards around it. It was released and for a moment nothing happened. Then displays came to life in the control room. They looked on as the Skimmer propulsion powered up and it slowly submerged below the surface and disappeared.

Ying Yue did not have much to do until the Skimmer was in position and the Xtracts deployed. Her father came over and congratulated her.

'Really, Father,' she said. 'I would wait until the trial is successful before congratulating me.'

'It's times like this,' he said, 'that I wish Chang had made more of himself and was here. Such an angry young man. What happened to his mother wasn't my fault. She chose to do what she did.'

'I know that, Father,' she said touching his arm.

'He despises me for it though,' he said.

'Right now, you should be more concerned about the Harvester and Sue and Lee. I don't trust them,' she said quietly.

'What do you mean?' he said. 'They report to me.'

'I know that, Father,' she said. 'But I feel very uneasy and they watch my every move. I feel like a prisoner here sometimes.'

Sue and Lee being the most senior officers on the Harvester had met Chang's crew during the previous incident. They were interested in the rumours going around about Connor's work and the technology.

'What about your other project, the mimic drones?' her father asked.

'A work in progress,' she said. 'Infecting other drones and taking them over to swarm is hard. Perhaps this Connor has some answers.'

'I have a good relationship with Jonah,' he said. 'From what I can tell, Connor is close to getting Xtracts to autonomously learn group behaviour.'

'That is why Sue and Lee are so interested,' she said. 'But it's Sue, she is connected to the Peoples Liberation Army. She is so ambitious. I am worried.'

Ying Yue had a pleading look in her eye.

'Don't worry so much,' he said holding her hand with both of his. 'I will ask some people I know about all this.'

'Sue and Lee will be overseeing offloading now,' said Ying Yue. 'A ship is arriving to off take nodules.'

'Yes, I know,' he said. 'I will head off and talk to them while this ship that has arrived is being loaded with nodules. Inform me when the Xtracts are released. I will be here for the day and fly out later on a transport drone.'

She nodded. Her father let go of her hand and went to find Sue and Lee. She turned back and looked at the control centre displays. Her thoughts drifted between her family, the operation being carried out and concern for her own safety. She felt nervous. A gut feeling something was not right.

***

Chang's father walked through operations to the off-take control centre.

He walked in and saw on the monitoring screens that the ship in question was now stationed alongside the Harvester.

It looked tiny.

The Harvester, a monolith in comparison dwarfed it.

They all watched as a conveyor belt arm rotated and extended out from the side of the Harvester. The ships nodule hatches opened, and tonnes of nodules slowly filled the hoppers.

'Sir,' said Lee as he walked in. 'I hope the Skimmer launch went well. We have been pre-occupied with this offtake. The ship arrived last night and is now taking on nodules.'

'I see,' said Chang's father.

They watched through the camera system as the nodules moved along the conveyor. It stretched out over the water for about fifty metres. From the edge of the Harvester, a riser with cables on it extended upwards from the drone deck to support it. It would retract and the arm would fold in once the hoppers were full.

'Have you heard anything more about this Skimmer crew you spoke to during that incident six months ago,' he asked cautiously.

Sue turned towards him, glancing briefly at Lee.

'A crew member called Connor is working on something,' she said. 'From what I can gather, a way to get Xtract mining drones to learn autonomous group behaviour. It is of interest.'

'Is it relevant to Ying Yue's work,' he asked cautiously.

'Ying Yue has one part of the puzzle,' said Lee. 'This Connor seems to have the other or is close to discovering it.'

They watched on as the conveyor continued to move from hopper to hopper and load nodules into them.

'How is your son?' said Sue. 'Perhaps we can arrange a visit with his sister next time they are here.'

Interesting comment, he thought to himself. I was going to ask them to arrange that.

Chang's father was careful to keep his thoughts to himself. His leading questions confirmed that Sue and Lee might be up to something. Or, that Sue may be up to something that Lee was not aware of. Were they both acting alone, was Sue acting along or was she doing someone else's bidding? No one on the subcommittee had said anything. Was it a group within the PLA and who were they reporting to? Was it outside his scope? How could he not have clearance?

'My son is where he needs to be right now,' he said. 'But yes, next time they are on a skimmer I would like you to arrange that for him.'

Lee walked forward and around Chang's father, turned and looked back.

'Let's go to the lab and get an update on the Skimmer operation,' he said. 'Being able to monitor these Skimmers remotely is of significant benefit to us.'

'Yes,' said Sue smiling as they turned and left the control room.

'A lot to think about isn't there,' she said looking at Chang's father.

Lee looked at him as well. His eyes piercing as if to say watch yourself. He dared not say anything in front of Sue.

They walked through the operations centre to the lab complex and hanger. On the way, Chang's father's mind was racing. His family seemed caught up in something bigger than all of them. How on earth did that happen. He would get to the bottom of it.

On the way, he collected his personal aide and security officer. They had been following him around but kept their distance. He wanted them close by for now.

***

They walked into the lab complex and greeted Chang's daughter Ying Yue. The Skimmer was now in position a short distance from the Harvester. SAI had deployed the communication streamer and the Xtracts.

'Just in time,' she said looking at the monitoring screens. 'I was about to send for you. We are going to run the disruption sequence to see how SAI responds.'

Ying Yue had got the technicians to rig an Xtract to malfunction. SAI would then have to recover it with no human interference.

When a skimmer had a crew, they worked with SAI to manually retrieve them. Another Xtract would be used to tow the malfunctioned one back to the Skimmer.

This time SAI would have to control another Xtract and use it to do the recovery itself.

'Your daughter is very talented,' said Sue as they watched on. 'It would not be good to lose her. She seems a little distant lately.'

'Family,' he said calmly. 'She worries about her family.'

They watched on as the malfunction sequence was activated in one of the Xtracts. At first, everything went smoothly. On the monitoring displays, SAI could be seen taking control of another Xtract and using it to hook up and tow the malfunctioned Xtract. However, once underway something un-anticipated happened. The loading bucket on the malfunctioned Xtract got caught in the communication streamer.

'Damn it,' said Ying Yue.

They all watched as SAI tried to manoeuvre the Xtract to untangle the loading bucket.

'Take over,' she said quickly to her team. 'We don't want to cut the streamer.'

She terminated the trial. The team was able to untangle the Xtract and then hand control back to SAI. It resumed towing the Xtract back to the Skimmer moonpool.

'That is fortuitous,' her father said. 'That is why the mimic drone program and this work of Connor's is all so important. The future of mining depends on it.'

'Unless these Xtracts are able to learn to deal with unexpected situations by themselves during mining operations,' said Ying Yue, 'and pass that learning collectively between themselves they will never be truly autonomous, and SAI will never be able to control a mining operation without a crew on board.'

'Still, it is progress,' said Sue. 'Let's finish this trial and get those drones and that Skimmer back to the hanger.'

'Right, I have to get going,' said Chang's father. 'I have some work to attend to and will meet you for a meal before I fly out.'

Ying Yue smiled and returned to overseeing the recovery operation. Her father, his aide and security officer walked off leaving Lee and Sue.

Lee and Sue walked out onto the observation platform overlooking the hanger and the moonpool below.

'I am worried that Ying Yue might go ashore to the naval facility for a break and not come back,' said Sue. 'It seems as though she wants to solve the problems between her family.'

'Her work is absolutely crucial to our success out here and what we intend for the future of mining in "the Area",' said Lee.

'What about defence?' said Sue. 'The PLA want to use her work to project maritime domain dominance.'

'If she ends up on the wrong side of all this, we will have nothing to show for all the work that has been done so far,' said Lee. 'Somehow we need to get hold of Connor's work.'

'Chang is the key,' said Sue. 'Failing all else, I have approval for the ultimate solution.'

'I'd prefer not to have to do that,' said Lee. 'It is not necessary. It's a short-sighted military solution.'

'It's the only way to secure what we are trying to achieve here without causing an international maritime incident in "the Area",' said Sue.

'Let's focus on reassuring Ying Yue that she is safe here,' said Lee. 'We will arrange for Chang to see her next time his crew is here. Then we can think about how to get Ying Yue to meet up with Connor and learn exactly what he is up to. That will be our opportunity to acquire the information we need. We can decide from there.'

With that, they left the lab complex and walked to the operations centre. As they left, across from them technicians were preparing the hanger to recover the Skimmer from the moonpool below. Ying Yue watched them leave, wondering what they were talking about.

***

Early that evening in the crew accommodation area next to operations, Ying Yue and her father caught up for a meal at the restaurant before he flew out. It had been a long day and he was looking forward to one last chat with his daughter. He wasn't sure when he would be out again. Often when his daughter got leave ashore, he was so busy that he missed the opportunity to see her.

'When will I see you again,' she said as they were eating.

'I am not sure,' he said. 'The company seems to highly value your work though. So does the PLA for that matter. They are reluctant to give you any more leave than you are entitled to at present. A long holiday and a chance to catch up would be good. But not right now.'

'What about Mother?' she said. 'Her illness is not going to go away. None of us have seen her for a while. I'll drag Chang there myself if I have to, no matter how angry he is with you about it all.'

'I have seen her a few times,' he said. 'She is not well. Not better, not worse. I suppose that is something.'

'You can't help what happened,' she said. 'It wasn't your fault.'

'I wish Chang would see it that way,' he said.

The conversation continued for a while.

They talked about days gone by.

Once their meal was finished Ying Yue accompanied her father to the drone deck. His secretary and security detail followed.

They walked to the lift and up to the drone bay.

Across from them was the hex, the large retractable control tower shaped like a hexagon.

'Such an odd shape,' her father said as they walked towards it.

'A symbol of greater understanding,' she said.

They walked across to it and into the foyer.

Others were waiting in the foyer for a flight out as well. The opening above it retracted, and it rose up.

The drone deck became visible.

The hex tower slowed and locked into position.

Above them and off to the sides were workstations for monitoring and controlling air and surface operations.

Ying Yue gave her father a quick hug while others were not looking so as not to embarrass him.

He smiled, gave her a kiss on the check and waved goodbye. He walked across the drone deck to the waiting transport drone secured on its docking clamp. Others walked up the stern ramp. He followed them in with his aide and security officer close behind. It closed and the four blades in their cowlings started rotating as it powered up. The docking clamp rose and released the transport drone. It hovered, then angled forward. It flew across the drone deck, over the edge and did a slow bank heading low over the ocean towards the horizon.

Ying Yue looked on, an uneasy feeling in her stomach. She felt it might be the last time she saw him. It wasn't a nice feeling at all.

Chapter 5

While Chang's father had been at the Harvester, out at sea in the Pacific Ocean some distance away the Sea Hunters were carrying out an inspection of a skimmer. They were some distance north of the Harvester.

A skimmer was in position a hundred metres below sea level. Its laser signal communication streamer was deployed. It was mining manganese nodules from the seabed four thousand metres below. Xtracts were coming and going, filling the trays along each side of the Skimmer with nodules.

Skimmers, looking a bit like a Chiton that you would find on the rocks in the intertidal zone, were about fifty metres long and thirty metres wide. On each side was a half-pipe recess the docking clamps were positioned from which drones had detached themselves. In front of this recess, the Skimmer trays were being loaded.

Inside the Skimmer and to the rear was the moonpool and airlock. Forward was the maintenance bay and Xtract monitoring bay. Further forward and behind a sealed bulkhead was the overdrive propulsion system, which extended up through the next level to the SAI console above.

The level above contained living quarters and amenities for crew. Forward of the rec area a watertight bulkhead and narrow esplanade went around each side of the sealed overdrive propulsion system that passed through to the SAI console on the level above. The narrow esplanade that skirted each side opened forward to a viewing area.

On the level above was the Skimmer Artificial Intelligence or SAI monitoring console itself. To the rear of this and in the centre was the information hub and another airlock. Either side was a passageway, propulsion and life support systems.

A Sea Hunter interceptor drone was nearby. A breaching pod with a boarding party aboard had detached from it. The pod was now docked with the topside hatch of the Skimmer above the airlock.

The boarding team had entered the Skimmer and were now standing at the SAI console. The outer hull shields were open, and they were watching the Xtract mining drones coming and going, loading nodules into the trays along each Skimmer wing.

An Xtract came into view, climbing up from the depths below with its loading bin full of nodules. As it came level with the trays it moved forward. Hovering over the trays it released its load, which dropped into the tray below it. As the nodules settled a small plume of muddy sediment drifted off. It joined the plume of muddy sediment that soon mixed with the marine snow that constantly fell from the photic zone to the seabed four thousand metres below.

Dotted over the Pacific Ocean these Skimmer plumes of resuspended mineral laden mud and silt had enriched the food web. This bottom-up iron rich remineralisation of the photic zone and explosion of the food web was attributed to a resurgence in the yellow fin tuna industry in the region.

They watched on as the Xtract reversed itself, changed its orientation and started descending again to the depths below. As it descended the communication streamer from the Skimmer could be seen alongside it plummeting to the depths below.

After watching the Xtract the boarding party Chief, Cameron or Cam for short turned to his two offsiders.

'Right, you go and check the maintenance and load logs in the Xtract bay,' he said to one of them. 'You go and check the Skimmer ones,' he said to the other.'

They nodded and each moved off with a skimmer crewmember to carry out their inspections.

'Can you get SAI to show me your movements and operations over the last month,' he said to the Skimmer communications and security officer.

'Sure,' he said. 'SAI show navigation logs starting from the day after the last inspection.'

While SAI displayed their previous movements in hologram in the middle of the circular SAI console, Cam recorded the log details.

'Everything looks to be in order,' he said.

'Standard mining runs,' said the Skimmer operator who was standing next to the Communications and Security officer.

Cam finished off looking over the navigation logs. He then walked through the information hub and then down each side of the rim driven propulsion and life support, checking system and status displays.

He was looking to make sure there were no breaches of discharge regulations or dumping of refuse.

In the information hub, he stopped and asked for the log of the seabed sampling regime they were meant to carry out alongside mining operations.

'Over here,' said the information officer. He showed him the log and then pulled out the samples that had been processed and stored for pickup by the Sea Hunters at Sea or at the Harvester. 'We missed one location. An Xtract malfunctioned so we didn't have time to get a sample before we left.'

'Noted,' said Cam. 'I will pass that onto "the Authority" in my report.'

They walked back to the SAI console and Cam placed the samples into a pelican case he had bought with him.

Soon after the others arrived back from carrying out their inspections on the levels below. Everything was in order, no contraband, Xtract logs were up to date and records of sediment plumes were within limits.

'Okay,' said Cam. 'We are good here, time to go. Thanks,' he said to the crew as they walked to the airlock.

The airlock closed.

Above them they opened the hatch and climbed the ladder. Above them the breaching pod hatch was opened, and they climbed back into it. The boarding party strapped themselves in and Cam activated the detaching sequence.

The Skimmer and Breaching pod hatches sealed and docking clamps released, and the breaching pod moved up and away from the Skimmer. It then turned in a wide arc, gained speed and headed off. The crew looked out of the pod at the Skimmer as it receded into the distance. It looked like some sort of giant creature from the deep, suspended in the blue green void.

They returned to the interceptor drone and docked. Cam then commanded the interceptor drone to return to the Sea Hunter vessel not far from them.

***

On the Sea Hunter vessel Max and Alex, the officers in charge were in the drone bay. They were discussing the status of their three aerial patrol drones with a technician. The three docking clamps arranged in a triangle each had a drone mounted on them. The clamping system moved the drones out to the rear of the vessel where they were launched. Depending on operational requirements they could be manned or unmanned.

'We need to replace the front left cowling on this one,' said the technician.

She was up on the cowling with another technician pulling it apart and dropping out the blades.

While they discussed how the cowling had been damaged SAI announced over comms, 'Interceptor drone and breaching pod boarding party inbound, docking in ten minutes.'

'Okay,' said Max as he stretched his arms and looked at Alex. 'Let's go down to the well deck. Let us know when this patrol drone is operational,' he said to the technician. 'Having one out of service is acceptable but not two.'

Max and Alex walked to the rear of the drone bay and down to the level below. The well deck was like an inverted version of the drone bay above them. Three interceptor drones could be suspended from their clamps and move out over the water in the well bay. A launch and retrieval well deck bay door was open. They could look out to the distant horizon.

One interceptor drone was in the dry dock suspended over its breaching pod, which had been detached for servicing. Hanging above, the interceptor drone defensive weapons system was being checked. It had a close quarters Acoustic Remote Cavitation or ARC array and a torpedo-mounted version could be deployed. The array was designed to disable a skimmer if needed and board it. They were also used to defend against piracy, which was now common in "the Area".

'We haven't heard from our contact at Xed Academy,' said Alex.

'You mean Rick,' said Max. 'Since the incident with the off-grid Skimmer six months ago and chasing after Ngarra's Skimmer it has been quiet. Rick still wants us to try and secure the technology this young Connor has developed though. He did say to sit tight until an opportunity arose to pursue his peoples' agenda again.'

Max was an imposing man of solid build. His relaxed demeanour hid a calculating mind that was always thinking about possibilities and options. Max folded his arms and watched as the technicians and a couple of deck hands got ready to receive the interceptor drone.

'That is going to be difficult now,' said Alex. 'We can't just board a skimmer and detain someone like we did last time. We had an excuse then. It has to be by the book and under our mandate to maintain security and compliance in "the Area" for "the Authority".'

'An opportunity will present itself,' said Max unfolding his arms. 'We just have to wait and be patient. I am picking that at some point our paths will all cross again on that Harvester.'

Alex just wanted to get it done. He could be impatient at times and was not as calculating and strategic as Max. It was a good match in terms of leadership though. They complemented each other's skills and expertise.

'Interceptor drone on final approach,' announced the control room operator over comms.

Alex and Max walked over to the control room stairs at the rear of the well deck. They walked up the stairs and in.

The control room operator was preparing to receive the interceptor drone. It was a calm day and the vessel was making way through the water. A technician on duty moved a docking clamp out over the well deck. As the docking clamp locked into position the interceptor drone surfaced. As it settled a wave slid off its topside. The docking clamp locked onto it. It was lifted slowly out of the water. The docking clamp moved the interceptor drone forward through the well deck dry dock and bay door entrance.

Once locked in position the breaching pod was detached and lowered to the deck cradle below it. Cam and his inspection team exited the pod.

Max and Alex watched on from the control room. Cam looked up and saw them. Walking over, Alex motioned that they were coming down to see him. The other two moved off.

'How did it go?' said Alex as they meet Cam at the bottom of the stairs.

They all walked over to the edge of the well deck and looked out through the open bay doors. They watched as the vessel picked up speed and headed off. The wake behind it extended out over a calm sea. It was one of those days where it was hard to tell where the ocean ended, and the sky began.

'Nothing out of the ordinary,' said Cam as they watched on. 'They missed a sample at one location due to an Xtract malfunctioning. All their logs are in order though. I will head off and collate the report.'

He walked off and for a time Max and Alex stood in silence watching the horizon out through the bay doors and the wake of the vessel astern of the well deck.

Their contemplation was interrupted by a message over comms.

'Alex and Max are requested to come to the SAI console for an external communication.'

'Let's go,' said Max. 'I wonder what that could be about.'

They walked off.

Entering the stairwell at the rear of the well deck they climbed the stairs. They came out in the drone bay and took another set of stairs to the operations centre above. From there they moved forward, walking past monitoring and control stations. They reached the bridge SAI console. The outer shields were retracted, and the duty officer was at the SAI console in the centre monitoring a navigation hologram.

'SAI, acknowledge external communication request and open message board,' said Max.

An image of Rick appeared on one of the console displays.

'Rick, what can we do for you?' said Max. 'We were just talking about you.'

'Things are moving again,' said Rick. 'On the upcoming crew change, Ngarra's crew will take over on the same Skimmer they used last time. They will carry out normal mining runs. But they are going to test the technology again.'

'Is the mission still the same?' said Alex. 'I mean, to secure the technology.'

'Yes, said Rick. 'But GlobeCorpMining will be poking their nose around. Chang's sister Ying Yue is working in that lab on the Harvester on both Skimmers and Xtracts. Something is going on. I'm not sure if Chang's father is even aware of it. I need you to monitor Ngarra's Skimmer and be in the vicinity of the Harvester when they are on it between mining runs.'

'We can come and go from the Harvester as we please,' said Max. 'No issue there. But getting hold of this technology will be tricky unless we have an excuse to do so under our mandate.'

'Be careful,' said Rick. 'Watch your backs around that Harvester and make sure you are always seen to be doing the right thing. I will be in touch with further details as they arise.'

With that, his image disappeared and Max and Alex stood silent for a moment.

'It seems things are back in play,' said Alex.

'Indeed,' said Max as they turned away from the SAI console and looked out over the ocean. 'Tomorrow we will head back towards the Harvester and carry out some inspections of Skimmers. For now, I want to head to that location in "the Area" where we have had a spate of piracy.'

It had been a long day, so Alex and Max left the duty officer to it and walked off to get something to eat and get some rest.

***

The following morning and not far from the Sea Hunter unit a skimmer was in position carrying out mining operations. Its communication streamer was deployed and Xtracts were coming and going from the depths below. They were halfway through loading the nodule trays along each side of the Skimmer.

The pilot was watching from the SAI console. The outer hull shields were retracted. The operator came in to catch up with him. Standing beside him they both watched.

'Proximity alert,' said SAI. 'Unidentified sub surface vessel approaching.'

They both jumped in surprise at the announcement.

'Shit,' said the operator.

The security and communications officer came running in.

'Piracy,' he said. 'Damn it. Nothing we can do except let them take what they want. SAI, confirm crew are at their workstations then close all watertight bulkheads.'

'Confirmed,' said SAI. 'Crew are at stations. Bulkheads are being closed and made watertight.'

'SAI send emergency assist request to Sea Hunter unit. Piracy incident underway.'

'Confirmed,' said SAI. 'Request sent.'

They watched as a diesel electric sub approached through the blue green void. It had two drones attached to it and the missile silos were open topside. It would deploy its drones to pick up nodules from their trays and drop them in the silos. Standard practice was to line the missile silos with a removable mesh funnel.

'Nothing we can do,' said the operator. 'As long as we do nothing, they will do nothing, take what they want and go. Damn it though! We will lose a good portion of our load to them!'

The watched on. All they could do was hope the Sea Hunters were near enough to catch them in the act and apprehend them.

Chapter 6

On the Sea Hunter vessel Alex and Max were in the mess having breakfast with the rest of the crew not on duty. Overnight three were on watch, one monitored navigation and communications, another engineering and the third oversaw operation of the two drone vessels accompanying them. All watches were standing watches, so time slots were fixed. Since most systems were monitored and controlled by SAI there was little to do unless they were operational.

'Good morning, folks,' said Cam as he walked into the mess for breakfast.

Max leaned back in his chair and looked Cam up and down, smiling and winking at Alex. Being the chief boarding officer, everyone looked up to him.

'Rough night was it,' he said.

'What do you mean?' said Cam.

The others in the mess started chuckling as Cam looked himself over and tried to figure out what they were all looking at.

'Missing your mum dressing you are we, Cam?' said Alex as he looked across at Max.

'Damn it!' said Cam as he whipped off his shirt and turned it in the right way. There was a shout and a few woof whistles amongst a chorus of laughter. Cam was a solid man with brutish looks.

'You lot had better watch your backs,' said Cam laughing and pointing his finger at his crewmates at another table. He raced over and messed up their hair, girls and guys alike as he went around the table hassling them all.

'Classic,' said Alex as he watched their antics.

'Indeed,' said Max.

They all continued eating and talking. For a moment, the atmosphere was relaxed. However, the light mood was soon disturbed by an announcement from SAI.

'Emergency Skimmer communication. Emergency Skimmer communication. Piracy incident underway. Assistance requested.'

'Damn it,' said Max as everyone jumped up. 'Right you lot know what to do, get to your stations. Arm our ARC array and torpedoes on all vessels, prepare an interceptor drone for deployment. Cam prepare a boarding team. And get a patrol drone in the air!'

Everyone raced off.

Max and Alex headed to operations.

A Sea Hunter unit, the main vessel and its two drone vessels, was largely autonomous. If a piracy incident was detected a lot of automated systems came online. The crew would run cross checks and make sure everything they needed was ready to go.

Max and Alex moved quickly through to operations. The full team were already there. It consisted of a duty operations officer, an ARC defensive array systems operator, an asset deployment coordinator and a communications and security officer.

The duty watchkeeper at the bridge SAI console looked after navigation and hunter unit safety.

'What's the situation?' said Alex.

'Distress signal from a skimmer ten miles northeast of us,' said the duty operations officer.

'Duty watchkeeper set course northeast and close Skimmer,' said Alex over comms to the SAI console. 'Maximum speed.'

'Confirmed,' said the duty watchkeeper as they got SAI to alter course.

SAI altered the Sea Hunter unit course and they picked up speed. They had been cruising at fifteen knots.

The operations team took up their positions. The SAI console duty officer carried on monitoring hunter unit navigation and safety.

'Listen up,' said Max to everyone as he stepped back and took everything in. 'Deploy an unmanned interceptor drone and close pirate sub and disable it.'

'Confirmed,' said one of the operations team. 'Deploy unmanned interceptor drone and disable pirate sub.'

'Launch unmanned patrol drone and circle location of Skimmer,' said Max.

He carried on issuing commands.

The duty team communicated with the vessel SAI and set in motion the automated launch sequences to deploy Sea Hunter unit assets. The asset controller worked with vessel SAI and communicated with both the drone deck and well deck personnel.

The operations team and duty watchkeeper at the SAI console team activated their displays. The ARC defensive systems array coordinator put on their interface lenses and worked with both the SAI console and operations.

In the drone bay and the well deck crew monitored the automated deployment sequence of both the unmanned patrol drone and the interceptor drone.

In the drone bay, a docking clamp activated and moved a patrol drone out onto the drone deck. The patrol drone's cowlings rotated outwards and the rotors spun up. Technicians in the drone bay control room monitored its deployment.

The docking clamp stopped in position and released the patrol drone. It rose and moved sideways across the deck into the head wind created by the ship. Once over the water it angled forward, moving slowly out and away from the ship.

Below in the well deck the bay doors opened. A docking clamp hanging from the bulkhead above moved an interceptor drone out over the water. Technicians monitored its deployment.

The docking clamp stopped and lowered the interceptor into the water. Its propulsion system powered up, the clamp released it and it moved out and away from the ship, disappearing the below the surface as it did. It slipped away heading towards the Skimmer in distress.

Meanwhile to the rear of the well deck Cam had assembled a small boarding party ready to apprehend the pirates. Success depended on being able to disable and force the sub to the surface so they could board it.

His team walked to one side of the well deck. A ridged hull inflatable was mounted at the top of a slipway. His crew got it ready for deployment. Cam briefed them.

Back at operations Max and Alex received confirmation from the control rooms in the drone bay and well deck and from the SAI console that everything was ready.

'Assets in play,' said one of the operations team. 'SAI has control, monitoring operation ringfence.'

Operation ringfence was a standard practice when dealing with piracy beneath the waves.

'Camera systems of assets in play activated,' said another team member. 'First person view on screen now.'

Displays around operations showed in first person view the status of each asset and real time images of their movements.

From the interceptor drone, they watched and waited.

A short time later it was on final approach. As it closed, they could see the Skimmer slowly come into view.

Looming in front of the Skimmer the operations team could see a modified diesel electric sub. Its two drones were being used to pick up nodules and tip them into the empty missile silos.

The Skimmer crew were helpless. With being tethered to the communication streamer in the middle of a mining operation, there was nothing they could do. To stay safe the standard protocol was to let the pirates take what they wanted.

A skimmer SAI would not allow crews to put their lives and the Skimmer at risk responding to a piracy incident during a mining operation.

'SAI,' said Max. 'Confirm hunter unit drone vessels are in position and track pirate sub movement.' 'Confirmed,' said SAI. 'Drone vessels are moving into position.'

The operations team worked with the Hunter unit SAI to monitor and execute commands. 'Great timing,' said Alex. 'First time we have caught them in the middle of a heist for a while.'

'They're not getting away this time,' said Max folding his arms and sitting in his command chair to take it all in.

They all watched the interceptor drone camera feed as it closed the pirate sub. Its two drones were now reattached to its hull. It had identified their approach and was starting to move away and make a run for it.

'Too late,' said Max with a wicked smile. 'Not this time.'

'SAI, close pirate sub. Confirm deployment of ARC array from interceptor drone at pirate sub propulsion system,' said Max.

'Confirmed,' said SAI. 'ARC array powering up and activating. Target locked.'

The interreceptor drone was within range. Angling outwards at close quarters its ARC array was deployed. A cavitation bubble was triangulated at the subs propulsion system.

'Damn,' said Max. 'Not a direct hit.'

'SAI deploy Hunter unit drone vessel ARC array. Target sub propulsion system.'

The Hunter unit drone vessels could deploy their ARC arrays from much further away.

'Confirmed,' said SAI. 'Hunter unit drone vessels tracking pirate sub. ARC array online. Target locked.'

The operations team monitored SAI as it locked a drone vessel ARC array onto the pirate sub.

'Hunter drone vessels have powered up their ARC arrays,' said one of the operations team.

Max nodded his head.

The pirate sub was trying to make a run for it between the two Hunter drone vessels.

It did not have a chance this time. It tried to slip past at 100 metres below sea level.

Two cavitation bubbles were triangulated at the sub's propulsion from the hulls of the Hunter drone vessels.

Max, Alex and the operations team watched through the interreceptor drone camera system. A slight delay was apparent as the laser communication signal transmitted the images.

A violent shudder interrupted the pirate sub propulsion. It stopped dead in the water. The sub started ascending.

'Yes!' said Max as he slammed his hand against the bulkhead. 'You're not getting away this time!'

The operations team let out a shout.

Often, they were too far way to get there in time. The pirates would get away with a load of nodules.

'Let's get this finished,' said Alex.

He contacted the well deck over comms.

'Cam deploy, board, apprehend and return sub crew to us.'

'Roger that,' said Cam in reply.

A moment later through the camera system they watched as a ridged hull inflatable could be seen moving out from the well deck. It sped up and moved alongside the ship, level with the SAI console.

Alex left operations and walked out onto an observation wing and gave them the okay signal. The sea boat moved off ahead, towards the circling Hunter drone vessels. Between them would be where the sub would surface.

'Duty watch keeper get SAI to come to a full stop,' said Alex over comms to the SAI console. It was a flat calm day so there was no need to be underway and the threat had been neutralised. 'SAI, drone vessels to close surfaced sub and come to full stop. Hold positions alongside surfaced pirate sub.'

'Confirmed,' said SAI. 'Drone vessels closing. Come to full stop and hold position alongside surfaced pirate sub.'

The duty operations team monitored SAIs control of deployed assets.

As they slowed down Max and Alex left and went to the SAI console. With the outer shields retracted, they had a good view.

The pirate sub surfaced.

After a short time, its crew climbed out onto the hull. They were now resigned to the fact that they had been caught. The unmanned patrol drone was hovering above them. The two hunter unit drone vessels had closed on either side and come to a full stop. Cams ridged hull inflatable had come up alongside the sub. His boarding party jumped onto it.

They watched on from the SAI console as his team rounded up the pirates.

Alex contacted the Skimmer crew and explained the situation.

He told them they had managed to apprehend the pirates and their sub. He explained to them that they had a crane that could lift the missile silo lining containing the nodules out. They would remove the nodules and return them to the Harvester and scuttle the sub. The pirate crew would be taken to the Harvester. They would be flown ashore by a transport drone to be dealt with by State sponsor authorities.

'SAI,' said Max while Alex was talking with the Skimmer crew. 'Recover all assets and set perimeter patrol for drone vessels.'

'Confirmed,' said SAI. 'Recover assists in play and set drone vessel perimeter patrol.'

In operations, the team worked with SAI and monitored recovery of deployed assets.

Through the camera systems at both operations and the SAI console everyone watched the interceptor drone and patrol drone make their way back to the ship.

Cams team and the apprehended pirates also made their way back in the sea boat, the ridged hull inflatable.

'Right team,' said Max over comms. 'Once we have our assets out of play move alongside that sub, secure it and offload the nodules then stand off and scuttle it.'

Everyone waited and monitored the situation while SAI recovered the assets in play.

The patrol drone flew up alongside the drone deck. It moved across and a docking clamp secured it in place. It powered down as it was lowered into place. The docking clamp then moved the patrol drone into the drone bay.

On the well deck below, the interceptor drone surfaced. A docking clamp arm lowered and secured it. The interceptor drone was lifted out of the water, moved to the well deck and secured in place.

Lastly, Cam arrived back at the well deck with the pirate crew. They were taken to the brig until they reached the Harvester.

At the SAI console, the duty watchkeeper worked with SAI and moved the vessel into position alongside the pirate sub. A crane forward of the drone deck was activated, and its arm extended out over the sub.

Two technicians had lowered themselves onto its hull and guided the cable and strops into place to pull out the lining filled with nodules in the missile silos.

The sleeves lining the missile silos were lifted out one by one. They were laid down along either side of the drone deck and secured in place.

While this was happening, Cam made his way to the SAI console to see Max and Alex.

'Well folks,' he said entering the SAI console. 'Our pirate crew is secure. Let's have some fun sinking this sub of theirs.'

'Too right,' said Max.

They moved out onto the SAI console bridge wing and watched the crane finish offloading the nodules.

'SAI, standoff sub, distance two hundred metres,' said Max once the crane had finished offloading the nodules and his crew were back on board.'

'Confirmed,' said SAI. 'Moving into position at two hundred metres distance from sub.'

The duty watchkeeper used his hand to pot a course on the navigation display that SAI would follow.

They got underway and moved into position.

'SAI deploy a percussion torpedo from each drone vessel and scuttle pirate sub,' said Max.

'Confirmed,' said SAI. 'Torpedoes deployed.'

The others watched as the two drone vessels targeted the sub with a torpedo. It had been some time since they had managed to catch one of the subs carrying out piracy in the region. It was satisfying to watch.

By the time operation ringfence was completed, the day had gone and the ship's crew were exhausted. Alex got them all together for a debrief.

Chapter 7

Ngarra and Chang were in the sim centre at the Skimmer crew monitoring and communications complex when the piracy incident occurred. An emergency communication request had come from a skimmer. A duty officer had pulled up the crew vitals display. They were spiking all over the place.

'Incoming laser communication signal,' said SAI. 'Grid buoy and Eel drone proximity is nominal, live feed available.'

'Open message board,' said the duty officer.

Ngarra and Chang came over to the workstation to see what was going on. They had each been overseeing a separate section of "the Area" where crews were currently on Skimmers and engaged in mining operations.

The Skimmer communications and security officer appeared on screen. He looked worried.

'We have a piracy incident underway,' he said. 'A pirate sub has found us and deployed its two drones. They are off-taking our load of nodules. We are following protocol. We have requested Sea Hunter assistance, halted mining operations and are monitoring the situation. Skimmer is at emergency stations and we are closed up.'

'Okay,' said Ngarra. 'SAI, request Jonah and Rick to come to the crew monitoring and communication complex. Piracy incident underway.'

'Confirmed,' said SAI.

'Ngarra,' said another duty officer. 'Communication request from the Sea Hunters.'

'Put it through,' he said.

Meanwhile the Xed Ocean Academy Sea Hunter liaison officer had been notified and arrived. He raced down the stairs and over to the workstation where the others were.

Ngarra transferred monitoring of the Skimmer and its crew to the large main display at the front of the complex. They were all now looking up at it.

'What's going on?' he said. 'I got a message from the Sea Hunters that they were responding to a piracy incident.'

'Correct,' said Ngarra. 'They are not on scene yet but will be shortly. We are communicating with the Skimmer crew. They are following protocol.'

At that moment, Jonah and Rick also came in, down the stairs from the enclosed mezzanine and over to the workstation. They both looked up and across at the main display.

'The Sea Hunters will be there soon,' said the liaison officer as they all looked at the crew vitals. 'We may be able to apprehend them this time. Usually, they are too far away to get there in time. They will follow standard operating procedures and deploy an interceptor to pursue and disable it. They will use the two drone vessels to surround it. ARC defensive arrays will target the pirate sub. A patrol drone will monitor from above the water. Once the sub surfaces a boarding party will apprehend the crew.'

'Sit tight,' said Rick to the Skimmer communication and security officer.

They were still on screen. Behind him another crewmember could be seen at the SAI console.

It wasn't uncommon for piracy to occur in "the Area" and loads to be stolen but Jonah was worried, nonetheless.

'We haven't had an opportunity to apprehend these people for a while,' said the Sea Hunter liaison officer.

'What if this sub and its crew get nervous and do something stupid?' said Jonah. 'It could endanger our Skimmer crew.'

'As long as they sit tight,' said the Sea Hunter liaison officer, 'they will be fine. The sub is not going to ram them or use its drones to do anything dangerous. All they want is the load of nodules and to get out of there.'

'Sit tight,' said Rick again to the communication and security officer on screen. 'The Sea Hunters are not far away this time. Do not do anything.'

'Roger that,' was the reply.

The liaison officer asked the duty officer to contact the Sea Hunter unit. The duty officer opened a message board and established comms for him. He sat down at the monitoring station and put a head set on.

'Not a lot we can do here,' said Chang. 'They're sitting in a tin can waiting for it all to pass and the Sea hunters will handle the rest. I'm going to check in on the other crews operating in that part of "the Area",' he said as he walked away.

'Good idea,' said Rick. 'Make sure they are aware of the situation and reiterate that they are not to respond or get involved and to stick to mining protocols.'

As he walked off Chang's smart watch activated. He looked at it and saw a message for him. It was marked urgent. The others were engrossed in the piracy incident.

Chang walked over to another work station. He talked briefly with a duty officer before stepping back and opening the message on his smart watch.

'How is your sister
When will you see her?
Never if you don't get hold of the technology
Wait to hear when and where
See you at sea'

Chang closed the message and looked up. Was it anyone here? Who was sending him these messages? It was happening again.

He was upset and angry.

He knew at some point it would all happen again. He walked back over to where the others were monitoring the piracy incident at sea.

Rick looked at him and wondered why he had come back so quickly.

'Not a lot you can do is there,' said Chang. 'If Skimmers didn't have crews, it wouldn't even matter. That Harvester is just an excuse to hide the fact that they want to automate everything and vacuum up the ocean floor.'

'What's up with you?' said Ngarra. 'Back to your usual grumpy self ay.'

'What's it to you anyway!' he said angrily. 'You got us into the mess we were in last time!'

'You didn't help the situation did you boy!' said Ngarra.

Ngarra was not one to have outbursts but Chang's accusations in the middle of an emergency triggered him.

'I'm not your boy!' said Chang as he barged past Ngarra and shoved him hard in the shoulder.

Ngarra grabbed him by the arm. Chang spun around and grabbed is shirt with his fist and pushed it up under his chin.

'Chang, cut it out,' said Rick as he jumped in. 'Get out of here now Chang. Go and get some fresh air!'

Chang walked off waving his hand at them dismissively.

'Whatever,' he said.

'I'll go and talk to him,' said Jonah. 'Something must be up. He hasn't been this angry in a while.'

Jonah took off after him.

Ngarra shrugged his shoulders and straightened his shirt.

The previous incident over six months ago on the Skimmer had shaken Ngarra's crew. Chang had been threatened about his sister then to. It turned out he had been asked to steal the technology Connor was working on. Ngarra's crew caught him doing it.

'I thought we had moved on from all this,' said Jonah to herself as she went after Chang.

Chang had raced up the stairs to the mezzanine. It was enclosed with soundproof glass.

'Chang what's going on,' she said catching up with him before he left.

'Nothing!' he said fiercely as he walked towards the entrance to pass through security.

'Rubbish,' said Jonah. 'Stop, listen. Whatever it is it must be bad. You haven't been like this for a while.'

Chang paused and turned around. He looked out over the floor below, across at the workstations and up at the main screen.

'I'm sick of being stuck here,' he said. 'We have been ashore for ages. I can't wait to get back out there, that's all.'

'Funny coming from you,' said Jonah. 'Last time you did nothing but moan about being stuck inside a skimmer.'

'Yeah well, shit happens,' he said. 'You don't have the family I do and between my father, my sister and my mother's situation how would you feel.'

Chang banged the toughened glass with his fist. A security guard at the entrance looked over and then at Jonah. She motioned to him that it was okay.

'Your crew is heading back out soon,' said Jonah calmly. 'You will be able to catch up with your sister on the Harvester between mining runs. I can even ask your father to make sure that it happens.'

'Yeah, well what would my father care anyway. He's the one that got my mother into the situation she is in now.'

'You never did tell us what that was,' said Jonah.

'It doesn't matter,' said Chang. 'I'm fine now. I just need some air.

Chang walked towards security and out through the entrance. He went off to find Connor and talk about his research. That would at least distract him for a while.

Jonah watched on and decided to talk with him some more later. Perhaps being back on a skimmer would help. She went back down to the stairs and across to the workstation to see how the others were going monitoring the piracy incident.

'The Sea Hunters are on scene,' said the liaison officer as Jonah got back.

They looked up at the main screen. The Skimmer crew vitals were still spiking, which meant they were anxious. The grid buoy and Eel drone proximity was nominal. It meant they had a live video feed from the Skimmer rather than recorded video or audio messages. An external camera feed from the Skimmer showed some detail.

'The subs drones are docking,' said Rick. 'I hope they don't get away.'

'Interceptor drone is on scene,' said the liaison officer.

They watched as the sub started to move off. It disappeared.

The duty officer checked in with the Skimmer crew.

'Skimmer crew is fine,' he said. 'They have stood down from emergency stations and will continue mining operations.'

'Right,' said Rick to the Sea Hunter liaison officer. 'Let's hope your guys get this sub and take another illegal operation out of the grid.'

They all waited patiently as the liaison officer communicated with the Sea Hunters. He gave them updates on the pursuit and what was going on. Finally, he confirmed that the sub had been disabled, had surfaced and the crew apprehended by a boarding team. There were some congratulations passed around and hands shock.

***

While the piracy incident had been going on Connor was at the research centre. Connor was not one for reading people's emotions very well. In some way, perhaps that was why his work was so important to him. He was trying to give a group of Xtracts a mind of their own; one he could interface with.

Over the last few weeks, he had become frustrated with the ocean bubble hologram he had got SAI to construct over six months ago. He was stuck with a group of Xtracts that just stored every response they made to a simulated task interruption in the mesh. No matter what he got SAI to try, he just couldn't get the Xtracts in the mining simulation to autonomously learn group behaviour.

The lab he was in looked a bit like the information hub on a skimmer but bigger. In the middle was his ocean bubble hologram. He walked around it talking out loud. SAI would pick up on key words and phrases and search code script libraries and databases for information on what Connor was talking about.

The advent of natural language processing had made it much easier to interface with AI technology. The key was being able to design system architecture that enabled SAI through natural language processing to construct what was needed. He didn't need to be an expert coder.

Around the lab were workstations displaying scripts of code and streaming data related to what Connor was talking about. SAI was running algorithms and projecting data analytics on results from trialling autonomous group behaviour in the Xtracts in the Ocean bubble hologram.

'It's so frustrating,' said Connor as he walked over to the hologram. 'Why is it that any simulation starts off okay and then breaks down. They just don't learn from multiple iterations of various scenarios. Something isn't right with this mesh. It's meant to be their brain; the mesh allows them to operate as individuals while also allowing any one of them to link with all others. Like a collective, but there is no link with stored experience or memory from which to learn by themselves and develop group behaviour responses. Something is missing.'

He looked around the lab. A couple of technicians were working with code scripts and data streams SAI had found. Connor walked over and looked at one that had come up and been put aside by the technician.

It was nothing spectacular, just a series of comparable data on competitive behaviour responses between species. It was cross-referenced against development of autonomous technology in drones. There wasn't much to look at.

Pre-determined or coded group patterning in drones was common. But few if any people in the world had gone beyond that to successfully develop independently learned autonomous group behaviour responses to interruptions.

Connor continued looking at the data that had been put aside.

'This data on competitive behaviour responses between species looks different than the others we have been using,' he said to the technician.

Connor had previously looked at group behaviour patterning in ants, flocks of birds, schooling fish and even regenerative properties and the non-centralised nervous systems in starfish. He had used all that data on behaviour patterning to get SAI to construct a set of layered algorithms to simulate analogous group behaviour by the Xtracts.

He would introduce a simulation into the hologram of Xtracts carrying out a mining operation and watch how they responded. They would adopt responses like those seen in nature by the organisms he had been researching. But over multiple iterations containing countless variations there was no learning or adaption of responses retained in the mesh. The simulations would fall apart. The Xtracts would wonder off randomly and not return to mining.

'It's data and algorithms from an old project,' said the technician. 'One where they tried to get one AI to compete with another AI and continuously try to optimise access to a resource; a game to win. They used data and algorithms that distinguished changes in group behaviour patterns between two species competing for a resource.'

'So not just one species then,' said Connor. 'But two different species.'

'Yeah,' said the technician. 'I got SAI to put it to one side for you.'

'SAI,' said Connor. 'Run the algorithms for this historical data.'

'Confirmed,' said SAI. 'Running algorithms and projecting output.'

They all watched. It was a script with a set of layered algorithms that distinguished the different ways each species responded to changes in its environment; trying to out compete each other to survive and gain the upper hand. A game of sorts.

'Maybe we have it all wrong,' said Connor. 'Instead of working with group behaviour patterning in one species and trying to get SAI to train the Xtracts to use that and learn by themselves maybe we need to look at two species simultaneously competing against each other for a resource. We force the AI for the ocean bubble hologram into thinking that the Xtracts represent two different groups.'

Connor thought for a few minutes then carried on talking out loud.

'So, it becomes an evolutionary game. Each time one side gets a slight advantage that's a generation. Each group of Xtracts wants more nodules because it means they get more energy in return from the Skimmer, which means they can collect more nodules for longer. The competition resets after each iteration.'

Connor paused again and looked at the streams of data, scripts and information SAI was displaying.

'Statistically, it's like maximum likelihoods, or logs of them in a softmax algorithm stack. Being loosely framed, it is probabilistic in nature. I think we are onto something here.'

Chapter 8

The next morning before heading out to the Harvester on a transport drone, all the crews were at a short briefing in the auditorium. They would then collect their belongings and head to the transport drone port. Ngarra's crew were sitting near the front.

'Finally,' said Jonny. 'Back in the saddle after a stint here. It's hard being so popular that you have to be sidelined until things calm down.'

'Yeah, the food hall will go out of business once you're gone little fatty.'

'Hey, that's harsh girl,' said Jonny. 'I'm not little. That seat wide enough for you?'

Everyone laughed.

Typical, Jonny and Stella were always hassling each other. Jonny, being the solid and tall Tongan Maori, he was and Stella the loud and outgoing Australian woman.

Both were very talented.

'Cut it out you two,' said Jesse as some of the academy leadership team stepped forward with Rick and Jonah.

'Right,' said Rick as he signalled and paused for them to be quiet. 'You've all been allocated to Skimmers and will swap out with their crews on arrival at the Harvester. We had a recent piracy incident. The Skimmer crew followed protocol and are fine. I reiterate, if you are the target of a piracy incident do not react or respond and escalate the situation. Besides, your SAI will not allow you to compromise the safety of yourselves or the Skimmer. Communications and Security officers are not to override mining protocols and go off grid unless an act of aggression occurs. Also, overdrive trials are not to be conducted without prior approval. If procedures are not followed correctly it results in overspeed on the rim driven propulsion system power train. Overdrive trials still require approval. Is that clear?'

Everyone responded with an enthusiastic 'yes sir.'

'How exactly does it work anyway?' said Jonny.

'Yeah, how exactly does it work?' said Stella. 'From the rec area you can walk around that esplanade either side of it to the forward viewing area. It extends from in front of the Xtract bay below to the SAI console above.'

'Shh,' whispered Jesse. 'Later, not now. I'll go over what I know with you lot and we can discuss it in more detail.'

Jonah looked at Rick and then she stepped forward to say a few things. Everyone quietened down again. She looked across at Ngarra's crew and smiled. Her hope was that Connor would make a real breakthrough trialling his technology at sea again on one of their mining runs.

'Our monitoring centre does a good job looking over and giving feedback on your vitals and your wellbeing. As I said at the last briefing, I have had reports of a few attitude issues at sea, and even some scuffles between crewmembers. That has been dealt with. Remember you are constantly being monitored so I don't want any more reports coming back on a lack of respect for other crew members.'

The leadership team turned to have a brief conversation amongst themselves. The crews started chatting.

'Guys,' said Connor. He was itching to say something. 'I've got a name for the technology, the mesh and ocean bubble hologram.'

He had been thinking lately what to call this technology of his. It had come to him late the night before. He was up late and couldn't sleep.

'Gilgamesh,' said Connor.

'Gilga what?' said Ngarra.

'You know,' said Connor. 'Heard of Gilgamesh?'

'Epic,' said Jonny. 'I have heard of that legend. The secret to life is death. An odd name to choose though.'

'I thought it was great,' said Connor.

'Connor,' said Jesse interrupting. 'Do you have everything you need to transfer your technology back to the information hub on the Skimmer,' said Jesse.

'Yes,' said Connor. 'I will load the source code for the ocean bubble hologram. All the additional work done will be loaded so SAI can carry on with our work. It's not a piece of self-contained hardware yet. It's going to be great. I think I have come across something that may overcome the memory problem with the mesh, or should I say Gilgamesh now,' he said smiling. 'That's why I called it Gilgamesh. Calling it the mesh is boring. We can get around the inability of the Xtracts to learn as a group.'

Connor was about to launch into what he was going to do but Chang interrupted him.

'Not again, Connor,' said Chang dismissively. 'It didn't work last time so what makes you think you will crack it now?'

Of course, Chang was very keen to learn more about what Connor was up to but for very different reasons to everyone else. He was still angry about the little message he had received. He would have to wait for an opportunity. They did say he would be told when to try to get hold of it and what to do.

'Okay, okay everyone, listen up,' said Rick as they quietened down. 'I want all crews at the transport drone port ready to depart at 1400 hours this afternoon. Off you go and Ngarra,' he said quickly, 'your crew stay behind briefly.'

The others got up and walked out of the briefing. They all headed off to get their belongings sorted ready to depart.

'I want you to be careful on that Harvester,' said Rick as he and Jonah walked over to them. 'Once you are away from it and on the Skimmer, it won't matter so much. Connor you need to get these trials of the technology completed. I am almost tempted to give you two security officers. However, that would look unusual and attract unwanted attention on the Harvester.'

'Yes, let's not draw attention to ourselves,' said Jonah. 'They know we are up to something. Connor, I want you to stay on the Skimmer. Don't go to the accommodation level on the Harvester between mining runs.'

'It is unlikely they will attempt to take the technology overtly and cause an international incident,' said Rick. 'It's more likely to be subtle and done under another excuse so be careful.'

'We'll be fine,' said Ngarra. 'Stop scaring my crew.' He avoided direct eye contact but knew they were all looking at him. That was his culture though, being indigenous Australian.

'This is serious,' said Jonah as she looked at them all intensely. 'Connor is onto something that has sparked a lot of interest. We still haven't figured out exactly why. I can't afford him or the technology to fall into the wrong hands. It could end everything we have built up around what you see here and you lot would be out of a job.'

'Not if I have anything to do with it,' said Jonny as he made one of his warrior faces.

'It's Gilgamesh,' blurted Connor. 'It's called Gilgamesh now.'

'How appropriate,' said Jonah. 'The Epic of Gilgamesh. Better than "the mesh", I suppose.'

The others had a chuckle, and everyone couldn't help but smile.

'I don't think any of it is funny,' said Connor. 'It's my work they want.'

'Where's Aamir?' said Stella. 'We haven't seen him much since coming ashore.'

'He will not be coming on this rotation with you,' said Rick.

Jonah jumped in before Rick could say anything else.

'Aamir is doing something for us here for a while. He may join your crew later.'

'But,' said Ngarra as he tried to ask why.

'Don't worry about why or what,' said Jonah. 'You just focus on helping Connor out there during mining operations. Off you go, and get ready for departure.'

Ngarra's crew said their goodbyes to Rick and Jonah and walked out. They headed off to the accommodation block to sort out their belongings before going to the transport drone port.

***

Back at their accommodation they packed what they needed for a month rotation on the Skimmers.

The accommodation complex was near the main administration building. Being elevated it overlooked the entire Xed and Ocean Academy campus and adjacent coastline. It was a series of interconnecting serviced villas. Leading to the beach below were a series of pathways.

'I'm going to miss my beach time,' said Stella walking through the common area for their villa and stepping outside.

Looking across and below them she could see other crews in their villas getting ready to depart. Most crewmembers were young and single or had a relationship with members of other crews. A few had young families, but they were slightly older and usually Security and Communications Officers. They were in separate villas.

'We all will,' said Jonny walking outside as well.

They all gathered outside for a while before heading off to the transport drone port in a driverless campus taxi. Everyone had finished getting their belongings together.

'What was all that about, Aamir?' said Chang.

'He hasn't stayed with us since we got back,' said Jesse. 'I guess he has another assignment.'

'We've hardly seen him,' said Connor.

'Well, whatever he is up to I am sure we will hear about it sooner or later,' said Jesse. 'Let's just focus on getting back on our Skimmer and completing those trials of the technology and our month mining rotation.

'Yeah,' said Jonny. 'But usually, communication and security officers do a number of years in the role before leaving the Skimmer program and moving on.'

'I will ask Jonah about Aamir at some point,' said Jesse. 'It can't be that big a secret surely.'

'Maybe,' said Ngarra. 'Anyway, let's head off to the drone port. The driverless taxi I booked is waiting outside.'

'I like the trip out on the transport drone,' said Connor. 'It's great travelling low over the water into an endless horizon of ocean. Gives me a chance to think about Gilgamesh some more.'

The others smiled at the name.

They walked back inside and grabbed their bags from the common area and headed out the front to the driveway. The taxi was waiting, and they loaded it and hopped in.

It moved off taking them to the transport drone port. It was a short distance from the accommodation, at the edge of the campus and adjacent to the coast. It was not far from the beach they frequented below the villas. On the beach crews would watch transport drones coming and going. It was quite a sight to see as they came in low to land.

As they drove through the narrow lanes connecting the Villa's the crew watched quietly out the windows. The driverless taxi turned onto the main concourse and proceeded to the transport drone port.

It wasn't long before they rounded the final bend and it into came into view. Three black transport drones were glistening in the early afternoon sun.

The driverless taxi arrived at the drop-off point and they all got out. They gathered their belongings and walked over to where the other crews had gathered.

They were all waiting to board one of the three transport drones. Everyone was early so they still had a bit of time before boarding through the stern ramp between the two rear blade cowlings above.

'How different is this compared to previous decades,' said Stella as they were standing around. 'Think about it, high school now only goes to year ten unless you are going to university. The rest of us enter learning academies funded by various industry organisations. The focus is on skills you need to work with technology in various roles. Look at Xed and the Academy, a world of robotics, drones and automation. Schools had a lot of catching up to do back in the 2020s.'

'Many didn't see what was coming though, did they?' said Ngarra.'

'And here we are,' said Jonny. 'Times have changed. We are the lucky ones. The 2020s saw a lot of unemployed people leaving high school without the skills to work in this new world. Education failed them.'

'It was worse for the Grey nomads,' said Jesse. 'Many could not retrain and retired very early. So much technology and so reliant on it now. The greys back then found themselves left behind. Perhaps integration with machines is an evolutionary dead end. Trying to get what you had back is not easy.'

They talked some more about how the world had changed so quickly; how education had been forced to change from pumping out students; forced to change from ticking the boxes in a broken system.

A security officer came over to where they had all assembled. He told them all to start boarding.

'Here we go girls and boys,' said Jonny.

Three crews per transport drone boarded, making nine crews of six people in all. Fifty-four to swap out on board the Harvester.

They picked up their bags and joined the queue walking up the stern ramp of one. They placed their bags for the technician to secure. Up the front two drone operators were doing pre-flight checks. They had their AI interface lenses on. Most of the process was automated unless they decided to take manual control.

'Love this part,' said Stella excitedly.

The other crews looked at her and agreed.

'She's got special needs,' said Jonny laughing and looking at everyone else.

'I'll put you back on your leash boy,' said Stella as she gave him a kick while he was strapping in.

Everyone laughed.

The transport drone powered up. The blades spun up and the stern ramp closed. Once the ramp was secured, they took off. Hovering, the transport drone tilted forward slightly and flew out over the adjacent coastline. Everyone looked outside at the beach below. A few were on the beach and looked up and waved as they left.

'I'll miss my beach,' said Stella. 'We had a long rotation ashore this time.'

The three transport drones flew out low over the ocean and into the distant horizon. They settled in for the flight out to the Harvester.

***

The flight had been uneventful and Ngarra's crew had either chatted amongst themselves or caught up with people they knew in other crews. Some of them had been up and about. There was a small canteen and ablutions forward and behind the operators.

'Attention Skimmer crews,' said one of the operators. 'We are fifteen minutes out. Take your seats and strap in.'

'Okay,' said Jonny as he seated himself and strapped in. 'About time. The hospitality on here is average. I mean look at the menu. Where's management?'

Others laughed at his antics. Typical Jonny, everything was about how good the food was.

'You lot should come to New Zealand and try some of our Kai,' he said. 'Ever had a hangi?'

He had to explain that kai was the Maori word for food, and hangi was like a BBQ in the ground.

Chang wasn't really listening to his antics. He was watching Connor talking to himself about his work. Chang thought about the message he had received, his sister, his father and his mother's situation.

'Round two,' he said out loud.

'What was that?' said Ngarra.

'Oh, nothing,' said Chang.

'Guys, this is it,' said Stella. 'We're back in black and ready to mine.'

'How eighties of you,' said Jonny laughing.

'What do you mean?' said Chang.

'The band,' said Jesse. 'ACDC I think.'

'Yep,' said Stella smiling.

'Here we go,' said Ngarra looking out over the water.

They sat back as the transport drones approached the Harvester drone deck. They flew in low over the side of it and reared up. Hovering over the docking clamp, it grabbed and secured them, lowering the transport drone into place. As the drone powered down, they looked out. A security detail was waiting for them. The hex tower was raised. Out on the observation deck two figures were watching.

'I am guessing that's Lee and Sue,' said Jesse. 'The two most senior officers. You know the ones we met with last time over that incident.'

'That's right,' said Connor as he looked out. 'Last time you didn't let me finish talking to them about my work and Chang's sister's research.'

'Same this time,' said Ngarra to all his crew. 'Remember nothing has changed. Someone is still after what you have developed with SAI's help and what you know. They will likely try again. Let's focus on our mining run and carrying out these trials with Gilgamesh as you call it now.'

Connor smiled. He thought it was a great name for it. The others weren't so sure.

'Yes, so exciting,' said Connor. 'You know…'

'Not now, Connor,' said Jesse. 'Wait until we are on our Skimmer.'

'Oh, okay,' said Connor glumly as they waited to get up out of their sets.

'Skimmer crews disembark,' said one of the operators.

The stern ramp opened, and they unbuckled and got up. Each crewmember collected their bags and walked down the stern ramp. Along from them they could see others doing the same. A couple of technicians were inspecting each transport drone.

'This way,' said one of the two Harvester security personnel assigned to each transport drone.

Ngarra's crew stuck together and followed the others.

Walking over to the nearest stairs exiting from the drone deck they went below to one of the lifts that would take them directly to the accommodation level on the Harvester. It took three trips up and down to get everyone below.

Once at the accommodation level they exited the lift into a large foyer. A steward gave them their room numbers and briefing notes on which Skimmer crew they were swapping out with. They went and put their belongings in their cabins and met in the common area.

Some of the crews swapping out were there as well; their Skimmers left in the moonpools below and secured by docking clamps. Tomorrow the replacement crews would take over and head out to sea.

'Do you think I might convince the Harvester crew to let me catch up with my sister?' said Chang as he walked into the common area.

'Not likely at the moment,' said Jesse.

The others were sitting down; about to go get something to eat from the buffet restaurant. It was late in the day.

'Besides,' said Ngarra. 'We are not to create any opportunity for Lee and Sue to question us. Remember last time. They know something is up. Your father seemed concerned about it all as well; I mean for both you and your sister. From what Jonah was saying anyway. In fact, like I said back at Xed Academy. After we have eaten, we will get our stuff and sleep on the Skimmer tonight.'

Everyone groaned, remembering that's what they did last time they were on the Harvester.

'Why do I care what my father thinks anyway,' said Chang angrily. 'He's the one that got my mother into the situation she is in, and my sister and I are literally worlds apart now.'

'At some point there will be an opportunity to catch up I'm sure,' said Stella.

'True,' said Jesse. 'But this is Chinese territory. We are on a flag state vessel in the middle of the Pacific. Chang, you are an Australian Chinese resident boarding a contractor Skimmer. Your sister is a Chinese national. The situation is dangerous so stick with us and let's get on that Skimmer tonight. We leave first thing tomorrow.'

'Okay, okay,' he said glaring at them and got up and walked off to get some food by himself.

Chang looked fiercely at everyone. Chang in Chinese meant free and unhindered and he was certainly that. The fierce face of a free and wandering canine; the face of two cultures with ancient histories.

'Let him be,' said Jesse. 'He will get over it. Let's just look out for each other.'

'On that note,' said Jonny as he got up. 'Foods up so let's eat.'

'Your belly calls,' said Stella chuckling. 'How do you fit that skin over everything hanging out.'

The others laughed.

'Skinwalker,' said Jonny as he tried to alter his shape and suck everything in.

It was comical and had the others laughing. Crewmembers from other Skimmers pointed and had a laugh at his expense as well.

'About the only shape changing you'll being doing is in the wrong direction,' said Stella poking him.

'My energy field needs stoking,' he said.

'What's its source?' said Stella egging him on.

'Tomato sauce of course,' he said.

Laughter erupted again from those around them.

'Cut it out kids,' said Jesse smiling.

They followed the other crews to the buffet style dinner where they could eat as much as they liked. Everyone got what they wanted and sat down together. For a moment everyone forgot what they were doing and enjoyed the time together. Meals were consumed, jokes were made, and the crew talked about family and life ashore.

Towards the end of the meal Jesse looked around at everyone. She couldn't help but think that they were walking into something big that was coming. She shivered and snapped out of her thoughts.

'Right,' said Jesse looking around at everyone. 'Time to get moving.'

'That it is,' said Ngarra. 'Let's go.'

They got up and returned their empty plates. After a few exchanges with other crews and some hassling about sleeping on their Skimmer and fearing the boggy man they went and got their belongings. They took the lift to the moon pools and boarded their Skimmer for the night.

Chapter 9

The next morning everyone was up early and running checks with SAI before departing. Stella was in the Xtract bay with Chang going over the operating systems of the Xtract mining drones. Ngarra, Jesse and Jonny were at the SAI console looking over propulsion, navigation and life support system displays. Connor was in the information hub loading his source code, setting up and running the ocean bubble hologram and synching it with SAI. It was now a mesh for the Xtract simulations. Gilgamesh as he called it. He wasn't far from building a containment system for Gilgamesh, housing its source code and hardware.

'What's this?' said Ngarra as he pointed to a flashing icon on the Skimmer propulsion hologram displayed in the middle of the SAI console.

Jonny looked up from what he was doing.

'SAI confirm propulsion system status is nominal,' he said moving his hands to enlarge and identify what it was.

'Starboard rim driven propulsion offline, system malfunction,' said SAI.

'Damn it!' said Ngarra.

'SAI identify problem and confirm time to fix,' said Ngarra.

'System calibration needed. Time to reboot, calibrate, test and try is 1600 hours.

'Oh well,' said Jesse. 'We are stuck here until later today then. I'll inform Harvester operations and contact Xed crew monitoring.'

'Stella, Chang,' said Ngarra over comms to the Xtract bay. 'Starboard propulsion is offline. Can you work with SAI to reboot and go through all the checks? We will be stuck here most of the day.'

'Got it,' said Stella. 'And bugger! Party tonight then,' she said over comms.

'Yeah right,' said Ngarra. 'We will use the time to make sure Connor has everything he needs to run the synch with the Xtract drones and test his technology when we get to our mining location.'

'Where is our latest assignment in "the Area",' said Chang over comms.

'Will brief you all on it later,' said Jesse. 'Just working on that now.'

Tenure holders in "the Area" including GlobeCorpMining kept locations for mining to themselves until the last minute. A skimmer contractor would get the coordinates for the next mining run when they got their briefing notes. This information was then passed to a skimmer and its crew.

'Party spoiler,' said Stella sarcastically.

At the Xtract bay console she got SAI to project the propulsion system hologram. They watched as SAI shut down starboard propulsion and initiated a reboot and calibration sequence.

If the power train was not aligned when the overdrive was used it would be interrupted and the capacity to maintain propulsion systems drained. If continued, eventually the system would have to shut down and reboot. A skimmer would be left motionless in the water column until the reboot was completed.

'I wonder why it would be in this state,' said Stella.

'Pirates maybe,' said Chang.

'Not likely,' said Stella. 'They usually arrive when a skimmer is stationary and with its communication streamer and Xtracts deployed. They wouldn't need to fire on a skimmer.'

'I guess our previous crew has conducted an overdrive trial,' he said shrugging his shoulders. 'And didn't adhere to protocol.'

'Good point,' said Stella. 'SAI, show power supply to propulsion and the speed log records for last mining run.'

'Confirmed,' said SAI as the logs and schematics were accessed.

They looked at the display on an adjacent screen. The previous crew had used overdrive after being delayed at their last mining position and didn't follow protocol.

'Idiots,' said Stella. 'Bunch of cowboys some of these crews are,' she said waving her hands around. 'They're meant to get approval to use the overdrive. It's still being trialled.'

Chang smiled. He had grown to like Stella. She was irritating at the best of times, but he found everyone irritating he thought to himself.

'Rules are made to broken or for those that need them,' he said looking behind him at the forward bulkhead. 'Don't ask for permission, ask for forgiveness.'

Through the forward bulkhead was the override propulsion system. They could go extremely fast when it was engaged or even jump to a location. Essentially it resulted in a highly polarised energy field around them. Relative to their surroundings it was as if they had no mass, no resistance, and no friction to deal with. Gravity had no effect on them, and they were able to overcome inertia. Inertial mass reduction. The trouble was, if the rim driven propulsion drive power train was not aligned when the overdrive was active resonance would occur and the vibration would disrupt the power train. They had not calculated the correct dampening required.

'Boys and girls,' said Stella over comms. 'Looks like our previous crew used the overdrive to leg it back to the Harvester after being delayed at their last mining position.'

'I'll check the crew logs to see if I can find out why,' replied Jesse over comms from the SAI console.

A brief pause followed as Jesse used her security level access code to open the Skimmer crew logs. She looked at them, swiping her hands across, separating out dates and times on the display in front of her.

'Found it she said to everyone. 'A pirate incident apparently. That explains it then.'

'Yeah, well now we are stuck here,' said Chang. 'Like I said, if these things were fully autonomous and could be monitored remotely, we wouldn't even need to be on them.'

Stella jumped in over comms and continued talking. 'If these damn Xtracts didn't need to be monitored then yes, we wouldn't be here.

'Thus, Connor's work,' said Jesse over comms. 'He might do us all out of a job though you realise.'

'Like I said,' said Ngarra over comms. 'That's why we have to be careful. There is a lot at stake. Connor's work has become of increasing interest to others.'

'Theoretically,' said Jesse. 'These Skimmers could move straight out of the water through the atmosphere and into space using the overdrive.'

'A tic tac,' said Jonny over comms. 'Remember those sightings decades ago.'

'Indeed,' said Jesse over comms. 'There is more to these Skimmers historically than meets the eye. But that's Rick's domain and not for me to say.

Something to do with retrofitting them with these overdrives. Now back to work you lot.'

The crew carried on with their work and chatted over open comms. It was going to be a frustrating day waiting for a system reboot.

***

Meanwhile on the drone deck of the Harvester Sue and Lee were waiting on the observation deck of the Hex tower. The Sea Hunters had arrived. Two patrol drones were making their way across. Sue and Lee had been informed that a piracy incident had occurred and that they had caught up with those involved. A transport drone had been prepared and was waiting, glistening in the sun. It would take the pirates back to shore for processing and prosecution by the appropriate authority. They had been briefed that the Sea Hunters had managed to apprehend them.

'At least we have taken some of those pirates off the grid,' said Lee as they watched the two patrol drones fly across to the Harvester from the Sea Hunter vessel.

'Yes,' said Sue. 'It has been sometime since the Sea Hunters have been able to catch them in the act.'

'We will get our loading cranes to off take the nodules they recovered before they leave,' said Lee.

'What about that crew of Ngarra's?' said Sue. 'They are back on rotation. They are here with the latest crews to swap out and continue with mining operations.'

'Yes,' said Lee. 'Chang's father did say they were back on a skimmer. We should keep an eye on them.'

'They are still developing the technology that youth Connor was working on,' said Sue. 'As discussed, it could be used or adapted to help with Chang's sister's work in our lab.'

'Yes,' said Lee. 'His sister Ying Yue seemed very interested in seeing what Connor was up to.'

They watched as the two Hunter unit patrol drones came in over the drone deck. They reared up and hovered over their respective docking clamps. Both were caught and secured in place. The docking arms lowered and the two patrol drones powered down.

Lee and Sue watched as the pirates they had heard about were taken under guard to the transport drone by a Sea Hunter security detail. While they were boarding through the stern ramp two officers walked towards the hex tower.

'Looks like Max and Alex,' said Lee.

'They can brief us on what happened,' said Sue. 'Their security detail will be carrying out inspections of Skimmers today and tomorrow as crew changes are made.'

The stern ramp of the transport drone closed. Two of their own Harvester security personnel would accompany the apprehended pirates on their trip ashore.

They watched as the transport drone powered up and the docking clamps released it. Rising and hovering briefly it tilted forward and moved out over the side of the Harvester. It headed off and banked, straightened up and flew low over the water into the distant horizon.

'Max, Alex, welcome back,' said Lee as the two of them came up the stairs to where they were standing.

'A bit different to the last few times,' said Alex. 'It's been a while since we have been able to apprehend a crew of pirates.'

'Congratulations are in order,' said Sue. 'Another piracy operation taken off the grid.'

'And more to come,' said Max turning to check on his team below.

The security detail had come over to the bottom of the stairs. Max waved them on to carry out Skimmer inspections. One of the Harvester security personnel was waiting for them at the entrance to the hex. They walked to the lift to go below. They would all be staying on board the night and head back to their vessel early morning after further inspections.

Sue, Lee, Max and Alex stood looking out over the drone deck. A few technicians were looking over a Harvester patrol drone. Another one arrived to dock; a regular occurrence. The security zone around the Harvester was patrolled using air, surface and subsurface drones.

'Let's go below and have something to eat and discuss inspections, compliance and monitoring,' said Sue.

Max moved his arm indicating after you and smiled casually at Lee and Sue. He looked briefly at Alex; eyebrows raised. They had another agenda; that's why Cam their chief boarding officer was below doing inspections with his off sider. They walked inside and the hex tower retracted into the drone bay below, sliding down around the lift and stairwell that was permanently in position whether the hex tower was up or down. They walked out of the entrance and across to an adjacent lift that would take them to the operations centre.

'Have you heard much about those crews that were caught up in that incident over six months ago,' said Sue cautiously as they descended.

'Not much,' said Alex.

He looked at Max as they exited the lift and followed behind Lee and Sue.

'Aren't they back at sea,' said Sue.

Now how would they know that, Max thought to himself. Alex shrugged his shoulders and mouthed 'later' to Max. Perhaps Jonah had told Chang's father, the GlobeCorpMining chief operations officer who had then told them about it.

They walked along the main causeway of the operations centre and through to the common area where everyone gathered to relax or eat when off duty. They entered a private room where a small buffet style menu was waiting for them.

'Please,' said Lee. 'Have something to eat and take a seat. Then we will talk.'

As always,' said Max. 'Your hospitality is second to none.'

They selected what they wanted and sat down. Silence ensued for a short time as they all enjoyed the selection of food presented.

'I gather they are back at sea,' said Max in reply to the earlier comment. 'Ngarra's crew I mean,' he said dismissively; as if he didn't care too much for it.

Sue looked briefly at Lee with raised eyebrows. *How would they know?* she thought to herself.

'I guess they have recovered from the previous incident,' said Alex.

'How is Chang's sister?' said Max. 'She must have been concerned about Chang, as would her father?'

'She is fine,' said Sue. 'In fact, we will try and arrange for them to catch up. Our operations centre informs us that their Skimmer propulsion is offline and must go through a reboot. They will not be leaving the moon pool until late today or early tomorrow morning now.'

'Chang will like that,' said Alex.

Perfect, Max thought to himself. Cam can inspect their Skimmer and then do what he must do. He looked over at Alex with calculating eyes. Sue saw him and smiled, glancing at Lee and nodding her head.

It was like a game cheese. Each party trying to figure out what the other may or may not know. It had been quiet for over six months since the incident, but plans were afoot none the less. It was all over the technology that had been developed. Word had got around that Connor had developed it further and was about to run trials at sea. Max and Alex's contact at Xed Academy had made them aware of that.

The question was, Max thought to himself, *how would this lot know about it or are they just bluffing to try and glean information?*

A brief silence followed as they finished their meals. The conversation relaxed. Small talk was made about life at sea and getting ashore for a break. Often those that worked in "the Area" would go ashore to the Cook Islands or other Pacific Islands for a break between rotations.

'Right,' said Max as he cut through the silence again. 'We had better get back to our ship. Our security detail will complete their inspections and stay on board overnight to catch those arriving early morning as well.'

'Thanks for the meal and conversation,' said Alex.

'You're welcome,' said Lee.

They got up and Lee and Sue walked to the lift with them. A security officer escorted them. Max and Alex briefly discussed when they would catch up again and then entered the lift. It stopped at the drone bay and they exited and walked across to the lift in the hex tower.

Max and Alex looked around the drone bay at the docking clamps. A few transport drones were being worked on. In the distance they could make out some patrol drones. One powered up and left, moving out a side entrance instead of being lifted to the drone deck above.

They took the lift to the drone deck above and the security officer left them to it. Max and Alex boarded one of their two patrols drones and they returned to the Sea Hunter vessel.

***

Later that day the two Sea Hunter inspection officers working their way along the moonpools arrived at Ngarra's Skimmer. Accompanying them was a Harvester security officer. He followed the two inspection officers as they walked up the gangway, over the conveyor belt and through the main entrance of the Skimmer into the rec area.

Off into the dimly lit distance on either side other moon pools were empty as crews had swapped out and the Skimmers had left. Offloading robotic arms stood idle on each side of every moon pool. They were used to lift the trays off the Skimmers and deposit the load of nodules on the conveyor. The conveyor belts were running. They never stopped.

'Welcome aboard,' said Jesse as they entered the Skimmer.

'Right,' said Cam. 'My offsider will go below to the Xtract bay and go through mining logs then do a cabin inspection. I will go to the SAI console and look over route logs for previous crew runs.'

'Stella,' said Jesse motioning to her.

'Coming,' she said getting up from a chair in the rec area.

The crew had been having some downtime while the rim driven propulsion system was recalibrated by SAI.

'Take our inspection officer below and show him what he needs to see,' said Jesse.

'Sure,' said Stella motioning him to follow her below.

Cam looked over at the rest of the crew in the rec area. He made a mental note on each one.

'Chang, come with me,' said the Harvester security officer as he stepped forward. 'A visit with your sister has been arranged.'

Chang jumped up and Ngarra grabbed his arm whispering.

'Be careful, don't say too much, just family,' he warned.

The security officer waved him over. Impatient to get going, Chang left walking down the gangway behind him.

Jesse looked at Ngarra and motioned that they would talk later.

'Right come with me,' Jesse said to Cam. They walked forward and up the stairs through the watertight bulkhead to the SAI console.

Jesse asked SAI to display the route logs for the previous crew. Cam checked off where the Skimmer had been and for how long. He went through the load logs as well and matched them with what was offloaded at the Harvester.

'All checks out,' he said. 'Now I need the water column and seabed samples from the information hub.'

'Of course,' said Jesse. They walked back through the SAI console, down one of the side passageways and into the information hub. Connor was engrossed in running the new simulations of Xtract group behaviour learning in his ocean bubble hologram.

Cam looked around at the technology and made mental notes of everything. *So, this is what our contact was talking about*, he thought to himself.

'Here's the pelican case with the samples,' said Jesse.

'Great,' said Cam. 'Show me the sample collection and processing logs and I will be done.'

'Got them,' said Connor as he pulled up the logs on a display across from them. Cam checked over the logs and recorded what he needed. Everything checked out. There were no breaches of International Seabed Authority regulations or Maritime Regulations for working in "the Area".

'Looks interesting,' he said to Connor as he pointed at the ocean bubble hologram.

'Yeah, it's Gilga...' Connor was about to say.

'It's nothing important,' said Jesse interrupting. 'I'm sure you have a busy schedule. She moved her arm and gestured that they were leaving.

Connor stared at Jesse. Being autistic, he found it hard to read emotions in such situations. He was keen to explain what he was doing but Jesse had interrupted him for no reason. He shrugged his shoulders and went back to his work.

I can't just take it, Cam thought to himself on the way out. It's not as if it is something physical. At least, not yet anyway; and how on earth did Connor come up with this anyway.

***

Meanwhile, Chang had been escorted to the common area in Harvester operations and was having a meal at the restaurant with his sister Ying Yue. They were sitting at a table together to one side.

'It's been a while,' said Chang. 'How do you stand being stuck out here for such long periods of time.'

'You get used to it,' said Ying Yue. 'It's massive, a monolith, and besides we still get to go ashore for breaks. I just don't get home to China very often.'

'Father came and saw me the other day. He seems happy enough, but worried about us, about you to.'

'He's never worried or concerned about me,' said Chang gruffly.

'Oh, I would say he cares more than you think,' said Ying Yue.

'Yeah right,' said Chang. 'He never talks to me and it's his fault our mother is in the situation she is in.'

'Don't you think it is more that you don't want anything to do with him, or make the effort to try and understand him,' she said.

'Whatever,' said Chang gruffly again.

'That's your trouble,' said Ying Yue. 'You just brush everyone off whenever they confront you about all this.'

'Our father is married to his job, it's his fault. He got our mother into the situation she is in.'

'Keep your voice down,' said Ying Yue.

Others were looking over at them.

'I'm worried about you,' said Chang. 'Your work puts you in great danger. Others want access to this technology Connor has developed. They will manipulate us. They will use our family against us.'

Damn it, thought Chang. He wasn't meant to talk about all that.

'What work and technology?' she said dismissively as if not interested. She was aware of the situation and pretended not to be interested.

'I don't know the details,' said Chang dismissively. 'I am just worried about you. Why don't you leave all this and carry on your work elsewhere?'

'It's not that simple,' she said. 'I am a Chinese national. You can't just walk away. What we are doing here, and off planet is all connected with mining. I don't know how. I just focus on my work. It is dangerous to start asking too many questions.'

'Exactly,' said Chang. 'You'd better hope Father knows enough to keep you safe.'

The conversation carried on for a while. They talked more about their mother. Chang relaxed a little and they shared a few memories of better times. Finally, Chang left and returned to the Skimmer for the night. He was escorted by a security guard to the lift and back to the moon pool and his Skimmer.

Chapter 10

It was late when Chang got back to the Skimmer. The security guard left him and walked back down the gangway. He disappeared into the distance along the boardwalk or walkway next to the conveyor.

The others were in the rec area relaxing. They would not be leaving until the morning now.

'How was it?' said Ngarra.

'It's hard seeing my sister and talking about family,' he said. 'I tried to convince her to carry on her work elsewhere rather than being stuck out here.'

'She's a Chinese national on a flag state ship,' said Jonny. 'As if she's got a choice. As if that's going to happen.'

'Didn't ask you, did I?' said Chang glaring at him.

There was still some animosity between Chang and Jonny over what happened during the incident over six months ago.

'Always so angry,' said Jonny. 'Look bro, I am only trying to help. I'm not trying to get you wound up about life all the time.'

'Sure, you are,' said Chang sarcastically.

'Come on guys,' said Stella. 'He got to see his sister, even if it was not under the best of circumstances.'

'I'm worried about her,' said Chang as he walked over and sat down. 'I don't trust these people.'

'Neither do we,' said Jesse. 'That's why we are staying on board and leaving first thing tomorrow. Our propulsion system is back online. The previous crew caused an overspeed of the rim driven system when they engaged the overdrive. Resonance and vibration disrupted the power train. They didn't check.'

'We need to get Connor and his work away from here,' said Ngarra. 'I'm sure Jonah is in touch with Chang's father about your sister's situation. Surely, he keeps a watchful eye on things.'

'Don't you get it! That's what concerns me,' said Chang angrily. 'How much influence does he really have out here. What if something else is going on under his nose?'

'You're paranoid bro,' said Jonny. 'Don't over think it.'

'Come on people,' said Jesse. 'It's been a long day. Let's get some rest and get out of here in the morning. Sleep on it.'

They got up and walked off to their cabins.

'I had better go and get Connor,' said Stella. 'He will be up all night if we don't make him get some rest.'

Stella ran up the stairs, through the SAI console area and down one of the passages adjacent to propulsion on either side. Leaping and bounding along she burst into the information hub startling Connor.

'Hey Connor, we are turning in for the night. Don't stay up, we need you alert tomorrow for those trials of yours.'

'Sure,' said Connor.

He was absorbed in his work and looked right through Stella. She shrugged her shoulders and ran off.

'Men,' she thought out loud and laughed. 'Autistic or not, they were all the same.'

For some time, Connor carried on with his work. He wanted to re-run the simulations he was going to use tomorrow when they actually launched the Xtracts.

'SAI, run Xtract simulation.'

'Confirmed,' said SAI. 'Running Xtract simulation.'

Connor had modified the algorithms. To overcome previous problems, the layered algorithms now simulated competitive behaviour between two groups. Like two colonies of ant species in competition with each other.

So far, the mesh SAI had constructed, or Gilgamesh as he liked to call it now would store any Xtract group response to a simulation, but no learning occurred. They did not return to a mining operation afterwards. The simulation fell apart and they wandered off randomly.

He thought out loud.

'In nature, competition for resources between groups of organisms leads to selection of traits that advantage one group over another.'

Makes sense, he thought to himself. He carried on thinking out loud.

'Those behavioural traits are the memory of the population; its genetic memory. It's not a conscious thing, it's a generational thing that is selected for. So, it's learnt but not directly, more like inherited from generation to generation.'

So, each iteration of a simulation, he thought to himself, *was really the next generation of Xtracts. They carry that learning over from competing against each other in the previous generation.*

He thought out loud again.

'What I need to do is get SAI to divide them into two groups of Xtracts in the simulation that then compete for the same resource.'

Up until now Connor had been trying to get SAI to find and modify algorithms that identified group behaviour patterns in nature and use them to get Xtracts to copy that behaviour during an interruption to simulated mining operations.

Now he had found an algorithm and source code for simulating competitive behaviour patterning in nature. He had got SAI to hack the code. Now he was ready to run a simulated interruption to mining operations over many iterations. This would represent generations of learning at a population level between two groups of Xtracts. This could be it, the answer to passing on learnt behaviour in a group of Xtracts, a collective memory coded for in the mesh that passed on any learnt behaviour.

A noise came from outside the information hub. Connor paused and listened. Something must have fallen over.

He yawned. It was late. There it was again.

'What is that?' he thought out loud.

Connor walked out of the entrance to the information hub.

Before he could even react, a hand went over his mouth and an arm went around his neck. His arm was pulled behind his back. He struggled but it was no good. His attacker was dressed in black and his face was covered. He was pulled back into the information hub. As he passed through the entrance, he managed to get his hand to a control panel. A small red icon changed colour. His attacker did not notice.

He continued to struggle violently.

From behind and in his ear, his attacker talked.

'Where is it,' he said.

'Where's what?' said Connor wide-eyed and terrified.

Connor was now in an extremely heightened state. He hated being touched. It was horrifying to him. He was freaking out. His attacker did not know he was autistic. His extreme response to the situation and the amount of adrenalin rushing through his body meant for a moment he was incredibly strong and difficult to restrain.

'The technology. Give it to me now!' said his attacker.

'No, no!' Connor motioned violently and shook his head.

His mouth was still covered. He was in an extreme state of physical distress.

At that moment, Jonny came rushing in. He was still up.

The icon Connor had put his hand across had set off a silent panic alarm that SAI responded to by alerting the crew.

Connor's attacker let him go and pushed him hard and fast straight into Jonny. They both fell backwards, and his attacker took off. Jonny ran after him. Sprinting up the passageway and down the stairs to the rec area. He yelled out to the others.

'Hurry up you lot! Intruder!'

Jonny lunged forward and tackled the intruder to the floor near the entrance to the Skimmer. The intruder's knee came up and caught Jonny in the face, sending him reeling back. The intruder got up. Jonny jumped up again and in a sweeping motion caught the intruder's leg with is. The intruder went down again, rolled and got up. Jonny came at him, but the intruder side stepped grabbed his arm and in a sweeping motion turned back on the direction of Jonny's motion. Jonny ended up in the air, landing flat on his back. It knocked the wind out of him.

The intruder took off down the gangway just as the others raced into the rec area.

'No!' yelled Jesse as the others came running in and were about to race after the intruder.

'I can get him,' said Jonny wheezing and panting. He tried to speak. He still had the wind knocked out of him.

Leave it!' exclaimed Jesse. 'Is everyone okay, where's Connor. Stella, go and check on him.'

Stella raced off.

Jonny sat down on the deck. He laid back for a while. The others gathered around.

'You okay, Jonny?' said Ngarra.

'Yeah, I will be. Give me a moment,' he said coughing.

'What on earth happened?' said Ngarra.

'An intruder had Connor,' said Jonny as he got his breath back and sat up. He must have crept on board without being noticed. I didn't see him. I was not in here. I got up to get some food. They could have slipped past.'

'Whoever it was wanted that tech,' said Jesse. 'We need to get out of here. We will post a watch for the night and secure the entrance.'

'What about calling Harvester security?' said Chang.

'No,' said Jesse. 'Let's keep this to ourselves. We don't know who it was and who they are working for.'

'Shit,' said Chang. 'I told you so. I didn't sign up for this.'

'I seem to remember you saying that last time,' said Jonny as he got his breath back.

'You did as well at one point,' said Ngarra.

A few nervous chuckles followed.

'Okay, okay drop it,' said Jesse. 'Just deal with it you lot. Chang, you keep watch for what is left of the night. Let's check on Connor and then get what rest we can.'

Chang moaned but stayed put. He secured the entrance and went and got a drink while the others went up to the information hub.

Stella had managed to calm Connor down. He was talking constantly about not giving anyone his work. He was on the other side of the ocean bubble hologram, distancing himself from the others and backing away when anyone tried to approach him.

'You okay, Connor?' said Jonny coming in behind the others.

'Jonny,' said Connor as he snapped out of his ranting. 'You saved me.'

'Suppose I did,' he said smiling nervously.

'Connor go with Jonny and Stella,' said Jesse. 'Make sure he's okay guys and then all get some rest. We're out of here first thing in the morning.'

With that, they all went back to the rec area. Reassuring each other everything would be all right they went to get what little rest they could for the remainder of the night. Chang sat down and stared at the entrance, half expecting a small army to bash it down and come rushing in.

***

A duty officer in the Harvester security monitoring centre in operations called for Lee. A moon pool camera motion sensor had been activated.

'What is it?' said Lee walking in.

'Here, sir, look,' he said replaying the footage. 'A person has gone up a skimmer gangway and entered it.'

They watched the recording.

A person entered the Skimmer. For a short while, nothing happened. Suddenly there was commotion at the entrance.

'It looks like an altercation,' said Lee.

The person then ran down the gangway and disappeared.

'What should we do, sir?' said the duty officer. 'He doesn't appear on any other camera feed so they must know where all our sensors are.'

'Hmmm,' said Lee thinking. 'Don't do anything at present. I don't want whoever it is to know that we saw this happen. I will talk to Sue about it. Whose Skimmer is it?'

The duty officer looked up the docking logs for each moon pool and the crew change logs sent to them.

'A crew headed up by someone called Ngarra, and another called Jesse?'

'We are definitely not letting anyone know about this,' said Lee. 'Keep this to yourself, understand. That's an order.'

'Yes, sir,' said the security officer as Lee left and went back to his cabin.

I think I know what this might be about and who it is, Lee thought to himself as he walked back to his cabin. An interesting development but not unexpected.

***

The next morning on the Skimmer everyone was up early. The incident during the night had made everyone uptight. Chang looked like death warmed up. He had stayed up on watch for the remainder of the night.

'Geeze, Chang,' said Jonny. 'You look like I feel.'

Jonny was a little bruised and sore from the scuffle with the intruder during the night.

'About time you were of some use around here,' said Chang yawning. 'Apart from eating a lot what is it you do again?'

It was hard to tell whether Chang was being serious or joking. He didn't take jokes or being hassled to well and often took offense.

'Bro, I'm hurt,' said Jonny clutching his chest. 'I thought we were pals?'

The rest of the crew managed a subdued laugh as they got something to eat.

'Technology,' said Jonny as he got his meal. 'Fermentation and protein manipulation of plant-based products ay. A range of meals to select from. No Chef but never without,' he said to himself.

'Where's Connor?' said Stella looking around.

'He's already back in the information hub,' said Chang. 'He got up early and went up there. I don't think he really slept. He said something about being onto something with his work. A breakthrough maybe.'

Chang pretended he wasn't interested. However, his mind was racing, and he was thinking about the threatening message he had got. Once again, he was worried about his sister. He hadn't told her about the threat. It was eating away at his mind. He looked at everyone else. They carried on with their meal and chatting about the incident the night before.

'I will contact Jonah about what happened,' said Jesse as she sat down with her food. 'Our vitals would have spiked at the monitoring centre. They will be wondering what happened when they look at the daily logs. Let's get out of here first.'

For a few minutes, there was silence as everyone quickly ate. They were eager to leave the moonpool and get as far away from the Harvester as possible.

'Right,' said Ngarra as he finished eating. 'Let's get watertight and get out of here.'

Everyone looked at him and nodded.

'I'm all for that,' said Jonny as he chewed on a mouth full of food.

Ngarra got up and the others soon followed suite, returning their empty plates.

The crew moved off and prepared to leave. Stella and Chang went to the Xtract bay. Jesse, Ngarra and Jonny went to the SAI console.

'SAI, secure Skimmer for departure,' said Ngarra as they walked into the SAI console. 'Disengage from docking clamps and transit to mining location.'

Ngarra pulled up the navigation hologram and confirmed SAI's transit to their destination some distance from the Harvester.

'Confirmed,' said SAI. 'Securing Skimmer and initiating docking disengagement sequence.'

Unless otherwise stated ocean transits to mining locations were all standardised to a set depth and speed. The only thing to enter was the location coordinates.

The main entrance closed and was made watertight. Internal watertight bulkheads closed for departure. Propulsion and life support systems powered up. SAI conducted a multitude of system checks simultaneously and very quickly.

Jonny put his SAI interface lenses on so he could monitor the Skimmers movements in first person view and cross check navigation. If needed, he could take manual control of the Skimmer or adjust what SAI was doing.

Ngarra checked the hologram of Skimmer systems in front of him. He enlarged the propulsion system and life support system displays and watched as SAI ran checks.

'SAI confirm systems check,' said Ngarra.

'Confirmed,' said SAI. 'Skimmer is watertight, propulsion and life support systems nominal,' said SAI.

'SAI depart for mining location,' said Ngarra.

'Confirmed,' said SAI. 'Departing for mining location.'

Jesse watched on. She checked security and communication systems.

Underwater they were totally reliant on the grid set up across the Area, which was maintained by contractors. Q-bit technology was used to transmit laser communication signals between the Skimmers, the Eel drones and surface buoys. Depending on their proximity a skimmer either had a live video feed, or slight delays meant recorded video or audio messages were used. It was all done through a digital message board.

Chapter 11

Rick was in early at Xed Academy. It had been five days since he and Jonah had talked with Connor about his technology. He needed to talk with his contact in the Sea Hunters. Rick headed over to the sim centre and walked through the learning hub to the Skimmer simulators. Passing between them he paused and looked around.

In his mind, he still wanted to separate Xed from the Academy and carve out the Skimmer crew training and monitoring program. Since it was largely funded by GlobeCorpMining he was increasingly concerned about the amount of pressure to share information. They needed to distance themselves, or so his people had told him. Jonah of course was convinced that everything be kept together. She actively promoted this to the council.

The advanced propulsion system installed on the Skimmers wasn't really the issue. It was patented technology and had been for some time. Combining rim driven electric propulsion with an overdrive had been a logical step forward, even if it was a big one. *A curious piece of technology*, he thought to himself; a mercury plasma vortex encased in iron spun by a magnetic semiconductor at its base and a capacitor discharge ring. His people had been key in seeing that patented technology retrofitted to the Skimmers. One wonders whether the Skimmers were designed with that in mind.

Rick moved on and passed through security and into the crew monitoring and communication complex. He said good morning to the duty watch team as he walked down the stairs from the mezzanine overlooking the monitoring consoles. He went to the rear, through security and into the room. *The room*, he thought to himself. Where the institute's AI was housed; a highly secure facility.

Walking to the rear and finding a workstation he used his smart watch to access a grid node in "the Area". Using an encryption, he then sent a message indicating he wanted to talk with his contact Max on the Sea Hunter vessel.

A pause followed and then Max's voice answered.

'Morning,' said Max. 'What's your update?'

'As you know our Skimmer crew is back at sea and going to run some Xtract trials using this technology that has been developed. My contact on the Skimmer has again been given some motivation to secure this technology.'

'Yes, same as last time,' said Max. 'Look at how that ended up though. It was very risky, and we exposed ourselves in the pursuit of all this. If we are found to be breaching our mandate operating in "the Area", all this could end.'

'It won't come to that,' said Rick.

'Not so sure,' said Max. 'We met with the Harvester officers in charge yesterday. I am concerned about their agenda. Chang's sister is in danger. I don't know how and in what way Chang and his sisters' father is involved. Things are changing, the situation is fluid and emerging. We have to be careful.'

'Anything done would have to be under the guise of the mandate you are required to operate by,' said Rick. 'That's the only way people will not question your authority and comply with your requests.'

'Okay,' said Max. 'Securing the technology has to happen on the Harvester though. We can't risk a repeat of last time. Chasing Skimmer's around the ocean on the pretence they have violated "the Area" regulations is too risky. We won't get away with it second time around.'

'True, but we don't want to cause an international incident on a foreign flag state vessel,' said Rick.

'We will look into it and keep monitoring the situation,' said Max. 'My inspection team will finish up on board the Harvester this morning. We will move off and stay in the general vicinity of this Skimmer and its crew carrying out these technology trials at their mining location.'

'Right, got to go,' said Rick. 'I will be in touch.'

Rick closed the grid node he had accessed and shut down the link from his smart watch.

The AI log will note his use of the grid node but not what it was for. Jonah was suspicious of his moves. He would have to be careful. Last time he had been cornered and they had an argument.

Rick left "the room" and passed through security and back into the crew monitoring and communications complex. He caught up with the duty watch and got a morning briefing on crew activity in "the Area". Ngarra's Skimmer crew vitals had spiked.

***

Later that morning Jonah was in her office in the administration complex. She had been catching up on cost projections for funding of the Skimmer crew training program.

She grabbed a coffee and looked out over the campus. If they met extraction targets GlobeCorpMining would continue to fund the bulk of the programme. However, Skimmer contractors always pushed to increase extraction targets because it increased their margins. She was always balancing contractors moaning about the crews and their ability to meet production demands with the fact that they were delivering loads above what was required anyway.

There was some dissention amongst the council lately about the influence GlobeCorpMining had on the Academy through funding the crew program. Rick was pushing to separate out the crew program. He wanted to ensure the security of Xed, the Academy and Skimmer technology was maintained into the future.

Financially, being overly reliant on a Chinese led majority funded crew program supporting mining in "the Area" was making people nervous. But Chang's father, the Chief Operating Officer of GlobeCorpMining seemed genuine enough and supportive. But how much influence and authority did he really have. What about the PLA Navy interests in "the Area"? The advances in technology they were working on had a potential military application. Thus, the rumours about mimic drones.

Her secretary came in and walked over to where she was standing. She looked concerned.

'What is it?' said Jonah.

'I have Chang's father on hold. He wants to talk to you. He seemed worried. At least from the look on his face and the tone of his voice he did.'

'Okay, put it through to my office,' she said walking over to her workstation and activating the message board.

Her secretary went back to her office and transferred the video call to Jonah's message board.

'Good morning, Jonah,' said Chang's father as his image appeared on screen.

'Good morning,' said Jonah as she sipped her coffee.

'How is the Skimmer program going,' he said.

'Fine,' said Jonah. We just had a crew change and your son's crew is back out there. They are doing some more trials using this technology of ours while at a mining location.'

'Interesting,' he said. 'I was out at the Harvester recently and caught up with my daughter, Ying Yue. Her research program is going well, although they have had a few setbacks. I am worried about her and the agenda of the two senior officers in charge of the Harvester though.'

'What do you mean?' said Jonah.

'A few things were said to me by them and by my daughter that concern me. It's almost as if she is a prisoner rather than a willing research scientist. It wasn't like that until other people became aware of this technology of yours. I think something is going on and I don't like it.'

'Surely, your daughter is safe enough,' said Jonah. 'She is your daughter and people will respect that. Although, in saying that Chang seems to think she is in danger as well. But from what and who?'

'That is what I am not sure of and why,' he said. 'But the PLA Navy is involved somehow. Whatever is going on, I think it has something to do with Chang and your lad Connor, the one that has developed this technology. It must have some bearing on Ying Yue's work.'

'Do you think we need to keep an eye on Chang,' she said.

'I would,' he said. 'Given our family situation he could be easily influenced again. No one would dare touch me given my links to the PRC Communist party subcommittee I report to. My business relationships with you and others are too important. Besides, no one wants to be blamed for causing an international incident in "the Area". We are a signatory to conventions regarding exploitation and extraction of resources in "the Area". But there are some smart people around. There are other ways to secure a technology that everyone wants to get their hands on. Why don't you just share the technology, Jonah?'

'Not possible,' said Jonah. 'We have something others want. Besides, given there is a move towards fully automating Skimmer's, so they don't require crews GlobeCorpMining could pull our funding. This technology gives us leverage and a way forward.'

'Fair enough,' he said. 'Much the same was said about the overdrive technology when it was retrofitted and combined with electric rim driven propulsion systems on the Skimmers. However, it's patented tech and not an issue now. But remember you owe me for the favours I did for you over that previous incident. It's been over six months since that happened.'

'I do indeed,' said Jonah. 'If it worries you that much, I will talk to Rick about your daughter.'

'I thought you had concerns about Rick,' he said cautiously.

'I do,' said Jonah. 'Leave it to me.'

'Hmmm, alright then,' he said. 'I have to go so keep me informed about your little project on the Skimmer.'

'I will,' she said.

His image disappeared and Jonah stood there for a while thinking. What was it about his family's situation that kept coming up and how did Chang's mother fit into the picture? Why was it so important that both Connor and Chang's sisters work be kept separate and quiet?

***

The Sea Hunter unit was maintaining position off the Harvester. Alex and Max were in the drone bay waiting for Cam and his offsider to return on a patrol drone. They had stayed on the Harvester overnight.

Alex and Max walked outside to the docking clamps on the drone deck. They looked across to the Harvester. They watched the patrol drone take off. It hovered, tilted forward and moved off. It banked to the right as it left the Harvester drone deck. It then headed straight towards them. Alex and Max walked back inside the drone bay and up the short flight of stairs at the rear to the control room.

'It will be interesting to hear Cam's debrief,' said Alex as they watched the duty officer prepare the deck for landing.

Max stretched his arms and looked out at the technicians working on drones mounted on the docking clamps in the drone bay.

'Indeed,' said Max causally. 'Cam is a slick operator, and his team have spent a lot of time previously scoping out the security on the Harvester drone deck and down in the moon pools.'

They watched from the control room. Looking out through the drone bay doors the patrol drone arrived. It hovered next to the drone deck. It moved across in front of the drone bay and positioned itself above the docking clamp. The docking clamp opened, and the arm stretched up, grabbed it and secured it in place. As it retracted the drone powered down and the rotors and cowlings folded inward. The docking clamp pulled the drone inside the bay.

Cam and his offsider got out. They watched as Cam spoke to him. He walked off. Cam looked up and saw them in the control room. He signalled for them to come down.

'What's that on your face?' said Alex as they walked down the stairs and across to him.

'I ran into a situation,' said Cam.

'Not here,' said Max. 'Let's discuss this over some food.'

They exited the drone bay to the rear and walked up the stairs and forward through the operations centre.

'So, you didn't succeed then?' said Max as they walked down the passageway to the mess.

Grabbing something to eat and drink they returned to the briefing room and sat down.

'We know how to get around security monitoring systems between the drone deck and the moon pools,' he said rubbing his jaw. 'But getting on board that Skimmer and doing what you asked, well what can I say.'

'Ran into some trouble did you,' said Max smiling and leaning back in his chair with his drink.

'I got on board the Skimmer all right. But I didn't expect this person you talked about to be in the information hub at that hour.'

'I take it you didn't get it then,' said Alex.

'No,' he said emphatically. 'I grabbed this Connor person you talked about and had him secured. As I grabbed him, I think he must have activated a security breach icon. I was asking him politely to hand over the technology.'

'I'm sure you did,' said Max having a little laugh with Alex.

'Anyway,' said Cam. 'Another rather solid chap came rushing in and it was all on. I had to get out of there, so we didn't compromise the project. There was a scuffle. Well trained he is. Anyway, I got away and they didn't identify me.'

'Well, that's good news then,' said Alex.

'Indeed,' said Max leaning forward and crossing his arms on the table. 'The Skimmer crew know something is up. They will ask the Academy crew monitoring and communications centre what to do. Our contact will hear about it. He will then reiterate to his contact on the Skimmer the importance of securing

Connor's work and keeping his sister safe on the Harvester. But how we bring all this together is the question.'

'I am worried about his sister,' said Alex. 'Lee and Sue were very pointed in their remarks about her.'

'I think they see Chang as a threat to her maintaining focus on whatever it is, she is working on,' said Max. 'It seems family ties have a strong pull on them all, particularly given their fathers' high-ranking position in the PRC Communist party and the subcommittee he reports to. Not to mention their mother's situation.

'Something else is going on though on that Harvester,' said Alex. 'I get the impression others don't have the same view as GloberCorpMining's chief operations officer or appreciate his concern for his family. They see it as a weakness.'

'You may well be right,' said Max. 'Anyway, let's get underway and head in the general direction of the mining location where this Skimmer crew is running these technology trials. Let's keep our distance and monitor the situation. That way we can move either way, back to the Harvester or toward the Skimmer.'

'Right you are,' said Cam as he nodded his head.

They had finished their meals and got up from the table. Cam left and went to find the others. He would brief his team on the situation. Alex and Max headed off to the SAI console to meet with the duty officer and arrange for SAI to get the ship and its two drone vessels underway. The Hunter unit was back in business.

Chapter 12

Meanwhile on Ngarra's Skimmer it would take the rest of the day to reach their mining location. Designated by Skimmer contractors, location coordinates were delivered to Skimmers at crew changes on the Harvester.

On board Ngarra's Skimmer Chang was alone in the viewing area. He was forward of the narrow esplanade that stretched around either side of the bulkhead within which the overdrive propulsion system stretched from the level below to the SAI console above.

The outer hull shields were retracted. He looked out into the blue green void. *It could be quite disorientating*, he thought to himself walking forward to stand right in front.

'Let's see,' he said to himself out loud.

Stella is still in the Xtract bay, Jonny is in his cabin and the others are in the SAI console. What about Connor, he's always in the information hub.

'That guy irritates the hell out of me,' he said out loud to his reflection.

Not as much as Jonny though, he thought to himself. A solid Tongan Maori, a smart arse, and lover of food. He certainly was a gun operating Skimmers though.

'I prefer hanging around with Stella,' he said out loud to his reflection again.

Last time when at sea on a mining rotation Jonny had got into a scuffle with Chang over his attitude towards Connor. Stella had tried to smooth it over.

She is what I would call a bubbly personality, he thought to himself again. Always seeing the best in everyone. Ngarra is always so serious and boring. As for Jesse, well she's just an enigma.

'I just can't figure her out,' he said out loud again to his reflection.

'What can't you figure out?' said Jonny walking along the esplanade and over to where Chang was standing.

Hearing his voice Chang jumped as Jonny walked up behind him with some food in his hand.

'What are you contemplating, standing there looking into that void?' said Jonny.

'Nothing really,' said Chang cautiously. 'My sister, I just can't figure out if she really wants to be on that Harvester.'

Chang had quickly changed the subject. He didn't want to get into a conversation with Jonny about other crew members.

'Well, that's her choice bro,' he said. 'Besides, even if you convinced her and she wanted to, it would not be possible for her to leave the Harvester.'

'I know,' said Jonny reluctantly. 'For once, I agree with you.'

'Wow,' said Jonny. 'Are you feeling okay. Where's that grumpy grimace you always give me.'

'I'm stuck with an idiot,' he said smartly. 'Might as well get used to it.'

'I'm hurt,' said Jonny stabbing his chest in an action with his hand as he took a bite out of the food he was carrying.

'I'll leave you with your three friends Jonny,' said Chang. 'Me, myself and I.'

'Ha-ha, very funny,' said Jonny. 'Coming from a person that has so many friends and all,' he said laughing and dropping some food which he quickly caught.

Chang flushed red and giving Jonny a grimace, stormed off. He walked back along the narrow esplanade through the bulkhead entrance connected to the rec area and up the stairs. He walked into the rear of the SAI console.

He could see Ngarra was busy doing something with the navigation projections and Jesse was at her communication sand security station.

He walked back through the rear of the SAI console and down the passage on one side past propulsion and life support systems to the information hub.

Still fuming about Jonny, he walked in. *Let's see what Connor is up to*, he thought to himself. Sometimes he felt like locking himself in the airlock behind the information hub and flooding it and just floating away into nothing. That's how frustrated he was with everything.

To the rear behind the information hub was the airlock used for boarding and inspections. When on location with the communication streamer deployed and carrying out Xtract mining operation, the Sea Hunters used a breaching pod to dock with it and enter the Skimmer.

'Hey, Connor, how is the work going?' said Chang.

The thought of what his contact had said weighed heavily on Chang. He remembered what it felt like last time. That was over six months ago now. Jonah and Rick had warned him it was not over, and he may be threatened again. He kept it to himself. He was past being coerced into thinking that if he did someone's bidding, he would somehow fulfil this ambitious desire to prove his worth by working for GlobeCorpMining. Yes, he wanted his father to hold him in high regard. He wanted to prove him wrong and to make him pay for their mothers' situation. But now all he could think about was the danger his sister might be in.

'Red Queen effect,' said Connor looking blankly at Chang.

'Red what?' said Chang.

'Red Queen effect, it's about nature,' said Connor. 'It's when two species are competing for the same resource. One adapts in some manner and gains an advantage, which is selected for. So, in turn, the other species comes up with a way to adapt that is selected for. Over multiple generations each species adaptations are selected for. So, each species must constantly adapt, evolve and proliferate in order to survive. But in a population and not at the level of the individual.'

'So?' said Chang. 'What does that have to do with your work?'

'Learning,' said Connor. 'It's about how a system learns by itself. We were overly focussed on trying to get the Xtracts themselves to learn from the simulations. The response was always the same for every iteration though. The responses were not carried over to subsequent iterations of the same simulation. They were not adapted or improved on. The simulation always fell apart because the Xtracts do not return to mining operations. The mesh within which the Xtracts operate was not functioning.'

Chang watched the ocean bubble hologram as Connor explained what he was up to. It looked different now. Instead of a clear ocean bubble hologram it was now more like a meshed sphere. Gilgamesh as he called it now. He pulled up a display and inserted a giant squid into the simulation running within it.

'See,' said Connor. 'An Xtract in the mining simulation is grabbed by the squid. The Xtracts above and below move towards it and surround it. As the squid tries to move away with it, they close in and push it. If the squid lets go, they return to mining. If it moves off with it or pushes back the simulation falls apart and the Xtracts wander off randomly. It happens every time.'

'So? Obviously, that's not this red Queen effect you are talking about,' said Chang. 'What on earth are you getting at?'

'Watch this,' said Connor.

'SAI, initiate Red Queen.'

'Confirmed,' said SAI. 'Red Queen initiated.'

In the ocean bubble hologram, another column of Xtracts appeared. Now there were two groups next to each other moving up and down from the simulated seabed to the Skimmer.

'The algorithm stack now determines which group wins each scenario, like a game. If the response results in a loss they do not use it next time, if it results in a win they do. Watch.'

A giant squid appeared between the two columns of Xtracts. It grabbed one of them. Other Xtracts gathered around the squid and it let it go, but that group lost the round. The other group mined more minerals. The simulation kept repeating itself. The same squid appeared and did the same thing but the Xtracts started altering their response, fewer surrounded the squid and others kept mining. The group tried to deal with the squid but also not compromise their ability to win the round by mining the most minerals. In one simulation, a couple of Xtracts even went and interrupted the adjacent group to slow them down. It was a behaviour that ended up balancing out the amount of minerals each group mined. They were learning.'

'Holy smoke,' said Chang. You just got a group of Xtracts to learn group behaviour by themselves. How do you do that out there though in the ocean. You can't have one group of Xtracts competing against itself.'

'That I am not sure of,' said Connor. 'It would be like programming the Xtracts to compete against themselves. They would be playing host to a mind that competes against itself to survive. I haven't figured it out, but we are going to try a few things during this mining run.'

'What if Gilgamesh' said Chang, 'records the entire run of each Xtract in an actual mining operation up and down once. Then, runs that sequence again alongside each of the Xtracts carrying out the next mining run down and up. So, the result of the previous run is pitted against the current run. It works out which run resulted in more nodules. There's your red queen.'

Connor listened intently. It sounded confused; he watched the ocean bubble hologram. SAI use natural language processing to convert Chang's thoughts into a simulation that it inserted into Gilgamesh. It went back to one group of Xtracts quickly going through multiple scenarios. But it didn't seem to work.

Chang watched as Connor worked to try and transfer what they had discovered using two groups of Xtracts to using just one group.

It was going to be impossible to get hold of this technology while on the Skimmer, Chang thought to himself. Last time he got caught and all hell broke loose. They said his sister would be fine if he could get the technology to them. Maybe he should wait until they were back at the Harvester. The crew would be in accommodation on the Harvester.

He couldn't use the encrypted site on the grid node he had set up last time. They would be onto him if he tried to upload anything for his contact. It had to be a physical transfer; copy everything and get it somehow to his contact. He needed to reach his contact. But he would have to wait for them to contact him. It was stressing him somewhat.

'I've had enough of this,' said Chang gruffly. 'It isn't going to work, just wishful thinking. You and Gilgamesh should marry each other,' he said sarcastically.

Connor looked at him, not understanding the harsh remarks. Autism had its advantages. Connor shrugged his shoulders and carried on with his work.

'What about a symbiotic or commensal relationship in nature?' Connor said out loud.

SAI started running data and scripts from the libraries it had accessed.

Chang walked off, out of the information hub and back along the passage to the SAI console.

'Damn it,' he said walking into the SAI console. 'How long is this going to take, testing this hair brained idea of Connor's, I mean? Can't we just do the mining run and get back to the Harvester.'

'What's got up your nose?' said Jonny.

Jonny had come up to the SAI console and had his interface lenses on. He was checking over the navigation systems with SAI. Both Ngarra and Jonny were looking at a detailed projection of the mining location.

'Shut it,' said Chang. 'You think you're so funny with all those smart remarks. Seriously, they couldn't have picked a bigger idiot.'

'Have you seen my serious face before,' said Jonny smiling.

Chang blushed remembering what happened last time. He was feeling angry about everything, the situation with his family, being threatened again.

'If you get any fatter, we're going to have to mine you as well,' said Chang with a vicious tone.

Jonny took his interface lenses off and walked over to Chang. Jesse couldn't help but smile. She stopped what she was doing and looked at Ngarra who was trying not to laugh at the comment. She then looked at Jonny and Chang. It was getting serious.

'Enough,' she said trying to keep a straight face. 'Chang, get out of here and go check yourself. Now!'

'You lot just piss me off,' he said angrily.

'Out,' said Ngarra. 'Now, go!'

Chang stormed off and went down the stairs and through the bulkhead to the rec area. He grabbed a drink and walked forward, around the esplanade. He looked out and up at the blue green void and down to the black depths below.

Back at the SAI console Jesse and Ngarra started laughing as did Jonny. They just couldn't help themselves.

'That was classic,' said Ngarra chuckling. 'Jonny, we're going to have to mine you.'

'I'm glad you see the funny side,' said Jonny.

Jesse laughed a little then straightened her face. 'But seriously, something is up with Chang. Remember last time.'

'Hmm, yes I do,' said Ngarra. 'Let's keep an eye on him. Maybe Stella can talk to him. He seems to have taken to her for some reason.'

'Good idea,' said Jesse. 'I will talk to her.'

'I hope he's okay,' said Jonny. 'I don't hate him that much,' he said sarcastically.

'We know that. Anyway,' said Jesse. 'I have to contact Jonah about a few things and will bring this up as well.'

Jesse walked back over to the communications and security console.

'SAI, laser communication signal request with Academy crew monitoring. I want to speak with Jonah.'

'Confirmed,' said SAI. 'Eel drone and grid buoy proximity nominal, live feed available.'

A pause followed as a link was established. The crew monitoring centre duty officer appeared on the message board live feed. They said they were transferring the connection to Jonah.

Qbit technology had come a long way. By controlling photon configurations, technology had been developed to send and receive messages using lasers. The only drawback was proximity to the Eel drones and grid buoys in "the Area". Sometimes a message had to be recorded due to the slight delay. Not this time though.

'Jesse,' said Jonah as her image appeared. 'How is the trial going?'

'We are enroute to our mining location now,' said Jesse.

'Any problems with security,' said Jonah.

'Well actually yes,' said Jesse. 'I don't know if crew monitoring picked up any spikes in our crew vitals at the monitoring centre, but last night on the Harvester an intruder boarded our Skimmer to try and get hold of the technology.'

'Damn it,' said Jonah. 'We were expecting trouble but not so quickly. Everyone okay?'

'Yes,' said Jesse. 'Connor was in the hub when the person came in and restrained him. Luckily, he managed to activate the silent alarm and Jonny was still up. There was a scuffle and the intruder got away. They didn't get the technology. Connor was pretty shaken up though.'

'Thank god for that,' said Jonah. 'I mean that everyone is okay. And yes, it is good the technology was not taken.'

Jonah seemed to play down the significance of the incident thought Jesse. But then again, she was a people person. Jonah was passionate about the wellbeing of all Skimmer crews. Underneath it though, surely Jonah was nervous about losing the technology. What if it got into the wrong hands? It could be the end of the Academy crewing program.

'Also,' said Jesse. 'Something's up with Chang again. He's acting like he did last time we had that incident and he tried to steal Connor's work under duress. I think it's happening again, but he won't talk. I am going to get Stella to talk with him. Seems he is freaking out about the safety of his sister on the Harvester. He had dinner with her.'

'Makes sense,' said Jonah. 'Keep an eye on him. If it's happening again, we might not get off so lightly this time. We still haven't identified the security breach here at the Academy either. Whoever it is has gone quiet. I'm expecting trouble again over all this. I think I know who it might involve. I will talk to Rick about the Harvester incident. Got to go. I'll have to report back to the Xed council on aspects of this. Keep me updated on any developments and on how the trials go.'

Jonah's image faded. Jesse looked over at Ngarra and Jonny. They heard what was said. In their eyes was that look. The look she had not seen since the incident at sea last time.

'Okay, I'll say it,' said Jonny. 'Not again!'

'Let's just keep our heads,' said Ngarra. 'Nothing is going to happen out here, not after last time. The Sea Hunters wouldn't even risk it. It would compromise their mandate under "the Authority". Rick made it go away last time. I don't think it will be so easy this time.'

'What about the security breach?' said Jonny.

'Don't concern yourself with that,' said Jesse. 'Out here let's deal with what is in front of us, our mining rotation, these trials of Connor's technology, protecting that technology and sorting out what's going on with Chang. I don't want all this getting out of hand again.'

'On that note,' said Jonny. 'We are close to our destination. Once on site we can deploy the communication streamer and start mining.'

The conversation continued. They discussed whether to activate the Xtracts to start work overnight or wait until the morning. Also, when to set up and run Connor's trials, which would briefly take the Xtracts away from mining. They would also have to collect the required samples and process them for the Sea Hunters to pick up during inspections or when they got back to the Harvester.

Chapter 13

It was late in the day and everyone had gathered in the rec area for a break before getting ready for the mining operation.

It was over an area rich in manganese nodules. Several other contractor Skimmers were also operating in the region. More than one contractor could purchase or lease a skimmer to mine a tenure holder's lease. It was up to a tenure holder to manage this as part of their license conditions.

'Approaching mining location,' announced SAI.

'Right folks,' said Ngarra as the announcement was made by SAI. 'We all know what to do so let's get to it.'

As usual, approaching a mining location within "the Area" was an automated process. SAI controlled getting the Skimmer into position and deploying the Xtract communication streamer.

Stella got up and went down to the Xtract bay.

Chang had calmed down a bit since having his little tantrum. He was sitting across from Connor keeping to himself. He got up and followed Stella.

Connor snapped out of his thoughts and took off to the information hub above. Jonny, Jesse and Ngarra followed him up the stairs. They walked into the SAI console.

The outer hull shields closed as did the watertight bulkheads between compartments.

At the SAI console, Jonny put his interface lenses on so he could see what SAI was doing in first person view.

'Xtract bay closed up,' reported Stella over comms.

'Information hub closed up,' reported Connor.

'SAI confirm Skimmer is watertight,' said Ngarra.

'Confirmed,' said SAI. 'Skimmer is watertight.'

'Love this part,' said Jonny. 'Back in the saddle in first person view and with holographic and virtual displays on demand.'

'Typical,' said Jesse smiling. 'Back in the saddle?'

She stood to one side at the security and communication console monitoring everything going on.

Ngarra managed a smile as he looked at Jesse. He watched Jonny's cowboy antics, briefing thinking about his colloquial language. He turned back, watching the navigation hologram in the centre of the SAI console. It showed the Skimmer moving into position.

They watched on as the Skimmer slowed, moving to the coordinates that had been entered. It completed a broad arc around the location. Sensor arrays scanned the area and made sure nothing was in the way or going to interfere with coming to a full stop and deploying the streamer.

The rim driven propulsion drive, adjusted speed and started slowing down. Jonny briefly looked at the schematics of the power train. The Skimmer straightened up and slowed to a few knots. The crew waited and watched. In the hologram, it showed the Skimmer stopping in position.

'In position,' said SAI. 'Sensor scans clear. Deploying Xtract communication streamer.'

In the Xtract bay, Stella and Chang were watching a camera feed and display of the communication streamer. To the rear, below and between the rim driven propulsion system was a cabling drum. They watched as it activated and started to deploy the long streamer.

'Cable drum clear,' said Stella over comms. 'SAI is deploying it now.'

The weighted cable started descending into the depths below. Qubit communication nodes were spaced at even intervals along it. These nodes sent and received laser communication signals to and from the Xtracts.

SAI was able to control and communicate with the Xtracts moving down and up from the seabed 4000 metres below.

Stella and Chang monitored the descent of the streamer. It took a while. On the end of it was a sampling device. That was how they collected the required seabed and water column samples, which were processed and stored for collection by the sea Hunters.

Something was bound to go wrong, Stella thought to herself. Sooner or later either with the cable, communications or with the Xtracts. If it weren't for these ongoing issues, Skimmers would not need crews.

Once the streamer was in position the Xtracts would detach and start their descent to mine the seabed.

'Stella,' said Ngarra over comms. 'Confirm Xtract status.'

'On to it now,' said Stella. 'Chang is checking operating system displays for each one.'

Chang looked at Stella and moaned about having to check every Xtract display. He reluctantly went, quickly moving down each side of the Skimmer checking power systems for each one was nominal. He moved along each side of the Skimmer.

The Xtract maintenance bay, airlock and moonpool were located between this passage that ran down each side. He was on the inside of the recess along one side. Outside, the Xtracts were docked on their clamps.

The control room and console where Stella was standing were forward. A watertight bulkhead entrance and exit was located between it, each passageway and the maintenance bay.

'Chang,' said Stella. 'I have an Xtract with a malfunctioning nodule collection system. Have you got it, number four?'

'Yep,' said Stella. 'It's power routing to the loader control is compromised. Looking at the display now.'

'SAI, confirm power distribution in Xtract four is compromised.'

'Confirmed,' said SAI. 'Power distribution compromised. Recovering Xtract four to moonpool for servicing by repair drone.'

'Chang,' said Stella. 'SAI is recovering it to the moonpool. Have you finished those checks?'

'Yep, done both sides,' he said walking back along the passage he was in and through the watertight bulkhead entrance.

She swiped the display. SAI pressurised the moonpool and airlock, disarming the entrance which opened.

Stella turned the external camera system on. They watched as Xtract four detached from its docking clamp. It moved out over the nodule trays along the leading edge of the Skimmer. It then descended and moved under the Skimmer towards the moonpool.

Through the moonpool camera they watched it ascend and surface. A robotic arm secured it and lifted it up and out. It guided the Xtract into the airlock which closed behind it. The airlock returned to one atmosphere of breathable air and opened into the Xtract maintenance bay. The robotic arm guided the Xtract through and into position, securing it on a docking clamp. The airlock closed behind it.

'Okay,' said Chang. 'Let's get in there and see what's up with this thing.'

Chang's mood seemed a little better Stella thought to herself following him through the watertight bulkhead entrance. I must try and find out what is going on in that head of his.

'Ngarra,' she said over comms. 'One of the Xtracts has malfunctioned. Power to the loader is compromised. SAI has recovered it. Eleven powered up and ready to detach for mining operations.'

'Okay,' said Ngarra.

'The streamer is close to touch down,' said Stella.

'Confirm when you know how long it will take to repair that Xtract,' said Ngarra.

In the SAI console, Jesse decided everything was under control. Her checks over communications and security were done. She exited through the now open watertight bulkhead to the rear and went to check on Connor in the hub.

'Touch down,' said Jonny as he got up and put his hand on the floor and then raised both in the air. 'Another one for the team.'

The streamer had reached the seabed some four thousand metres below.

'Always the joker,' said Ngarra smiling. 'I guess Stella doesn't need to confirm it then does she.'

Jesse turned and looked at them both. Shrugging her shoulders, she walked out.

'SAI,' said Ngarra. 'Open outer hull shields.'

'Confirmed,' said SAI. 'Opening outer hull shields.'

Ngarra and Jonny turned around and walked forward.

The shields covered two levels. One on their level and one on the level below. When they were both opened a person in the SAI console could see a person standing at the front of the rec area below in the viewing area. It was forward of the narrow esplanade that skirted each side of the enclosed overdrive propulsion system.

From both the SAI console and forward viewing area below, a person could see down either side of the Skimmer.

'Here we go,' said Jonny. 'Bets on, which Xtract makes it away first.'

'I always loose these,' said Ngarra. 'Ever since we told SAI to randomise detaching and descending for our own amusement.'

'Well, it took on amongst the other crews,' said Ngarra. 'It's now an ongoing competition between crews to guess correctly. We were on the leader board for a while.'

'Horah!' said Jonny with a fist pump. 'Number seven is away.'

'Damn,' said Ngarra.

Xtract lights came on. The Skimmer mine lights also came on. They watched as each Xtract detached from their docking clamp within the recess. Along each side Xtracts slowly moved out over the nodule trays. They hovered briefly then started to descend in a line adjacent to the communication streamer. From above, they could see the pilot lights of each one as it descended into the depths below.

'Right,' said Ngarra over comms. 'Everyone, SAI has this now. Mining operation started. Let's meet in the rec area. Jonny can be on duty first and keep an eye on things.'

'Aww boss,' he said jokingly. 'You always pick on me. I need sustenance first,' he said rubbing his belly.

'You need more than sustenance,' Ngarra said.

'Ouch,' said Jonny as they walked to the rear and through the watertight bulkhead entrance, down the stairs and to the rec area.

Being on watch was a flexible arrangement. A person didn't have to be at a station. If SAI reported on anything, the person on duty checked it. They also responded to any alarms that went off.

In the rec area, Jesse was engaged in conversation with Connor about his work. The trial tomorrow was important. He would hide away in the information hub and forget to eat. She had managed to convince Connor to continue talking with her if he came and got something to eat.

She dropped a hint into the conversation about how he might be feeling after being restrained by the intruder that tried to take the technology he had developed.

Stella and Chang came up from the Xtract bay after checking on the malfunctioning Xtract. The repair drone was fixing it.

A conversation ensued amongst the crew about Chang's frustration and anger. Now that he had nothing to do Chang's mood had quickly changed. As usual Chang was dismissive, especially to Stella. Stella didn't take it personally.

'Looks like a counselling session in here,' said Jonny as he returned with a plate of food and sat down. 'My solace is sitting here on my plate,' he said licking his lips at the food he had in front of him.

'Funny guy,' said Ngarra. 'If you can call fermentation and protein manipulation 'solace' in food and think it's great cuisine, then you're easy to please.'

'That I am,' said Jonny. 'Still, it's a bit different not having Aamir with us this time though,' he said waving his knife at Ngarra. 'Now there's a man that knows about Cuisine.'

'If you really want to know, he's on another Skimmer,' said Jesse. 'They needed a Communications and Security Officer at short notice.'

'What about at the Academy?' said Chang. 'He wasn't around there either.'

Chang had managed to stop being grumpy about everyone asking him why he was so angry all the time.

'You ask too many questions Chang,' said Jesse. 'Anyway, it's not our concern is it. I'm sure he is fine.'

Chang relaxed a bit and continued eating. The light conversation and banter went on for quite a while. It had been a long day given the events of the previous night.

'Right,' said Stella as she finished her meal. 'I'm up for a game of something in the holo room before getting some sleep. It's getting late and we have a long day tomorrow.'

'For you maybe,' said Chang. 'What's to do tomorrow, stand and watch a bunch of drones doing their thing. I'm off for some me time,' he said getting up and slamming his plate into the collector. He walked off up the stairs to the SAI console.

'What is it with him?' said Jonny.

'He has issues,' said Stella.

'Leave it to me,' said Jesse.

'Let's go then,' said Ngarra.

'Nothing hard out,' said Jonny rubbing his belly. 'I'm full.'

'Full of yourself,' said Stella.

'Hey,' said Jonny. 'She's a hard woman to please.'

The crew laughed and made their way to the holo room. SAI was able to project a variety of interactive games.

While the others were in the holo room having some fun, Chang was at the SAI console. He stood in front of the retracted outer hull shields and look down one side of the Skimmer.

'Some of those Xtracts should come into view with their loading buckets filled with nodules soon,' he said out loud.

He watched and waited, trying not to think about his family situation. The anger subsided.

His smart watch activated.

He looked at it.

He had been expecting his contact to get in touch. He opened an encrypted message from a site linked to a node on the grid.

Proceed with plan
At Harvester secure the technology
Wait for contact to ask for it
Sister is in danger

Chang closed the link and clenching his fists looked out into the darkness. Alone, in the middle of nowhere. He wished the void would just take him. It was all just a dream, a nightmare he would wake up from.

As he contemplated what to do a pale light appeared from below; an Xtract was coming back.

His thoughts wandered. Much about human history had been manipulated through religion initially and then through science and later by industry. The pieces of the puzzle were all there if people bothered to look hard enough.

He watched the pale light and his imagination ran wild. *The Elohim, the Powerful ones, the Anunnaki had come back*, he thought to himself. They had come for him.

He watched on mesmerised.

The pale light rose out of the depths below.

An hour down, an hour on the seabed and an hour back. Had it been that long already?

'Hey, how's it going?' said Stella walking in behind him.

'Thought you lot were gaming,' said Chang.

'Short-lived,' said Stella. 'Too tired and Jonny got the stich. A belly full of food.'

'It sucks,' said Chang.

'What sucks?' said Stella.

'Family history, human history, all of it, that's what. It all sucks. A file full of paperclips holding the pieces of my life together. Paperclips and family ties.'

'Very deep of you Chang,' said Stella.

'Well, the space in my mind is deep,' said Chang. 'For better or worse, those paperclips bind us to how things are now. That's family for you. What I think is going on and what is actually happening don't seem to add up. It's like living in two worlds. One we are led to believe is our reality and the other.'

'Suppose you are right,' said Stella. 'It's all just perception, isn't it? Despite everything, you're stuck with your family no matter what you think of the situation that surrounds them.'

They watched the Xtract unload its nodules and descend back down into the depths of the ocean.

***

The next morning everyone was ready for the trial. They would be in position for another day or so until the trays were full.

Overnight the Xtracts had continued to descend and ascend from the seabed with loads of nodules. In between runs at set intervals, they would dock and recharge.

Stella was up before the others. She had got SAI to position all the Xtracts either side of the Skimmer adjacent to the nodule trays, temporally halting mining operations. Chang joined her.

Jesse and Ngarra were in the information hub with Connor. Jonny was at the SAI console. He had his interface lenses on.

'If anything goes wrong,' said Ngarra over comms, 'SAI will take back control of the Xtracts and return them to their mining operation.'

'Okay,' said Connor over comms. 'Here's what will happen. SAI will synch the Xtracts with the ocean bubble hologram simulation. Gilgamesh will take control of the Xtracts. Then we will run the simulation for "Red Queen". That's what I call it now, Gilgamesh and the Red Queen. It wasn't working before. It was basically a storage device. "Red Queen" changes all that. The Xtracts will be in two groups of six. They will compete against each other to mine the most nodules. Anything that interrupts that will initiate a competitive response.'

'How?' said Ngarra. 'I mean, if they are just going up and down mining nodules.'

'Easy,' said Connor. We use Gilgamesh; the ocean bubble hologram. Out there they will be responding to an imaginary situation that has been encoded.'

'Don't you wreck our Xtracts,' said Jesse.

'We won't,' said Connor smiling.

Connor often said we; as if SAI and the ocean bubble hologram; Gilgamesh and the Red Queen as he now called it was alive.

'It's taken us months to figure this out,' said Connor. 'We started by looking at all this colony and hive behaviour in animals. We also looked at non-centralised nervous systems in organisms. We identified patterning in data on all this. We found scripts of code that had been used to try and get drones to do the same. From online libraries, we put together a set of layered algorithms that we hacked. But group responses and learning were always user defined or guided. There wasn't any autonomous learning of group behaviour; no collective memory from which to draw. Red Queen takes it one step further, competition over many iterations. The iterations are the multiple generations over which the Xtracts evolve collective behaviour responses rather than just react to an event. It's retained memory at the level of the population, not the individuals within the group. It's a massive step forward in autonomous group behaviour in drones. One small step for us, one giant leap for them.'

'Right let's do this then Connor,' said Ngarra over comms.

'SAI,' said Connor. 'Initiate Red Queen.'

'Confirmed,' said SAI. 'Red Queen initiated.'

'Okay, okay, okay,' said Connor excitedly. 'This is good, great. SAI has initiated "Red Queen".'

Connor looked at the displays linked to the ocean bubble hologram.

'I got SAI to make the Xtracts descend to a depth of 200 metres below us and then come back up again,' he said over comms. 'They are in a loop and will do it continuously. Red Queen either disadvantages one group or gives an advantage to the other.'

'Hey, the Xtracts are moving off in their columns,' said Jonny over comms from the SAI console.

He was looking out at what they were doing. All Xtracts moved off, descending in two columns like ants looking for food.

In the ocean bubble hologram, the giant squid Connor loved to use appeared. It grabbed one of the Xtracts descending in a column. The Xtracts either side of it stopped and closed in on the squid. They pressed against it. That column was now delayed from mining nodules. The other column of Xtracts completed the round trip first and loaded the most nodules.

The simulation carried on. They watched as the giant squid reappeared in the ocean bubble hologram and grabbed one from the same column again. This time the same two Xtracts closed in and pushed on the squid but something different happened. The deepest Xtract moved out of the column and got in the way of an Xtract in the other column. It had to deviate. The Xtract then moved back into position and continued mining. As Red Queen progressed the simulation continued to alter by itself.

Outside, the Xtracts responded accordingly; as if the giant squid was there for real.

'Geeze,' said Jonny over comms as he looked out from the SAI console. 'These Xtracts are doing lots of crazy things out here.'

'They are doing exactly what is being down in the ocean bubble hologram,' said Connor 'Gilgamesh and the Red Queen is working.'

'Yeah, but what if you don't have this ocean bubble hologram and the communication streamer,' said Ngarra. 'I mean, your Gilgamesh would then have to be inside every Xtract wouldn't it?'

'I was stuck on that issue for ages,' said Connor. 'No central hub or centralised control. Perhaps it's both. I have to figure it out.'

'And you don't want them to actually do all this,' said Jesse. 'It would interrupt mining operations.'

'It would have to be like each Xtract was competing with itself,' said Connor. 'Self-competition, but not at the expense of group. Would it still be Red Queen? Red Queen works because two species compete for the same resource in a changing environment.'

Connor paused for a minute and thought about what he had said.

The others looked on, a little lost trying to figure out what on earth he was talking about.

'There would have to be a sub routine,' he said. 'It would always try to optimise nodule extraction in its own group of Xtracts without inhibiting the other group. But that must not override the need to assist another Xtract that runs into trouble.'

'Well,' said Ngarra. 'We have taken the next step. It works.'

'Okay,' said Jesse. 'Let's get the Xtracts back to their mining operation Connor. You have what you need to carry on. Break the synch with Gilgamesh and the ocean bubble hologram and return the Xtracts to SAI's control for mining.'

'Right,' said Connor. 'SAI terminate synch with Xtracts. Return Xtracts to mining.'

'Confirmed,' said SAI. 'Synch terminated, Xtracts returning to mining operations.'

'Thanks, Connor,' said Jesse. 'I will report the success to Jonah and Rick.'

'Everyone,' said Ngarra over open comms. 'Technology trial is finished. Return to mining operations.'

'I'm off to catch up on some work at the SAI console,' said Jesse.

'I'm going to the rec area,' said Ngarra. 'We have some time until the nodule trays are full. Let's hope no Xtracts malfunction.'

They walked out of the info hub and left Connor to his work. In the ocean bubble hologram, the simulation was reset and continued. Gilgamesh was now running Red Queen permanently.

Connor was engrossed in all the data generated from the simulation. SAI had also projected a range of information, data and scripts for Connor to look at based on his comments. The advantages of natural language processing.

Chapter 14

On the same morning that Ngarra's crew were testing Connor's technology, at the Harvester Lee had arranged to meet Sue at the lab complex. They wanted to talk to Chang's sister Ying Yue about progress with the project.

During the incident that occurred over six months ago, they had tested remotely operating a skimmer. The Academy sim centre had been able to do it successfully by synching their simulator SAI with the Skimmer SAI. But what they really wanted was to eliminate the need to remotely monitor a skimmer at all. They just wanted to send it out there to mine the seabed with its Xtract drones autonomously.

Walking towards the lab complex Lee thought that since catching up with her brother Chang, Ying Yue seemed a little distant and off task.

'Good morning,' he said walking into the lab. 'Another successful crew change.'

'Except for that little incident,' said Sue looking over at Lee.

'What incident?' said Ying Yue.

'Nothing really,' said Sue smiling. 'Just problems with logistics. Now that Lee is here let's talk.'

Sue, Lee and Ying Yue made their way to the observation platform overlooking the hanger. A skimmer was suspended over the large cavity that reached down to the moonpool below.

'How was Chang?' said Lee.

'Grumpy as usual,' said Ying Yue. 'But he was glad to see me.'

Ying Yue was careful not to say too much; it could get her in trouble, and she was worried enough about her situation. She didn't trust Sue.

'It seems Chang wants a lot out of life,' asked Sue. 'He thinks the world owes him something.'

'He blames Father for everything,' she said. 'Including our mothers situation. He has never got over that.'

'Perhaps he feels hard done by,' said Lee. 'I mean look at how successful you are. Your father favours you.'

'No more than Chang,' she said. 'If he would let Father into his life more, he might see that it is him pushing his family away not the other way around.'

'Perhaps when they return from their mining run you would like to catch up with him again?' Sue enquired.

'That would be nice,' she said cautiously.

'We could even invite Connor and you two could talk,' said Sue. 'Perhaps you could get some insight into this technology they have.'

'From what Chang has said, I don't think Connor would be allowed to do that given his personality and project security,' at least that is what Chang said.

Ying Yue thought she was starting to say too much and needed to change the topic. Her father had said he was worried, worried about the Harvester and other people's agendas. She had to be careful.

'That's right,' said Lee. 'We wouldn't want to cause an incident at sea that would reflect badly on us. Perhaps when you see Chang, you could just ask him for a tour. A tour of their Skimmer. Perfectly innocent and you can report back to us.'

'I suppose I could,' said Ying Yue. 'Innocent enough and harmless. I'm sure that because it is me, they wouldn't mind. You know unauthorised personnel are not allowed on those Skimmers though. They could get in trouble.'

'I am sure they will be able to get approval if it's family,' said Sue. 'They don't have to show you any of the secure areas do they.'

'Sounds like a plan then,' said Lee as he looked at Sue.

'So, on another note,' said Sue. 'How is the project going.'

'Since testing remote monitoring of the Skimmer, we have been trying to break it,' she said.

'What do you mean by break it?' said Lee.

'Well,' said Ying Yue. 'Run all sorts of mining scenarios where something goes wrong with the Xtracts. An automated mining operation is fine until something goes wrong. SAI was put together to run the actual Skimmer. It also has control over the Xtracts and directs them until something goes wrong. That's why if something does go wrong, they still need crews. SAI just can't think the way we need it to.'

'It's disappointing that Connor isn't working with us,' said Lee.

'Yes,' said Sue. 'From what we hear, this youth Connor has something we need.'

'It will be good to at least get a tour with Chang,' said Lee. 'A picture paints a thousand words. Isn't that why they say.'

Sue smiled at his analogy all the while thinking about how to get hold of Connor's technology.

Lee reminded her of Chang's father, to emotional and far too interested in family, western ideals and their way of thinking. She wondered why the CCP thought so highly of their father. Perhaps because he was so well connected with people in the western world. *A liability*, she thought to herself.

They all looked out over the hanger bay. Four large docking clamps held the Skimmer in place. It was suspended high above the moonpool below. Around it several technicians had various equipment hooked up. It looked like spikes or lances piercing the side of some caged animal. It looked like electrodes connected to a brain, or in this case linked to the Skimmer SAI. If a skimmer SAI had feelings, perhaps it would be in pain.

'I have to get back to work,' said Ying Yue as she walked off.

'Certainly,' said Sue. 'And Ying Yue, thanks for the brief on your work.'

Ying Yue walked off to check in with her team and continue her work.

Lee was admiring the scene in front of him. He thought of an old star trek movie. In it, was a large gateway station orbiting the earth. Starships were docked in it for maintenance. Not much different from what now orbited the earth. The staging gateways that serviced the off-planet mining outposts.

'I have an idea,' said Sue.

'What would that be?' said Lee.

'We plant a device on Ying Yue before she meets with Chang,' said Sue. 'If she does get a tour, then we can get hold of the information we need without her even realising.'

'Where would you put it though?' said Lee. 'What if she doesn't go on this tour straight away?'

'It's a risk but easy enough to do,' said Sue. 'The device would detect and synch with any open data feeds. Assuming Connor is in the information hub and working on his project, anything open and running will be copied.'

'A family tour seems innocent enough not to arouse suspicion,' said Lee. 'However, I don't know if their father would agree with what we are doing. He wouldn't want to jeopardise the relationship he has with Xed Academy and with

Jonah. GlobeCorpMining provides most of the funding remember. If that was compromised, it would have a major impact on mining in the area. Contractors that lease or purchase the Skimmers would take legal action against us. If the Xed council pulled away from allowing GlobeCorpMining to be the majority funder of the crew program there wouldn't be enough crews for the Skimmers either. We still need them. We are not ready.'

'But if we have Connor's technology, we wouldn't need the crews anymore,' said Sue. 'Combined with the mimic drone program we would have it all.'

'It's a big if,' said Lee. 'What if the technology is not advanced enough, the lag time could be huge?'

'We could save GlobeCorpMining hundreds of millions of dollars funding the Skimmer crew program,' said Sue. The CCP would praise us for it.'

'Or make us disappear,' said Lee looking concerned.

'Lee, you worry too much,' said Sue smiling. 'They tolerate Chang's father's weakness for his western ways. If it doesn't work, we can find someone to blame.'

'What's that supposed to mean?' said Lee. 'I'm not sure it's the right thing to do. In saying that, let's do it and see what we can come up with. We may get enough information to determine what this technology is capable of.'

'There is the other project Ying Yue is working on to,' said Sue. 'The mimic drones.'

'Yes, but that is dangerous,' said Lee. 'Drones copying behaviour patterns of species including humans, but to what end?'

'It's just a concept,' said Sue smiling. 'Who knows what the end point and application is? It's infectious isn't it, if you know what I mean.'

'That's because you want to weaponise it,' said Lee sternly. 'Anyway, I will get our security team to get this device to attach to Ying Yue's uniform. It will then be on her person when she catches up with Chang on their return from mining.'

'The day is getting on,' said Sue looking out over the hanger and suspended Skimmer. 'Let's continue this discussion over a meal.'

They walked off the observation platform and back through the lab complex and out into the passage. They moved forward along the passageway, passing technicians, operations personnel and a few security officers. Other crew stopped briefly as they passed and acknowledged their presence. Protocol demanded it as they were the two most senior officers on the Harvester.

Walking into the restaurant they ordered a meal and were served automatically a selection of Asian cuisine. They sat down in a secluded area off to one side.

'What about the Sea Hunters?' said Lee as they sat eating.

'My suspicions are that within that agency, someone is doing the bidding of another organisation or person,' said Sue. 'No one else on board here would even bother or have the need to attempt to get on a skimmer undetected. Besides the Skimmer crews, the Sea Hunters were the only other people on board.'

'That means someone else is interested in Ngarra's crew and most likely Connor's technology,' said Lee.

'Or someone is playing all of us at the same time,' said Sue.

'Don't you think that when Ngarra's crew returns to the Harvester and the Sea Hunters turn up as well that we should have cause for concern,' said Lee. 'Perhaps we should delay trying to get hold of this technology.'

'No!' said Sue slamming her utensils down.

Lee jumped back in surprise. A few others looked over. Lee gathered himself and sat back looking Sue in the eyes.

'No,' she whispered. 'I don't think you understand just have valuable this technology is. If Skimmers and Xtract mining drones are able to look after themselves, don't you see the implications of that?'

'What do you mean?' said Lee.

'Other applications that are not so innocent, that's all I'm prepared to say.'

Lee carried on looking at Sue. She was PLA Navy. He didn't trust her.

Sue went back to eating her meal.

They were nearly finished.

Lee decided to change the topic.

Sue was a dangerous woman to get on the wrong side of.

'What about Chang's mother?' he said. 'Is that not driving his anger? Isn't that what makes him so susceptible to persuasion? At least that is what I have heard. He talks too much and has these outbursts.'

'His father isn't to blame for what happened to his mother, Chang just thinks he is,' said Sue. 'His father didn't make her work in that lab when the accident happened. She wanted to work there. He just encouraged her.'

'Isn't that why Ying Yue is so interested in mimic drones?' said Lee. 'I mean understanding how a virus works and what they do to cells. Isn't that the point;

mimicking the same process in a drone that takes over other drones by replicating itself using another drones AI system. A drone virus if you like.'

'Yes of course. Weaponised mimic drones, but let's keep that quiet,' said Sue. 'The point is that when Chang was little; back in the mid-2020s the world changed. Chang's mother was working in a lab. They had just started looking at this whole concept. She got exposed to something that made her sick. She recovered from it but was never the same afterwards. Always weak. That's where his anger comes from.'

'Some people made a lot of money out of all that,' said Lee. 'A global shift in power and economies. Look at where we are now both on and off the planet. And look at the energy technology and interest in the planet by the others. It is much more open now and talked about now.'

'Enough,' said Sue quietly. 'You should mind what you say about the others.'

'Okay,' said Lee. 'Anyway, Chang will easily be swayed into thinking he is doing something noble.'

'Exactly,' said Sue.

They had finished eating.

'I will organise this device to put on Ying Yue's uniform,' said Lee as he got up.

'Let's go to operations,' said Sue. 'A ship is arriving alongside to load nodules.'

So much going on, Lee thought to himself as they made their way to the operations centre. *It was mind blowing*, he thought. He felt like he was in a movie.

They walk out of the restaurant and down the passageway to operations.

'I'll leave you to it,' he said. 'I'm going to sort out this device to plant on Ying Yue and go over our security protocols with the team.'

'See you later then,' said Sue as she turned away and walked over to the duty staff.

She got an update on the ship that had arrived.

'The ship has cleared the security perimeter,' said the duty officer.

On a large navigation and pilotage display, they watched the ship come alongside, get into position, and prepare for loadout. Schematics were being displayed.

'Initiate loading sequence,' said the duty officer.

They watched what was going on through the external camera system display.

On one side of the Harvester drone deck, a large riser column extended upwards. It rotated outboard and a large conveyor dropped down and extended out over the water. It was a relatively calm day.

A duty officer bought up the display of the nodule storage system on the Harvester. The storage and conveyor system activated. The loading technician used his hands to swipe across the displays and bring up various icons to monitor the loading sequence. Once everything turned to green the loadout would begin.

'Automated loading system deployed and clear for loading,' he said. 'Nodule storage system online. Ready to load. Waiting for go from ship.'

Everything on the Harvester was ready. They waited for the ships hopper silos to finish opening.

'We are green for go,' said the duty officer. 'SAI, load nodules.'

'Confirmed,' said SAI. 'Loading nodules.'

SAI controlled the loading of the nodules along the conveyor system and into the ships silos. They all watched as the nodules started streaming out along the conveyor system. The nodules exited the Harvester, moving along the conveyor extended out over the water. They started spilling into the ship's silos.

Chapter 15

On the same day Ngarra's crew were conducting mining operations, Rick and Jonah were at Xed early for a council meeting. Jonah had heard from Jesse about the intruder incident on board the Skimmer at the Harvester and told Rick about it. The council needed to be informed.

She was in her office looking out over the campus. It felt like it was all happening again. It had been quiet for some time. No attempts had been made to get hold of the technology. They had still not identified the breach in security, but she had her suspicions.

'Right,' said Jonah as Rick walked into her office. 'Let's go into the meeting room,' it's time.

'Morning to you to,' said Rick smiling.

'Oh, sorry, yeah,' said Jonah. 'A lot on my mind with all this.'

'Tell me about it,' said Rick.

They walked into the meeting room. Jonah's secretary followed behind. Around them the images of council members appeared. They all greeted each other.

'Thank you for responding at such short notice,' said Jonah. 'There was an incident at the Harvester. As you know Ngarra's crew is on a skimmer rotation. They are running trials using the technology. Last night at the Harvester an intruder tried to board their Skimmer and remove the technology. The intruder tried to restrain Connor. Luckily another crewmember was awake and saw the emergency duress alarm go off. He managed to stop what was going on, but the intruder got away.'

The council members erupted into conversation about who or why they would be there. Jonah waited a short time and then refocussed the meeting.

'Okay everyone. Listen please,' said Jonah.

She looked at Rick who motioned her to carry on.

She waited for the council members to quieten down.

'Does this mean GlobeCorpMining is behind it?' said the council member for Australia.

'I don't think so,' said Jonah. 'They would not want to jeopardise their relationship with us, funding of the Skimmer crew program or breach any regulations in "the Area".'

'That doesn't mean someone within GlobeCorpMining is not involved,' said Rick.

Jonah stared at him. He was doing it again, undermining her in front of the council.

'We should move to secure the technology before it gets into the wrong hands,' he said. 'We came close to losing it last time.'

'Yes, and to the Sea Hunters,' said Jonah.

Rick went slightly red in the face. *Got me there*, he thought to himself trying not to look at Jonah.

'Wasn't the whole point to give the technology to the Sea Hunters for safe keeping?' said the council member for the UAE.

'Yes, exactly,' said Rick. 'Last time they thought they were doing the right thing. This time they will stand off and keep an eye on things. The Sea Hunters have left the Harvester after doing some inspections.'

'How do you know that?' said Jonah.

I'm sure he is up to something again, thought Jonah. Last time he wasn't upfront either. He's up to something again.

Rick quickly changed the subject.

'If we have what they want, why don't we double down on it,' he said. 'I mean, Chang's sister is on that Harvester and she knows a lot more than we think about all this. Perhaps we can get Chang to find out what she knows.'

'Is that wise?' said the council member for Australia. 'We are not even sure who "they" are. Besides Chang is volatile. He could just as easily spill the beans to his sister about Connor's work.'

A discussion ensued amongst council members about what course of action to take to protect development of the technology.

'Back with me again,' said Jonah. 'Listen everyone.'

She paused and waited for them to refocus.

'No one out there is openly going to jeopardise their right to operate within "the Area" under "the Authority" and maritime regulations. The situation the Sea Hunters were in last time was passed off as a legitimate pursuit in order to board and inspect a non-compliant operation of Skimmers. It was all made to go away by State sponsor agencies and nothing more was said about it.'

'True,' said Rick. 'Whoever "they" are will not look to expose themselves openly just to protect the interests of another party in a technology being developed for mining in "the Area".'

Rick decided to play down the importance of the Sea Hunters working in "the Area" and their involvement. Work still needed to be done and his people wanted some progress towards the next stage of the project.

'This is what I propose,' said Jonah. 'I will ask Chang's father, Chief Operating Officer of GlobeCorpMining to keep a watchful eye on what is going on out at the Harvester. Rick will contact the Sea Hunters and inform them about the risk to Ngarra's crew given the incident on the Harvester that has happened. I will also talk with Jesse about Chang and his sister and what if any risk there is.'

'What about the security breach?' said the member for Oceania. 'We have not been able to determine how it occurred or what the implications are for Xed or the Academy.'

'They are safe out there for now,' said Rick. 'We monitored Connor and Chang when they were here. The best we can do is as Jonah has said, inform the Sea Hunters that they may be in danger and to keep an eye on them. Also, to talk with Chang's father the Chief Operating Officer of GlobeCorpMining.'

'Right,' said Jonah to everyone. 'I will inform you of the outcome.'

With that, the council member images disappeared.

Rick and Jonah stood quietly and somewhat uncomfortably for a moment. They had been avoiding each other lately. Each suspicious of the other but both with the future of Xed and the Academy in mind.

'I will go and check in with the Sea Hunter liaison officer on campus,' said Rick.

'Okay, yes good idea,' said Jonah glad that the silence had been broken. 'And I will touch base with Chang's father.'

Rick walked out of the meeting room and Jonah's office.

'I'll catch up with the liaison officer later,' he thought to himself out loud.

He made his way down through the admin building, across the large centre foyer that stretched up to the roof high above, out of the entrance and across campus.

'Better get hold of Max,' he said to himself out loud. 'He will have a good handle on what's going on out there. I'll catch up with our liaison officer later.'

It was a clear sunny day. He enjoyed walking through the grounds between the buildings. The sim centre loomed large in front of him. As he entered it a few students said hi. Pausing briefly to chat he then passed through the learning hub. He walked between the Skimmer simulators in the crew training facility adjacent to the learning hub.

On the way, he kept thinking about the Harvester. From what Max said, he thought something was going on out there. There was the family connection with Chang to consider as well. His people were concerned about bringing Connor and Chang's sister together. It wasn't just about Connor's work.

The walk was always the same, he thought to himself along the way. He passed through security and into the Skimmer crew monitoring and communications complex. He crossed the floor between monitoring stations. He went through security again and into "the room". He knew it so well now he could do it with his eyes closed.

He walked to the rear of "the room" and stood in front of a workstation. Using his smartwatch, he opened a grid node and using a secure link sent an encrypted message to Max to make contact. He waited a few minutes for a reply.

'Rick,' said Max. 'What's the situation?'

'Did you get the technology,' said Rick.

'No,' said Max. 'Currently lingering with intent while Ngarra's crew is mining.'

Damn, thought Rick to himself. I will have to rely on Chang to try and get hold of it now.

'The risk of losing the technology to the Chinese has increased,' said Rick. 'You must monitor any movement on the Harvester. Especially between Ngarra's crew, Chang's sister and her minders. Find a way.'

'I will,' said Max. 'We will shadow Ngarra's Skimmer. Between mining runs we will make sure we are on board the Harvester for inspections.'

Rick thought quickly. I need to get Chang to secure Connor's work and give it to his sister on board their Skimmer. That's the excuse to take them both into custody and off the harvester. The Sea Hunters will write it up as a breach of Skimmer protocols; having a non-crew member on board. Harvester security won't be able to do anything about it.

'Got to go,' said Rick. 'I will be in touch.'

With that, he closed the link.

He hoped the spot checks by security of "the room" access would not flag his use as abnormal. Even if it did, no details of what was done would show, just who accessed a grid node, when and for how long.

Rick walked out of "the room" and through security. He returned to the crew monitoring and communication complex and continued with his day. He went and got a briefing from the duty officer on any Skimmer crew updates.

Looking up at the main status screen to the front he could see where every Skimmer in the area was operating. He went to a workstation and using his hands swiped through Skimmer crews until he found Ngarra's one. He swiped the crew icon so it appeared on the main screen at the front of the centre. Using a drop-down menu, he opened the crew status and vitals display. He then told the duty officer to keep a watchful eye on Ngarra's crew until told otherwise and pass on the request to any duty watch handover.

***

Meanwhile, in her office Jonah stood looking out over the campus. With a coffee in hand, and her secretary back in her own office, she pondered the situation at hand.

'I'm sure Rick is involved in all this,' she said out loud to herself. 'We can't afford to lose this technology Connor has developed. It represents our future if the Skimmers become crewless. Whether crewless or not, I am sure Rick has another agenda.'

Jonah carried on thinking.

'What about the rumours?' she thought out loud again. 'Rumours about something called mimic drones and what was the connection with Chang's family.'

She knew they were working on something else out at that Harvester.

'Right,' she said to her secretary as she turned and looked at her through the office door. 'I'm going to get in touch with Chang's father.'

'Okay,' her secretary said. 'Anything I can get you.'

'No, I'm fine thanks,' she said.

Jonah turned back to look out over the campus again. She swiped her smartwatch and used her message board to link with Chang's father. She hoped he was not busy. Most of the time she was on a priority line to him. He usually stopped whatever he was doing to talk.

After several minutes, her smart watch message board activated, and his image appeared.

'Jonah, nice to hear from you,' he said. 'How are things going?'

'I'm concerned,' she said. 'Ngarra's crew is back on a mining rotation and Connor is running trials using the technology. But your son Chang is unpredictable. I'm worried. Seeing his sister again may be problematic. Given how angry he gets he could say too much. Why is he always so angry?'

'I've known you for a long time,' he said. 'Chang blames me for his mother's situation. It was a long time ago and she never fully recovered. His sister is now involved in that research out on the Harvester.'

'What happened and what research?' said Jonah.

She tried to keep her tone even and almost uninterested.

'It's complicated,' he said. 'His mother was working in a lab in China when she was younger. It was back in the early to mid-2020s. She got exposed to something that made her sick. She recovered from it but was never the same afterwards. Always weak. That's where his anger comes from.'

'What research was it?' she said.

'AI, viruses and biopolymers and metallurgic nanotechnology for drones. They were looking at viruses as a model for AI development in drones. A model of how to infect, mimic and then take over drones and develop swarming hives,' he said. 'Can't say much more than that. Other than the fact that my daughter has carried on with aspects of that work.'

'Thus, the term mimic drones then,' she said. 'Why is she doing that on a mineral Harvester.'

'Just an opportunity,' he said. 'GlobeCorpMining had an interest in its application in mining operations. That's all.'

Jonah decided not to press him about it. But it rung some alarm bells in her head. Connor's work on learning autonomous group behaviour in drones. Chang's sister work and this rumour about mimic drones. *What happens when you bring the two together*? she thought to herself.

'Anyway,' she said. 'If something goes wrong, are you able to help us get Ngarra's crew off that Harvester and back here.'

'Like I said last time,' he said. 'We cannot be seen to contravene any regulations, codes and standards for working in "the Area". I report to the CCP subcommittee. Their agenda and their mandate are different to mine, but I have their full support. The research program my daughter is working on does not come under my control. I can however keep an eye on what is going on. Between Chang, my daughter Ying Yue and Connor it is certainly complex. The last thing I want is an incident that jeopardises our mineral processing and production operation.'

'Thank you,' said Jonah. 'I want my crew back in one piece with our technology intact. I will be in touch when I know more.'

His image disappeared and Jonah stood thinking. So, that is why Chang is always so angry about his family. His mother's accident and his sister's success. That makes him volatile and a liability when it comes to Connor's work. He was threatened last time and maybe he has been threatened again.

Jonah wished she was out there in the Pacific at the Harvester. She had to trust Jesse. Communication and Security Officers were highly trained and picked for their emotional intelligence. She would know what to do. If that lab out there was not directly under Chang's father's control, then it made sense that something else was going on. And how much does Rick really know about all this anyway. A lot it would seem.

Chapter 16

Early in the morning Connor was back in the information hub on their Skimmer going over the results from the day before and continuing with simulations in the ocean bubble hologram. Tomorrow they would return to the Harvester with a full load of nodules to offload.

The Skimmer had been in position for two nights. The day before they had run the technology trial with the Xtracts. It had been successful but there were still problems to solve. The Xtract drones continued mining nodules from the seabed.

He watched Gilgamesh; the ocean bubble hologram simulation continued to run Red Queen. Two different groups of Xtracts were competing for seabed resources. They were learning to outdo each other and load more nodules.

He had shown using Red Queen that by altering the environment between mining runs the Xtracts would adapt their behaviour patterning to optimise their chance of extracting more nodules and gain an advantage over the other group.

Originally, at its most fundamental level the Xtracts carried out mining operations under the control of SAI. If something went wrong with one of them, assistance could be provided by any of the Xtracts. But that was just coding responses for given situations involving malfunctions not learning autonomous group behaviour.

Next, overlaying this Connor had got SAI to construct a mesh using a layered sequence of algorithms to create a stack of decision-making feedback loops for deep learning. This enabled all Xtracts to respond to an event that interrupted a mining operation. That was where the simulations fell apart and the point at which no learning occurred. No memory as Connor liked to put it. Red Queen had changed that.

He thought back to the swarm he had got the Xtracts to make during the incident over six months ago now. In the ocean bubble hologram, he had got SAI to synch the simulated Xtracts with the Xtracts outside and to also make the

Skimmer a member of the swarm. At his direction, they all then moved like a school of fish, reacting and responding to the Skimmers every move.

Connor then thought about the giant squid simulation. It would grab an Xtract. Others would close in on it and push it. The squid sometimes released it and sometimes didn't. But the Xtracts didn't learn or return to mining. They just wandered off randomly. Somewhere between swarm behaviour and reacting to an intrusion but wandering off was the missing link. The ability to react, respond and return to their task and then to improve on it next time. Red Queen seemed to be part of the solution but not all of it.

***

While Connor was absorbed in his work in the information hub, the others had gathered in the rec area to relax.

Stella was now on duty watch and responded to any situation that might arise during mining operations.

'No Xtract malfunctions so far,' she said standing up and walking off, 'I will head off and check over the propulsion system.'

'Good idea,' said Ngarra. 'Make sure that problem with the power train overspeed on the rim drive doesn't come back and bite us.'

'It only happened because the previous crew didn't check the power train was aligned when the overdrive was engaged,' said Chang. 'The surge of energy and resulting resonance disrupted it.'

'How does that overdrive work anyway?' said Jonny. 'I'm no physics expert but it seems a bit unusual.'

'Not really,' said Stella. 'Ay Jesse.'

'True,' said Jesse. 'The concept is straight forward but why it works can be hard to grasp.'

'What do you mean?' said Jonny.

'Well, when they installed them below the SAI consoles, they also had to be able to contain and shield it,' said Stella. 'If it ruptured, we would be done. It would rip us apart.'

'Great,' said Jonny. 'That makes me feel better, not!'

The others laughed at his facial expression and hassled him about being a jockey sitting on top of an overdrive.

'So, what's stopping that from happening then,' he said.

'A magnetic semi-conductor at the bottom of the column. It spins the core material and an extremely high speed. That way when it forms a plasma it cancels out the enormous outward pressure placed on the column.'

'What do you mean by that?' said Jonny.

'Well,' said Jesse jumping in. 'The pressure is directed inwards. Around the base are a series of capacitors that discharge a high voltage current at set frequencies across the mercury plasma vortex column being rotated at an extremely high velocity. It strips electrons from their atoms. Using the high voltage current the perpendicular circulation of charged particles are polarised, producing an electromagnetic field around us that reduces our mass to zero relative to our surroundings. Inertia is cancelled out since it relates to the reduction in our mass. Relative to our surroundings we don't have any. It means we don't get squashed against the bulkheads when we take off. Alignment of the rim driven power train and overdrive means we can travel at extremely high speeds. And that's because of inertial mass reduction. With zero mass or close to it, we can also potentially disappear from this physical dimension and jump into what is essentially all that space between atoms and subatomic particles. Four-dimensional scalar space. The fourth dimension created by angular momentum. The empty space that is everywhere and occupied by all this energy, the source of the four fundamental forces. Potentially we could go anywhere in a very short space of time, as in compression of time in four-dimensional scalar space. Crossing the point of light as they say.'

'Cool,' said Jonny, looking a little confused and lost in the explanation. 'Why Mercury though, what's so special about it.'

'Another time,' said Jesse. 'Similar concepts regarding inward spiralling vortices of charged particles and polarised energy fields and inertial mass reduction can be observed in nature. Right now, we've got things to do.'

'Always wanted to know how these things work,' said Jonny.

'Well,' said Stella. 'Now you a bit more cowboy.'

'It's still being tested,' said Jesse. 'That's why we have a strict overdrive protocol to follow. The previous crew used it incorrectly and disrupted the rim driven power train. If it's used, everything must be documented for review. I expect once we come out of the trial period it will become standard practice. Imagine the time we will save running around this vast ocean.'

'Well, now that we know more about how this thing works,' said Stella pointing at the column around which the esplanade went to the forward viewing area, 'let's eat.'

'Best thing I have heard you say all day Sister,' said Jonny getting up.

'Geeze,' said Stella. 'I haven't seen you move that fast in a while.'

The others laughed as they went to choose what they wanted from the menu. The day was gone, and everyone sat back down and talked about getting ashore again and enjoying the beach next to campus accommodation.

***

That evening after Stella did the rounds and checked over systems with SAI, she caught up with the crew gathered in the rec area again. The Xtracts would carry on mining overnight, completing the filling of the nodule trays.

The conversation turned to Connor's technology. The Xtract trials and insertion of what he called "Red Queen" had sparked a lot of interest amongst the crew.

'Thanks to you Connor we might end up with a bunch of crazy Xtracts running around by themselves at some point in the future,' said Stella as she sat down and poked a face at Connor.

'From what I saw,' said Jesse, 'the trials are advancing. You've come along way with this whole concept Connor.'

'We have,' said Connor referring to the fact that it was the use of SAI and natural language processing that was key. "Red Queen" was part of the puzzle. Like accelerating an evolutionary process except in drones not animals.'

'Can you show us where you are up to?' said Chang.

'Sure, yeah come on then,' said Connor. 'Let's go and see Gilgamesh.'

'I think what you are uncovering is dangerous,' said Jonny. 'What if humans were cut out of mining in "the Area" all together? We'd become guests in our own back yard to some AI running the show.'

'What do you mean?' said Connor. 'We work together. It can't do it by itself you know. It all relies on me.'

'That may be so for now,' said Jesse. 'But the result could be greater than the sum of its parts. Ever heard of that saying Connor?'

Connor looked blankly at them all not understanding what their point was. It was a project that infatuated him, and he was obsessed with it. A world he lived in where the only goal was to make Xtracts think for themselves. To make them act as a group where the only criteria was not to let anything interrupt collecting as many nodules as possible.

That was where "Red Queen" came in. It was inserted into the mesh by SAI. It sped up the process he had developed in the ocean bubble hologram. The ocean bubble hologram was still isolated though; Gilgamesh was like a baby learning to walk.

'I agree with Jonny,' said Chang. 'It sounds dangerous. What happens when it learns to walk? Does it then wake up as well? I think you are fooling around with something that you have no idea about.'

'What do you mean?' said Connor.

'You could do us out of a job,' said Chang raising his voice. He had become irritated by Connor's single-minded focus.

'Sorry about that,' said Connor. He was a little confused by the comment and couldn't make the connection.

'Yeah, well sometimes you should think more about the impact of what you are developing on others,' said Chang.

'What do you mean?' said Connor. His expression had changed to one of concern that he had done something wrong.

'You can be such an idiot sometimes,' said Chang.

'Hey, cut it out,' said Jesse. 'Do you want to see what he is up to or not.'

'Oh yes, of course,' said Chang as he calmed down.

He remembered the message from his contact and what he must do. *Didn't want to compromise that,* he thought to himself. My sister is in danger.

'I'm still hungry,' said Jonny. 'I had better get some sustenance.'

He got up and went to get some more food.

The others laughed.

Jonny could always calm tense situations with his antics and make everyone see the light side of things. Between him and Stella they injected some fun and comradery into the crew at the toughest of times.

'Speaking of you two,' said Ngarra as he looked at Connor and Chang. 'I am worried about returning to the Harvester with our load of nodules.'

'I am too,' said Jesse. 'We need to be careful. No one is to be alone at any time okay. And you must ask me if you want to go anywhere. A lot of things were not solved from what happened last time out here. It's been over six months now, but Connor is still in danger as are you, Chang.'

Jonny returned and sat down with a plate of food. The others looked at him and then at Stella, waiting for her baited comments that they knew were coming.

'Geeze,' said Stella. 'Eating for two are we.'

The others burst out laughing and Jonny went red in the face.

'It takes just one of me to keep you lot in line,' he said laughing. 'Imagine if there were two of me, man what I could achieve.'

'Spare us,' said Ngarra. 'Anyway,' Stella if you are checking propulsion, I will take your duty and be on call overnight.'

'About time you did some work,' said Stella.

Everyone got up from the table except Jonny, who got stuck into his food.

Connor headed to the information hub.

'Connor wait for me,' said Chang. 'I'm keen to catch up one what you were doing.'

'Okay, let's go,' said Connor. 'It's so cool, you should see our ocean bubble hologram now. It has changed.'

Connor had a captured audience. His enthusiasm bubbled over. He may have been socially awkward but if you engaged him in his work he would talk for ages. Sometimes it was difficult to stop him talking. The crew would find an excuse and walk off. Connor didn't seem to mind though. He would look blankly at them; at times right through them, shrug his shoulders and carry on with his work. Autism had its advantages and its drawbacks, but the crew was pretty used to it now.

Chang followed Connor up the stairs, through the watertight bulkhead, along the rear of the SAI console and down one of the passages either side of propulsion to the information hub in the middle.

'Over here,' said Connor as they entered. He almost dragged Chang to Gilgamesh, the ocean bubble hologram. To the sides around the hub displays showed data streams and analytics. Various source code was running, and SAI was searching script libraries. One display was now red.

'See, Red Queen,' said Connor. 'SAI has constructed a unique algorithm. Gilgamesh is in a constant battle with itself. The goal is to optimise nodule extraction. Not a risk optimiser though, that's just a bunch of code and algorithms to improve performance. This is different. "Red Queen" is like a game, an evolutionary game that accelerates development of autonomous learning in group behaviour. You can't just program this, it must evolve over thousands, if not millions of iterations. Here look at Gilgamesh. In this iteration, which has evolved from many previous versions a group is trying to take the nodules from the other group, which is mining them. It will change eventually but change by itself. Don't you see?'

'I think I get it,' said Chang as he looked carefully at some of the source code, algorithm stacks and outputs.

'Look at the ocean bubble hologram,' said Connor.

'Yes, yes,' said Chang. 'But how is each iteration altered. I mean, is it purely random.'

'That's the key to control,' said Connor. 'It's still me, I inject if you like to call it that, the variations that alter the responses. SAI then plays them out thousands of times. Each variation is added to its library. It has a feedback loop. If equilibrium is reached, one of my variations is injected. I maintain control.'

'It makes sense,' said Chang. 'So "Red Queen" it is then.'

He looked over at Connor. He was absorbed in what SAI was doing with the latest injection of a variation. Chang pulled a device out of his pocket and inserted it into the console running Red Queen.

'What are you doing to Gilgamesh?' said Connor coming around the ocean bubble hologram to see.

'Nothing,' said Chang. 'Thought you should back all this up.'

'It is backed up,' said Connor. 'Give me that!' he yelled and went to grab it off Chang.

'Don't worry, Connor,' said Chang as he pushed him away. 'I can help with all this.'

He was about to use the icons to start the process.

'No,' said Connor as he grabbed Chang's arm. Chang pulled it away and carried on with what he was doing. He pushed Connor off again.

'You can't do that to Gilgamesh!' he said yelling at Chang. 'SAI, lockout Red Queen.'

'Confirmed,' said SAI. 'Red Queen lockout initiated.'

'Give it to me,' said Chang fiercely as he went to grab Connor.

'Give me the technology!'

Connor backed off.

'No!' he yelled.

Chang launched himself at Connor and grabbed his arm. He pulled it behind Connor's back and grabbed the front of his hair and pulled his head back. Forcing Connor over to the console.

'What the hell is going on!' said Ngarra racing into the information hub.

He had been in the SAI console checking on the status of the Xtracts and loading of the mineral trays.

'Let him go Chang!' he yelled.

Ngarra moved quickly.

Chang backed away, holding onto Connor. Connor had gone white in the face. Panicking, he struggled to break free.

Ngarra grabbed Chang's shirt and tried to pull him off Connor.

'I need this!' he pleaded. 'I have to get it for them. My sister will be okay, that's what they said. It's my father's fault. He made it like this, my mother and all. Now my sister is involved.'

Jesse came racing in with Jonny behind her.

'Bro, not again,' said Jonny. 'Look what happened last time. We told you to trust us.'

'No,' said Chang. 'She's in danger, my sister I mean. How can she be helped? It's the Harvester, she'll never get off it.'

'There is always a way,' said Jesse. 'Now let go of Connor and we can talk it through.'

'That's not what you did last time. You injected me with a sedative.'

'Not this time,' said Jesse. 'Just let Connor go and come with us to the rec area.'

Jonny had moved around to the side. Last time he had punched Chang over what happened between him and Connor.

Jesse motioned him to stand off. He grimaced at her. He was all fired up and wanted it to end.

Chang collapsed onto the deck sobbing. Connor raced around the other side of the ocean bubble hologram, gripping the console like it was his baby.

Jesse raced forward. Stella heard all the commotion and had come running in as well. She motioned to Jesse to leave Chang with her. Chang had a connection with Stella. An odd one but he would talk to her. Perhaps because Stella reminded him of his sister.

'Okay,' said Jesse. 'Let's go everyone. Out!'

'You okay, Connor?' said Jonny.

'Don't touch me,' he said backing off as Jonny reached out to him.

'No worries, bro,' he said.

'Connor,' said Ngarra. 'Come on. Update us on how all this Red Queen stuff works.'

Connor looked up.

'Okay,' he said calming down. You could see his mind instantly grab something familiar to him.

'It's like I was telling Chang.' He looked back at Chang not understanding what had just happened.

As Connor talked, they walked back to the rec area and sat down. Jonny and Jesse moved to one side and talked quietly about what had happened. By the time Jesse and Ngarra had got everyone settled, it was late. They all turned in and got some sleep.

***

The next morning Ngarra's crew prepared to depart for the Harvester with a full load of nodules. Everyone looked a little tried from the night before. Despite what happened with Chang and their apprehension about returning to the Harvester, they were keen to get going.

The last of the Xtracts had ascended from the depths below. The communication streamer had been retrieved as well. The collected sediment and water column samples would be loaded into the sample collection port and retrieved.

Ngarra watched from the SAI console as the remaining Xtracts placed their loads into the trays. They moved across the Skimmer wing and into the recess, securing themselves on the docking clamps.

'SAI confirm Skimmer is watertight,' said Ngarra.

'Confirmed,' said SAI. 'Skimmer is watertight.'

The samples attached to the streamer were recovered and the moonpool entrance was sealed and armed. The airlock was also armed.

'All good here,' said Stella over comms.

They checked off the Xtracts docked and looked at status reports as SAI ran system checks on each of them.

Chang went down along the inside of each external recess either side of the maintenance bay and airlock and checked the docking displays of each one.

Chang seemed a bit better than yesterday, Stella thought to herself. Jesse had said they would arrange for him to see his sister when they got back to the

Harvester. Maybe he would calm down a bit if he saw she was okay. He had been coerced into trying to get hold of Connor's work again. Last night, he was convinced that his sister wasn't safe. Maybe he was right. Jesse would contact Jonah about it again.

'Xtracts docked and communication streamer secured,' said SAI.

'SAI proceed to Harvester,' said Ngarra.

'Confirmed,' said SAI. 'Proceed to Harvester.'

At the SAI console, Jonny had his interface lenses on and was monitoring control of the Skimmer.

Ngarra checked the holographic projection of their route back to the Harvester.

The outer hull shields were still retracted. Ngarra watched as the Skimmer started moving off.

The rim driven propulsion system powered up and they gained speed. The endless blue green void started sliding past them. The Skimmer slowly turned in a wide flat arc and straightened up. As usual, the marine life that had gathered around them started to move away. A small school of yellow fin tuna moved past.

Chapter 17

While the Skimmer completed its mining run and returned to the Harvester, the day before Jonah was in early at Xed Academy. She had just arrived at work and was getting herself organised. She had a meeting later with Rick about the next lot of crew placements. It would provide an opportunity for her to confront him about his difference of opinion. She was thinking about the meeting Rick and she had with the council.

She walked through her office and over to her secretary thinking she might bounce a few ideas off her.

'Morning,' she said as Jonah walked in.

'Hi,' said Jonah. 'You heard that conversation with Chang's father the other day right. A complicated family, but it interests me. I mean the fact that Chang's sister is on that Harvester. There is a link back to his mother's work. There is more to all this than we think.'

'Perhaps Chang just needs to spend some time with his sister to talk about what happened. She can make him see it wasn't their fathers' fault.'

'True,' said Jonah. 'It would be great if it was that simple. But Chang is being used to try and get to Connor. It concerns me that it may well happen again.'

'Maybe if the family issue is resolved the rest will take care of itself.'

'Chang's father seems to trust my judgement,' said Jonah. 'Perhaps if Chang shows his sister what he gets up to and the relationships he has with his crew he will calm down. It's against protocol but I'm sure the Harvester operators would love the chance for Ying Yue to board Ngarra's Skimmer. I can bet they would coerce him into looking into what Connor was up to. Why don't we use that to our advantage?'

'What do you mean?' said her secretary.

'Well, we arrange a visit on the Skimmer. Harvester security would see that as an opportunity. I mean there is no way they would let Chang visit his sister in her lab now.'

'But how is that to our advantage?' said her secretary.

'Think about it. If there is a security breach here at Xed and the Academy, then word will spread. We could have all three of these people in one place at the same time. Like a decoy to flush out whoever is involved in all this.'

'You would use one of our crews to find out who is behind all this then?' her secretary said.

'This is my life,' said Jonah. 'Someone or something is going on to undermine everything we have achieved. Obviously, what Connor has developed means more than we know to some people. I want to know why.'

'You're taking a big risk,' she said. 'I mean, it's a breach of protocol to have a non-crew member on board a skimmer outside of any arrangement made for maintenance. Even worse if it happened to be a Chinese national on board the Harvester. What about the Academy Skimmer crew program, its future and the technology Connor has developed? What about the overdrive trials that have to be completed for Rick's people?'

'I have something in mind,' she said. 'I owe Chang's father for his help with that incident over six months ago. He is worried about his family. Even more so than last time.'

Jonah turned and walked back through to her office. She looked out over the campus. Her thoughts turned to what was going on out at the Harvester and how Ngarra's crew were going.

The council was on her case about pushing ahead with developing the technology to its full potential. They did not like the fact there was still an unsolved security breach within the Academy either. She was sure Rick had something to do with it but no direct proof. She was due to catch up with him later.

She sat down and got to work catching up on a pile of reports she had to review.

***

Around lunchtime she left her office and went to meet with Rick at the crew monitoring and communication complex. She exited the admin building and crossed the campus.

As she entered the sim centre and walked through the learning hub a few students said hi. She stopped and chatted briefly with them. Moving on she got a quick update from the instructors training crews in the two Skimmer simulators.

Passing through security she entered the crew monitoring and communication complex. In the large glass enclosed mezzanine overlooking the crew monitoring stations and main display below was a board room annex and table and chairs. She walked in. Rick was there waiting. He had pulled up displays of crew progress training in the Skimmer simulators.

'Hi,' he said looking up from his work. 'I got all this ready before you turned up.'

'Great,' said Jonah. 'Let's see then.'

'These crews here are ready to graduate from simulator training and be placed on Skimmers,' said Rick.

He swiped across the displays and arranged the crews that were ready.

'These ones need more time. Over here I have several individuals to place on separate Skimmers. They will be understudies for specific roles.'

'I see,' said Jonah as she looked over the profile of each person he pointed out.

'What about students coming out of the learning hub into the simulator program? Have we got that sorted?'

'Both,' said Rick. 'Those coming out of the learning hub and the ones coming from Xed that want to go into the Academy Skimmer crew program.'

Jonah looked through the numbers and matched them with contractor Skimmer numbers currently working in "the Area". She then looked at load logs, which checked out. This gave her an idea about current and future crew to Skimmer ratios. They were easily meeting requirements. No one else had the capacity or capability to run such an extensive program or gain the ongoing support of the likes of Globe Corp Mining. Besides, it wasn't as if Skimmer contractors had a choice.

'Great,' she said. 'It looks like we are up to date as always. I am getting pressure from contractors to keep crews on Skimmers for longer and do more runs. Not that we need to. They are just getting greedy. We meet the load requirements for the Harvester. That's what we really need to worry about.'

'Agree,' said Rick. 'And we have not had any breaches of regulations in "the Area" lately either. All inspections by the Sea Hunters have come back clear over the last few months. Sampling results show we are operating within the set environmental thresholds as well. As for that incident out their over six months ago with the off-grid Skimmer and the threats against Connor. Well, Chang seems to have been a bit calmer since then. However, with what's going on I am worried it is all going to flare up again.'

'Speaking of that,' said Jonah. 'Why do you always contradict me in council meetings. What's with that?'

'What do you mean?' said Rick cautiously.

'You go on about the Sea Hunters taking care of things and looking after some very sensitive information as if they were our allies.'

'Not really,' he said. 'They have a monitoring, compliance and enforcement role in "the Area".'

'Last time when emergency administration orders were issued by the Authority two of our Skimmers were being chased around the ocean by them,' she said. 'I wanted Ngarra's crew to find that off grid Skimmer and get our rogue crew back before the Sea Hunters found them. You undermined everything I said last time. You even thought we should let someone else secure the technology Connor had developed and hold it for us.'

'I'm just looking out for Xed and the Academy,' said Rick. 'GlobeCorpMining is the major funder of the Skimmer crew program. It's a tenuous position to be in. They are aware that we have this technology. Your relationship with Chang's father exposes us, Jonah.'

'Rubbish!' exclaimed Jonah as she frowned at him. 'He is very professional. All he has done is offer to help. I have known him a long time Rick.'

'Chang is compromised,' said Rick angrily. 'He has an issue with his father, he wants to prove himself. He misses his sister and is somewhat envious of her. He is consumed with anger about his mother's situation.'

'I know that!' said Jonah as she walked up to Rick and got in his face.

Rick stepped back. He knew how pissed off Jonah could get with him at times. He could see it in her eyes now.

'What is it with you, Rick?' she hissed at him.

Getting in his face she waved a finger in front of him.

'What is it you are not telling me?' she said. 'I have spoken with Chang's father. Something isn't right with all this. Something else is going on. He is worried. He thinks he is not across all this and something more sinister is going on.'

'It's nothing!' said Rick aggressively, backing off. 'My people are just concerned about where all this is going,' he said waving his hand around at the monitoring and communications complex.

'What do you mean!' said Jonah angrily as she stepped forward.

'If you must know we have been watching Chang's sister,' he said harshly. 'When Connor stumbled across his little discovery and started to figure out how to develop it, we became concerned. Concerned that others want these two people together to achieve some other purpose. You don't realise the danger in front of your own nose!' he said angrily. 'Plus, we are still in the trial phase for the overdrive propulsion system. A zero-mass drive, or inertial mass reduction and its integration with the rim drive propulsion system needs a lot of trialling. In overcoming inertia and keeping our crews safe, we still get overspeed in the power train if our crews don't follow the protocols correctly. What's more, the energy field from the magnetic semiconductor that spins the mercury plasma vortex and the capacitor ring discharge into it have to align with the power train to control transits and arrival at set coordinates. If not, they could potentially be at zero mass and jump into trans-dimensional space, or four dimensional space, that space between atoms and sub atomic particles where the energy of angular momentum lies, without having a set point at which to emerge. It's scalar, so they could be lost and emerge anywhere. So it's not just about overspeed.'

'Your people wanted all that integrated into the Skimmers when they were built. I'm not that stupid,' she said. 'Retrofitting a skimmer designed to incorporate these drives is one thing, but you seem to want to offer up the Academy Skimmer crew program to these people of yours.'

'Damn it, Jonah,' he said angrily. 'Only to protect what we have. I wanted to separate all this entirely from the Academy as a standalone enterprise,' he said waving his arm around. 'It's a national security risk in its current format. A global risk to my people even. It could all blow up in our faces, literally.'

'Why?' said Jonah. 'You are still not telling me something here.'

'Artificial intelligence,' he said. 'It could compromise project Cygnus. Do I have to spell it out for you? A danger exists that if Connor figures this all out with the Xtracts, and Skimmers become crewless and remote monitored, and Chang's sister is in fact doing what she is rumoured to be doing and links up with Connor then all could be lost!'

'Okay, okay I get your point,' said Jonah. 'But you're still hiding something. No one knows what project Cygnus is for a start!'

'In time you will,' said Rick. 'Give it time, geeze woman!'

She stepped back from laying into Rick. He was not being upfront with her about what was really going on. She wasn't going to get a straight answer. At least, not yet anyway. She had picked up on where his thinking was heading though. Carving things up was not what she wanted to see happen.

Makes sense, she thought to herself that Rick would be so concerned about the potential danger of these technologies if they were bought together. But he was still not telling her something. It made her even more worried about Chang, Connor and the rest of the crew.

If Chang's father was that worried, then something else really was going on. Chang's father had explained their family situation to her. Rick didn't know that Chang's father had probably said more to her than he should have about his daughter's work.

'Well,' said Rick after an uncomfortable silence. 'I suggest we proceed cautiously on all fronts.'

'Exactly,' sighed Jonah. 'We may disagree on the way forward, but we both have the protection of this place and what we have developed here foremost in our minds. Let's wait to hear from Ngarra's crew about the trials and how their mining run is going.'

'Okay,' said Rick as he relaxed and gathered his thoughts. 'I'm finished with these crew profiles and need to catch up with the duty officers down there,' he said pointing at the monitoring and communications complex below.

Rick closed the displays and walked out of the mezzanine and down the stairs to the floor below. Jonah watched him go. *So much for monitoring crews on Skimmers carrying out mining operations in the area*, she thought to herself. Holding onto this technology Connor had come up with was proving difficult.

Chapter 18

It was late in the day as Ngarra's Skimmer approached the Harvester. They cleared perimeter security. As they looked out into the water a sub-surface patrol drone went past them.

'SAI prepare for final approach,' said Ngarra.

'Confirmed,' said SAI. 'Preparing for final approach.'

The outer hull shields closed. The watertight bulkheads sealed shut for pilotage under the Harvester and up through the moonpool.

Stella and Chang were in the Xtract bay, Connor was in the information hub and the others were at the SAI console.

The external camera system activated, and they watched as the Skimmer approached the Harvester.

Jonny had his interface lenses on and could see everything in first person view. His arms and hands moved as he swiped and altered displays in front of him.

Ngarra was switching between watching the view from the camera system and looking at the SAI console navigation hologram of their approach.

The Skimmer slowed and moved into position under the giant Harvester hull. It stopped mootness for a while directly below a moon pool. Then slowly, it started to ascend.

A school of yellow fin tuna that circled the Harvester came into view. Then, as they entered the moon pool the surrounding marine life started to disappear.

Suddenly they were surrounded by rows of dim lights that illuminated the surface.

With a final thrust upwards, the Skimmer slowly emerged from the water. A large wave gently rolled off its top and surged around the moon pool, settling as the Skimmer came to rest.

On either side, a docking clamp moved across and secured them in place. The external camera system switched off and the outer hull shields opened.

Off into the dimly lit distance on either side of them stretched the conveyor belts and robotic arms for offloading nodules. It was always dimly lit unless maintenance was being carried out.

Some of the other moon pools had Skimmer's in them.

Jonny took his lenses off, stood up and turned around. He moved forward to look out at the view with Jesse and Ngarra.

'Something you never get over looking at,' he said. 'It's just so vast. Like something out of a movie. I could gaze out at all this for hours.'

'It is indeed,' said Ngarra. 'Like being inside a giant organism, swallowed whole. Like the story of Jonah and the whale.'

They watched as the robotic arms on either side of the moonpool activated. Moving across they started to offload the mineral trays full of manganese nodules. They watched one side as a tray was lifted out, up and across to the conveyor belt. A lever in the tray was pressed and the robotic arm slowly pushed the noodles forward and out the chute on one end. The nodules slowly spilled onto the conveyor in a narrow line and moved along it, disappearing into the dimly lit Harvester. It took some time to unload the entire load of nodules from the Skimmer.

'Right,' said Jesse. 'I have to get hold of Jonah about what's going on.'

'Okay,' said Ngarra. 'We've finished here with SAI. The Skimmer is secure, so let's meet in the rec area for a briefing.'

'Sounds good to me,' said Jonny stretching and patting his stomach. 'My system is definitely not nominal and requires sustenance.'

The others laughed and turned to walk out.

'Always the comedian,' said Jesse.

'SAI,' said Ngarra. 'Skimmer wide communication. Meet in the rec area now for a briefing.'

'Confirmed,' said SAI as a request to meet in the rec area was announced.

It was something that could be done either manually or by getting SAI to make an announcement. The Skimmer maintained the flexibility to communicate directly using the comms system or request SAI to communicate with the crew.

Jonny and Ngarra walked off and left Jesse to it. They met Connor on the way and went down to the rec area.

'SAI,' said Jesse. 'Send a request to crew monitoring to speak with Jonah.'

'Confirmed,' said SAI. 'Request sent.'

Jesse watched the message board at the console and waited. A few minutes passed. She was about to walk off and try again later when Jonah's image appeared.

'Hi Jesse,' she said. 'I was hoping to hear from you. How did it all go?'

'Good and bad,' said Jesse.

'Well let's hear the good first then,' said Jonah smiling.

'Connor's trials had some success. Red Queen works but it needs refining. He has come a long way with all this. The use of SAI and natural language processing has helped enormously. That mind of his is rather unique though. We get lost sometimes when he tries to explain where all this is coming from.'

'Great,' said Jonah. 'Once you've unloaded, he can run some more trials then?'

'Yes,' said Jesse. 'It's hard to keep him away from the information hub to eat and sleep. He's so obsessed with making it all work. It's like it's part of him now. He even uses the term we, as in SAI and him working on it.'

'Look after him won't you,' said Jonah. 'Remember being on the spectrum gives him a rather unique view of the world.'

'Speaking of that,' said Jesse. 'Now for the bad news.'

'Alright,' said Jonah. 'Let's have it then.'

'It's Chang; he tried to copy the technology again. Like last time. He lost it. Jonny had to pull them apart. He's been threatened again, or should I say his sister has.'

'Damn it!' said Jonah. 'We thought this might happen again. I've argued with Rick yesterday about all this. Chang's father is worried about his daughter as well. Whatever she is working on has something to do with all this as well. Is Connor okay?'

'He is,' said Jesse. 'His work consumes him though.'

'You're back at the Harvester I assume,' said Jonah. 'It's a dangerous time. Chang will want to see his sister and Connor is exposed. You need to be careful.'

'I know,' she said. 'The Sea Hunters will be back as well.'

'Correct,' said Jonah. 'Rick said they have been hanging around expecting trouble. But don't trust them. I'm sure our security breach here has something to do with them. Just like last time.'

'Do we let Chang see his sister then?'

'Of course,' said Jonah. 'No one is going to want to compromise working in "the Area". Nothing overt is going to happen. But it will happen, nonetheless.

Be careful out there. Something bigger is going on. Something to do with what we have and what Chang's sister is working on. Someone wants to bring it all together. I still haven't worked out why, but Rick knows something.'

'Okay,' said Jesse. 'We will watch things carefully and act as normal. Once offloading has finished, we will have some downtime and then be out of here on our next run.'

'Right,' said Jonah. 'Keep in touch. I will question Rick and Chang's father again. Got to go.'

Jonah's image disappeared. Jesse was left thinking about what it all meant. She left the SAI console and went down to the rec area to talk with the others. They had to come up with a plan. In the rec area, everyone was having a meal and joking about 'holiday island'. That's what some of the crews had started calling the Harvester back at the Academy.

'Right everyone, we need a plan,' she said walking over to the table and sitting down. 'Chang, you want to see your sister. You've also been threated again. Or should I say your sister has. Why don't we use that to our advantage? I mean, pretend that you have got Connor's work for whoever it is.'

'Not again,' said Jonny. 'We are not meant to run around the ocean wheeling and dealing. Remember last time. We are just a bunch of youth monitoring a skimmer and its Xtracts during seabed mining operations.'

'True,' said Ngarra. 'But what if Chang brings his sister down to the Skimmer on a tour and she catches up with Connor as part of it. While she has Connor's attention, you could secure his work.'

'No one's getting my work,' said Connor standing up.

'That's right, Connor; they aren't,' said Jesse.

'But you said they are,' said Connor.

'It only looks like it,' she said. 'What we give to Chang's sister is fake. But she will think it's real enough. She will see Chang's attempt to secure it and think it is real.'

'If Chang's sister is in danger, this solves two things,' said Ngarra. 'It appeases whoever is threatening her while also thinking that they now have the technology.'

'We then flush out who the contact is and expose them,' said Stella excitedly. 'We haven't lost your work Connor and Chang's sister is safe again.'

'Makes sense,' said Chang. 'We expose them and get whoever they are bailed up by the Sea Hunters, and by GlobeCorpMining.'

'It's still too dangerous,' said Jonny. 'It is probably someone within those very organisations. We have no idea what we are getting ourselves into. Someone could get hurt.'

'So, if we can't trust anyone,' said Chang. 'How is it going to work then?'

'Because we will know when they expose themselves,' said Jesse. 'We get behind everyone else who isn't involved. The accused will have nowhere to run.'

'Sounds overly simplistic,' said Jonny. 'I still don't like it. I didn't sign up for this either.'

'That's what you said last time,' said Stella trying to make light of the situation. 'You big baby.'

'I don't want my sister to get hurt,' said Chang with a worried look on his face. 'I don't want her in any more trouble than she might already be in. It all sounds very risky.'

'It would be great to meet your sister,' said Connor interrupting everyone. 'I can ask her about mimic drones.'

'Can't you get it into that thick head of yours, Connor?' said Chang. 'This is my family you're talking about not some piece of code bubble boy.'

Everyone turned away and smiled. They just couldn't help it and laughter ensued.

'Chang, you're killing me,' said Jonny laughing.

'Hey cut it out,' said Jesse. 'Remember what this is all about. He's just as much a part of this as the rest of us.'

Connor looked at them all blankly.

'What's so funny,' he said. More laughter followed and Connor even managed a smile. Although, he wasn't quite sure what he was smiling at.

The mood lightened and the discussion carried on for a while. Everyone finally agreed on a course of action. Jesse went off to contact Harvester security to arrange a time the next day for Chang to catch up with his sister and to see if that was even possible. She knew they would be breaching Skimmer protocols which strictly forbid non-crew members to board a skimmer.

***

At the Harvester operations centre, Lee and Sue were talking about the conversation they had just had with Jesse about Chang and his sister catching up.

'That was an interesting development,' said Lee.

'It's perfect,' she said. 'We convince Ying Yue to try and get information off Chang about Connor's work. We also put a device on her uniform, which she will be unaware of. All she must do is stand near whatever this technology is. Even if she refuses to this device will still give us an idea about what exactly Connor is up to.'

'Seeing as it's family,' said Lee. 'Chang may be quite willing to engage Connor in sharing information with his sister about this technology. But what if the device is found or detected?'

'Then they will know something is up,' she said. 'Either way, I or should I say we will be heroes for getting hold of this technology. We can use it in the lab for our project.'

'I'm not so sure about that,' said Lee. 'There are relationships to consider long term.'

'Nonsense,' said Sue. 'That's weak. Just like family.'

Lee frowned at her. He wasn't one to agree with such comments and was concerned about Sue's motives.

'Why are you so adamant that we get hold of this technology at the expense of other things going on?' he said.

'I'm not,' she said. 'It's an opportunity that shouldn't be passed. That's all.'

'Fair enough,' said Lee. He knew not to press her on the issue. She was a dangerous woman to get on the wrong side of.

'Right,' she said. 'Let's go and brief Ying Yue. Then she can meet Chang tomorrow and go to visit his Skimmer.'

They got up and walked out of the meeting room. Passing the operations centre and various monitoring and control rooms they walked through to the lab complex.

On the way, a duty officer interrupted them and said the Sea Hunters had arrived back at the Harvester to do some more inspections of Skimmers. Max and Alex wanted to meet with Sue and Lee tomorrow to discuss concerns about the increase in piracy activity in "the Area".

'Tell them to meet here tomorrow morning straight after we have briefed Ying Yue,' said Lee. 'Get a security detail to escort them from the drone deck.'

'Yes, sir,' said the duty officer as he left to organise the request.

Lee and Sue entered the lab complex. The prototype Skimmer was still suspended over the moon pool below. Technicians were moving around it. To one side another lab was positioned. Inside were several Xtract drones.

'There she is,' said Lee pointing over to the enclosed lab.

'Working on her pet project, mimic drones,' said Sue. 'Something we don't want to get out.'

They walked into the lab and waited in the small foyer. Ying Yue saw them. They watched as she took her lab gear off.

'Hi,' she said walking over to them. 'What is it?'

'Your brothers Skimmer is here,' said Sue. 'They are between mining runs. He wants to see you and show you what he gets up to. We arranged a tour of the Skimmer for you.'

'That's nice,' she said. 'I appreciate that. Chang will be thrilled, I'm sure.'

'However,' said Lee. 'We want you to do something for us.'

'Depends what it is,' said Ying Yue with a worried look.

'We want you to convince Chang to explain and if possible, get hold of or copy Connor's work for us,' said Lee. 'It may help you here with the project you are working on.'

'What if I get caught, or what if Chang gets found out?' she said nervously.

'You won't,' said Sue. 'Look and listen, copy if you can.'

'Do you really think his crew would let me into their information hub to look at a sensitive project? I doubt it,' said Ying Yue. 'And it's a breach of strict protocols regarding non crew members boarding a skimmer.'

'That's the whole point,' said Sue. 'Chang will do it for family if you plead with him enough. And if you get Connor talking, he won't stop.'

'I don't like it,' Ying Yue said. 'I don't think my father would like it either. It could compromise the relationship GlobeCorpMining has with Xed Academy.'

'Rubbish!' said Sue defensively. 'This has nothing to do with your damn father! He has no authority over the research and your lab. It's PLA Navy!'

'Hey,' said Lee. 'Let's keep things in perspective here. 'Ying Yue will do what she can, and if it works great. If it doesn't, we will regroup and come up with something else later.'

'It will work,' said Sue with a wicked smile. She calmed down.

Lee was becoming increasingly concerned and worried about Sue. Ever since the previous incident and becoming aware of this technology Sue had become aggressive and unpredictable.

'I will do what I can,' said Ying Yue.

'Right, tomorrow morning be at the meeting room,' said Sue. 'We will get security to escort you down to the moon pool to Chang's Skimmer. A security detail will wait at the gangway for you. We will be catching up with the Sea Hunters afterwards about piracy reports in "the Area".'

'Okay,' she said walking off back to her lab to continue with her work.

Sue and Lee left.

They walked back through the research complex and past operations to the meeting room they had come from and sat back down again.

They talked about Ying Yue's work and the importance of Connor's work. The conversation turned to linking the two technologies together and what that might mean for mining in "the Area".

***

On the Skimmer, Jesse caught up with Chang. Now that the whole crew was in on it, they needed to get him to message his contact. It was up to him. His sister's visit would provide the distraction Chang needed. Connor would be engrossed in talking about his work. That would give him time to access it. *Second time around*, he thought to himself. Last time he got caught out as well. At least this time, everyone was in on the plan.

At the communications and security display in the SAI console, Jesse watched as he used his smart watch to activate the grid node he was using. He sent a message to his contact briefly outlining how he was going to secure Connor's work and waited for a response.

He wanted to know who he was going to give it to or how to upload it. A short time later his contact replied.

Message received
Hand information to your sister
Job done; sister safe
If you fail
Sisters' safety compromised

He disconnected from the grid node. It didn't make sense using his sister. How was that going to flush them out. And what would his sister do with the information anyway. He had an uneasy feeling that something wasn't right. He was even more concerned now for his sister's safety.

'What is it?' said Jesse. She had been quietly watching.

'It doesn't make sense,' said Chang as he stopped looking at his smart watch and put his arm down.

'My contact wants me to hand the technology to my sister?'

'Strange indeed,' said Jesse. 'That's what we are going to do to flush out whoever is behind this. If this contact of yours wants the same thing and it keeps your sister safe, then that is what we must do. Fortuitously, both our plan and your contacts request are the same. The only difference is that it will be corrupted.'

'That's what we did last time,' said Chang. 'Don't you think my contact will know we might do that. We should give them the technology. But then the Chinese have everything. Jonah will be pissed, and the council could remove her.'

'There has to be more to it than that,' said Jesse thinking. 'Someone is playing all of us. I wish we could figure it all out. Let's go back to the rec area and update the others.'

They walked back down to the rec area to explain what was going on to the others. Jesse couldn't help thinking that they were all being manipulated into a situation that forced things out into the open.

Chapter 19

The next morning on the Sea Hunter vessel Alex and Max along with two members of their inspection team got ready to fly across to the Harvester in a patrol drone.

'Did you confirm the meeting?' said Max as they stood in the drone bay.

'Sure did,' said Alex. 'A security detail of theirs will escort us from the drone deck to a meeting room.'

'Sir,' said a duty officer coming over to them from the control room. 'You have a message from Xed Academy to contact them immediately.'

'Right,' said Max. 'You lot board and strap in. I won't be long.'

He walked off to the control room.

Alex watched.

He could see Max talking to someone over comms.

'This is Max,' he said while looking over at Alex and giving him the thumbs up.

'Max, its Rick. Chang's sister Ying Yue will have the technology. She will be touring the Skimmer. You must apprehend her under the pretence of breaching of Skimmer protocols. It is strictly forbidden for non-crew members to board a skimmer. Debrief her on the Sea Hunter vessel, remove the technology and return her to the Harvester. Prepare and submit the breach of Skimmer protocol report. Got to go.'

Comms went blank and Max looked out the window over to the drone.

Alex was watching and could see Max now looked a little concerned. For someone usually so relaxed, it was unusual.

Max exited the control room, walked down the stairs and back over to the drone, boarded and strapped in.

'We have to get the technology off Chang's sister,' he said. 'Damn it, Murphy's law this is going to get messy.'

'Should we be prepared for something,' said Alex.

Max turned back to look at his security and inspection team. 'Look sharp boys,' he said. 'This could all go pear shaped quick. Be prepared to get out of there fast and back here.'

'Yes, sir,' they said looking at each other apprehensively.

'I'm not flying today,' said Max.

'Neither,' said Alex. 'Let's go auto.'

They checked in with the automated control system run by the drone AI. Sitting back, they got the all clear from drone deck control for an automated take-off.

The docking clamp moved out from the drone bay to the deck. The cowlings unfolded and the rotors spun up. The docking clamp lifted and released them. The drone hovered, moved off the side of the vessel, tilted forward and then speed off and banked out over the water heading towards the Harvester.

On the way, Alex contacted the duty watch keeping officer at the Sea Hunter vessel SAI console and explained the situation. He wanted the Hunter unit ready to leave quickly if things went awry on the Harvester.

In no time, at all they flew in over the Harvester drone deck and hovered over a docking clamp. It grabbed them and lowered into place. The drone powered down and they unstrapped themselves and got out.

'You two go with one of them and start inspections,' said Alex pointing at the officers approaching them.

A Harvester security detail walked over and one of them motioned to follow. They walked off, making their way to the moon pools below. The other officer escorted Max and Alex below to a meeting room in the operations centre.

As they followed the security officer Alex looked at Max. He had not often seen Max uptight about anything.

They entered the Hex and it took them below to the drone bay. They exited and followed the officer to a lift that would take them to operations.

Max's intuition was usually spot on. If he was apprehensive, it meant something was going to go wrong.

They walked into the meeting room. The security officer waited outside.

'Greetings,' said Lee standing up as they came in.

'Hello again,' said Max trying to act causal. 'My team are doing a few inspections. We need to discuss what to do about the increase in frequency of piracy in "the Area".'

'Welcome,' said Sue as she stood as well. 'Take a seat and let's discuss what's going on.'

They all sat down at the table. Lee and Sue were on one side and Alex and Max on the other.

'The increase in activity is concerning,' said Lee. 'If it starts to impact Xtract mining operations, we will not be able to meet production quotas. It has a big knock-on effect. We have scheduled offloading times for ships that arrive. It could cost us a lot of time and money if all that was put out.'

'A pattern is emerging,' said Alex. 'It shows these pirates are focussing on specific regions. We intend to deploy our drone vessels further afield. We will spread out the task force and use the drone vessels as a deterrent. It will mean less frequent visits to the Harvester for moon pool Skimmer inspections though. We will have to do more sub surface boarding's at sea using the breaching pod. Of course, this won't affect loading of Skimmers with nodules by Xtracts. It doesn't impact your scheduling.'

'Unless of course a skimmer crew has done something non-compliant within "the Area",' said Max. 'Then they will have something to answer for and be held up by us.'

'It sounds like a necessary move,' said Sue. 'Given the changing situation with Piracy in the Area.'

The security officer outside knocked on the door and came in.

'Ying Yue is here to meet with you before her tour with Chang,' he said.

Alex shot Max a quick look. Max nodded his head slightly in response. Sue looked at them both then back at Lee and smiled briefly.

Max saw the brief exchange between them. It wasn't often he felt uncomfortable. He trusted his instincts. Something was going on.

'Please come in,' said Sue getting up and going to the entrance. She motioned for Ying Yue to come in. 'This is Max and Alex,' she said. 'They control the Sea Hunter unit.'

'Hi,' she said greeting them both.

'Nice to meet you,' said Alex. 'We've heard…'

He stopped himself and Max glared at him. Alex managed to catch himself, but Sue noted the stumble.

A security detail was waiting outside to escort her down to the moon pools. Ying Yue was dressed casually.

'Okay,' said Sue as she stood in front of her. She put her hand on her shoulder and whispered so Max and Alex would not hear. 'Make sure you look and listen as much as you can and get inside that information hub. You have to insist on it with Chang.'

While Sue was talking, she slipped a small device under the collar of her top. It attached itself to her clothing.

Ying Yue said goodbye to Max and Alex and left. She walked through operations with her escort to a lift that would take them down to the moon pools. The others watched her leave and for a moment there was an uncomfortable silence.

'Let's get something to eat,' said Sue as she moved towards the entrance and gestured for them to follow her.

'Sounds good,' said Max as they got up and followed her out, glad to be on the move.

On the way walking behind Alex, Max swiped his smart watch and sent a quick written message to his inspection team.

Move to Ngarra's Skimmer
Inspect Skimmer
Locate Chang and his sister
Breach of Skimmer contractor protocol
Apprehend sister
Buzz me when done
Return to drone with her
Power up and standby

Sue and Lee could not see what Max was up to. They reached the restaurant just as he finished. They all moved to a side room.

'Help yourselves,' said Lee as he gestured for them to get what they wanted to eat and return.

Sue went and had a brief word with an off-duty security officer eating at one of the other tables.

Alex and Max watched as he got up and left in a hurry.

'Somethings going down,' whispered Alex as they selected various items of food from the buffet.

'I don't think Lee is fully aware of it,' whispered Max. 'It seems to be more about Sue. She is up to something.'

Sue stood watching them and then came over and got some food herself. They returned to the side room and sat down opposite each other to eat.

'So,' said Sue. 'Bit of a family affair, isn't it?'

'Meaning what?' said Alex.

'Well, poor old Chang has had a bit of a rough time,' said Sue. 'I mean, he hasn't seen much of his sister and blames his father for his mother's situation.'

'I wouldn't know about that,' said Max. 'Our focus is monitoring, enforcement and compliance in "the Area".'

'Yes, yes, it is,' said Sue. 'You certainly would not want to contravene your mandate as agreed to by signatories to the convention. Ensuring activities in "the Area" under the regulations are compliant is important.'

'We wouldn't want an international incident now would we,' said Max pointedly.

'No, we wouldn't,' said Sue. 'We look after our own here on the Harvester. That is the limit of our jurisdiction on a flag State vessel under international maritime law. That also includes the disciplining of our own crew under Chinese law.'

Lee looked at her curiously and then at Alex and Max. What was she getting at? He wished Chang's father was here right now. He had a bad feeling.

Max felt his smart watch vibrate silently. He looked quickly at Alex and then at Sue and Lee.

'Right,' he said pushing his plate away and standing on Alex's boot hard. He stood up quickly in response.

'Yes,' said Alex. 'Time is getting on and we have reports to write. Let's get going.'

Max and Alex thanked them for their hospitality and turned to leave. They didn't take their plates back to the buffet. Sue and Lee looked at each other questionably.

'Yes,' said Sue. 'You must have a lot of work to do. Let's get you back to your drone as quickly as possible to so you can get on with the day.'

They moved off with the security officer.

They walked through operations to the lift and up to the drone bay.

The atmosphere was tense.

Max noted Sue tuck her arm inside her tunic and reach for something.

Her hand came back out again.

He looked quickly at Alex and while Sue and Lee were not looking signalled with his hand.

It meant weapon.

***

At the moon pool, the mineral trays had all been offloaded from Ngarra's Skimmer.

The security officer that escorted Ying Yue waited at the bottom of the gangway.

She walked across it and entered the Skimmer.

Everyone on board was now in on the plan to pass to her what she would think was a copy of the technology Connor had developed with SAI's help.

Little did they know that Sue had planted a device on Ying Yue's clothing to try and copy the technology as well.

'Sister,' said Chang as she boarded the Skimmer and entered the rec area. 'Great to see you again. I was moaning so much about catching up with you that they relented.'

'Chang,' she said greeting him with a hug. 'How is Skimmer life going?'

'Could be better,' he said gruffly.

The others looked at him and smiled.

Typical Chang, thought Ngarra.

'This is the crew,' said Chang. 'Jesse, Ngarra, Jonny and Stella.'

Ying Yue did the rounds and greeted everyone.

'And where is Connor,' she said.

'Where do you think?' said Jonny. 'With the love of his life of course.'

The others laughed and joked about Connor's affair with SAI.

'More love than you'll ever get Jonny boy,' said Stella.

'Says the most eligible bachelorette in the Academy,' said Jonny.

'My standards are high,' said Stella.

'Just ignore them,' said Jesse smiling. 'Anyway, Chang, I guess you want to show Ying Yue around,' she said with a wink.

'Let's go,' said Chang.

Ying Yue followed him down to the Xtract bay to start with. The others stayed in the rec area and either relaxed or went to their cabins for a while.

'I hope this works,' said Jonny. 'What happens when Chang's contact figures out that what we have given Ying Yue doesn't work?'

'By then, we will be out of here,' said Ngarra.

'But Chang's sister will still be in danger,' said Jonny. 'It doesn't make sense to me. Why not give them what they want.'

'It's not what Jonah would do,' said Jesse. 'There is no way she would want to lose that technology to someone else, especially the Chinese. Even if it puts Chang's sister in danger. She is not Australian; she is Chinese remember. Besides their father will look out for them.'

'But he isn't here,' said Jonny. 'I still think she is in danger and this is not good.'

'What do you want us to do about it?' said Ngarra getting grumpy.

'We are just a skimmer crew. Hang on, I sound like you now bro,' he said trying to lighten the situation.

'You do bro,' said Jonny smiling. 'Hard not to want to be like me though.'

Jonny made one of his Tongan Maori warriors' faces and tensed.

The others laughed.

'Still,' said Jonny. 'On a more serious note. I am guessing that Chang's sister is valuable to anyone that gets hold of her or her work. I mean given the work she must be involved in; if the rumours are true that is. I just don't understand why this family of theirs gets used as pawns by other people. It's sick.'

They quietened down as Chang passed through with his sister. He seemed happy enough given the situation.

'Great piece of kit these Skimmers,' she said. 'The prototype we used for that previous incident we helped you out with has improved on much of the AI technology inside them. For remote monitoring of Xtract mining operations without the need for crews I mean.'

'Just what we need,' said Jonny sarcastically. 'Out of a job because of some woman.'

Everyone laughed. For a short time, the tension amongst everyone lessened.

'Okay,' said Chang to his sister as they passed through the rec area. 'Let's go up to the SAI console and then catch up with Connor last. I'm sure that's what you'd really like.'

'Definitely,' she said. 'I've heard a lot about this person and look forward to meeting him.'

'Oh, he's a character all right,' said Jonny. 'A barrel of laughs, not. Go easy on him.'

Chang and Ying Yue walked up the stairs and through the watertight bulkhead entrance into the rear of the SAI console.

'Let's go straight back to the information hub,' she said. 'I know these things inside out. I'm just glad we have an excuse to catch up again.'

'Good idea,' said Chang. 'Then we can relax and talk about things.'

They walked down the passage to the information hub. Connor was running some simulations.

'Connor,' said Chang as they walked in. 'This is Ying Yue, my sister.'

Connor didn't reply straight away.

He was talking out loud about the simulation that was running in the ocean bubble hologram, or Gilgamesh as he now called it.

SAI was using natural language processing to identify key phrases from what he was talking about and searching for more data, scripts of source code and algorithms that could be hacked.

'So, this is it,' she said walking around the ocean bubble hologram. 'Impressive. It's like an entity constructing a hive around itself.'

'A mesh,' said Connor looking at Ying Yue. 'Gilgamesh. I have used data on patterning of group behaviour in nature, coding scripts and algorithms which we hacked. It was the basis for developing group behaviour responses in Xtracts when mining operations are interrupted. The simulation kept falling apart until now. I mean, there was no learning from responses, no memory stored in the mesh we created.'

Chang watched and took his chances. He inserted the device he used last time into a port and stood in front of it. He watched as Connor carried on talking to or should he say at Ying Yue.

'That is until we developed "Red Queen". That's from nature you know. An evolutionary arms race. Inherit memory built into a species across generations. They are always in competition with each other to get the most nodules. We created an algorithm stack; deep learning. It took ages, but we got there in the end. Trouble is we can't have Xtracts pitted against each other all the time out there. That's where I am stuck now. I've been thinking about parasite host relationships.'

'Wow Connor,' impressive she said thinking about her own mimic drone work.

She walked around the ocean bubble hologram. Little did she know that the device under her tunic collar had activated and was searching the data stream and source code running the ocean bubble hologram. It found a way in and started downloading.

While Connor was talking to Ying Yue, he glanced behind him. The icon showed the copying as complete. He took the device out and walked over to where Connor and Ying Yue were standing.

'Great isn't it,' he said. 'Anyway, I guess we had better get going. We are off Connor. I have some catching up to do with my sister.'

Connor had already lost interest and was back working with SAI on the simulations.

'Thanks Connor,' said Ying Yue as they walked out.

'Here,' said Chang as he grabbed her hand on the way out. He placed the device into her hand. On the device was a hack that would corrupt what he had copied. It would run but not make any sense. It would take whoever it was a while to figure out it was fake.

'No questions,' he said as she was about to ask what he was up to. 'Just hold onto it. Someone will ask you for it. You must give it to them okay. You are in danger if you don't.'

'That means more than you think,' she said as they walked back down the stairs to the rec area.

'What do you mean?' said Chang.

Ying Yue didn't get to answer that. The two Sea Hunter inspection officers had arrived to carry out an inspection.

They saw Ying Yue.

'What is she doing on board a skimmer? Does she have clearance? Have you got clearance?' one of them asked as they moved towards her.

'What do you mean?' asked Ngarra pleading innocence.

'A foreign national on board a contractor Skimmer,' he said. 'There are rules. Where is your security clearance?'

Damn it thought Jesse to herself. That wasn't meant to happen.

The Harvester security officer waiting for Ying Yue had seen the commotion through the Skimmer entrance. He raced up the gangway and came in behind the two Sea Hunter officers.

'What's going on?' he said.

'This person can't be on here, she must come with us for questioning back on the Sea Hunter vessel.'

'Not possible,' he said.

'Under our mandate for monitoring, compliance and enforcement in the Area it is,' said one of the Sea Hunter officers.

Chang panicked and grabbed his sister pushing her behind the other crewmembers. The Harvester security guard went to grab her and prevent the Sea Hunter officers taking her away.

A scuffle ensued.

The Harvester security officer tried to leave and get some help.

'Grab him,' said one of the Sea Hunter officers.

The other grabbed his arm as he passed and pulled him around in a semicircle before bending is arm quickly up and back and sweeping his foot under his leg to drop him to the ground.

The Harvester security guard anticipated the move and as he hit the deck bought his leg up and kicked him in the face. Jonny jumped on him as did Ngarra and they held him down.

The other Sea Hunter office grabbed Ying Yue while everyone was distracted and pushed Chang away.

Jesse grabbed her stun rod and yelled across the commotion.

'Stop! Stop this. Let them take her away for questioning.'

'No,' said Chang yelling.

'Think about it,' said Jesse as she tried to calm everyone down. 'Let her go with the Sea Hunters. They will question her, write an incident report and release her.'

'You lot need to leave now,' said one of the Sea Hunter officers.

'Not without my sister,' said Chang.

'She can't be on here,' said the other Sea Hunter officer as he pulled the Harvester security officer up off the deck.

They all stood around breathing heavily from the struggle.

'You,' he said to the Harvester security officer who now stood there brushing himself off and correcting his uniform. He looked rather embarrassed about the whole situation.

'Move in front of us and take us back to the drone deck,' he said.

The Harvester security officer reluctantly did as he was told.

'The cameras will pick up our movements,' said the Sea Hunter inspection officer. 'Report that we are taking Ying Yue for questioning about being on a skimmer without clearance.'

He nodded his head. They headed off and he contacted Harvester security.

Ying Yue looked at Chang and then at Jesse.

'Don't worry everything will be fine,' she said. 'Sometimes things are just meant to be Sue if you know what I mean.'

Ying Yue looked intensely at Jesse and nodded her head. Jesse looked at them both. Something else was going on; why would she call her Sue.

They watched them walk down the gangway and head for a Harvester crew lift. It would take them up to the drone bay and drone deck above.

'Let's go!' yelled Jesse. 'Now! Everyone to your stations let's head for our next mining location. Ahead of schedule but away from here. I need to speak with Jonah and Rick at Xed Academy.'

'SAI,' said Ngarra. 'Prepared to leave moon pool for next mining run.'

'Confirmed,' said SAI. 'Prepare to leave for next mining run.'

The entrance to the Skimmer closed and SAI started system checks before powering up.

Stella and Chang took off to the Xtract bay to monitor SAI's checks of Xtracts and their operating systems, nodule trays, and moon pool and airlock systems.

The others raced up to the SAI console. Connor had remained in the information hub absorbed in his work.

Jonny put his interface lenses on and synched with SAI to monitor moon pool exit protocols. Ngarra got SAI to show the navigation hologram and check their next mining location.

'All systems nominal and Skimmer is watertight. Propulsion online and mining location confirmed,' said SAI.

'SAI exit moon pool and transit to mining location,' said Ngarra.

'Confirmed,' said SAI.

There was a pause and then an alarm went off.

'Unable to depart,' said SAI. 'Docking clamps locked. Require manual release.'

'Damn it,' said Ngarra. 'SAI, go to standby and hold.'

'Confirmed,' said SAI. 'Skimmer on standby.'

'What are we going to do?' said Jonny.

'Hey guys,' said Stella over comms from the Xtract bay. 'What's happening, why aren't we leaving?'

'The docking clamps are locked,' said Jesse in reply.

'Bugger,' said Stella. 'Need my lock picking skills do you.'

'You can unlock them manually can you,' said Ngarra.

'That I can,' she said.

'That would be right,' said Jonny. 'Got to watch those hands of hers. Gets her into trouble. Remember last time in the airlock and moon pool.'

'Well, your fat little hands aren't going to get us out of any tight spaces are they Jonny boy,' she said laughing.

'Damn it this is serious!' said Jesse. 'All meet in the rec area now. Let's go over what to do before we get stuck here and tied up in all this mess,' said Jesse.

SAI was now in standby. The watertight bulkheads were open, and the crew could move freely about the Skimmer.

'What about my sister?' said Chang over comms from the Xtract bay.

'She's still up there with everyone. Let's get her.'

'Dreamer,' said Jonny laughing. 'You think a bunch of youth monitoring a skimmer are the 'A team' or something boy.'

'Cut it out you lot!' said Jesse over comms. 'Get to the rec area now.'

Jesse, Ngarra and Jonny walked to the rear of the SAI console, through the watertight bulkhead entrance and down the stairs. They didn't think to grab Connor. Amidst all the panic everyone had forgotten about him.

Stella and Chang walked up the stairs from the Xtract bay, through the watertight bulkhead entrance and into the rec area. They almost walked into each other as they all came into the rec area.

Chapter 20

At Xed Academy crew monitoring and communications a duty officer was at a monitoring station. Crew vitals had activated an alarm for the Skimmer Rick had tagged and placed on the main display at the front. He opened the icon and called over the supervisor.

While they looked at the crew vitals, an urgent request came through on the message board to speak with Jonah. It was from the same Skimmer.

'Get a message to Jonah now,' said the supervisor. 'And Rick to.'

'Right away,' said the duty officer as he sent a message to Jonah and Rick.

'Open message board,' said the supervisor.

An image of Jesse appeared.

'We're in trouble,' she said. 'Chang's sister was on board, and the Sea Hunters came across her. They took her way for questioning. There was a scuffle. Chang is beside himself.'

'Is everyone okay?' said the duty officer.

'Yes,' said Jesse. 'We tried to leave but the docking clamps are locked. We are stuck here.'

'What about the manual override?' said the duty officer. 'Did any of your crew violate "the Area" regulations?'

'No, well they did jump on a Harvester security officer and hold him down. But no, no mining regulations were violated. Well except for having a non-approved person on board a contractor Skimmer.'

The conversation continued over what to do.

Rick and Jonah arrived and came running down the stairs from the mezzanine and over to the monitoring station.

'What's going on?' said Jonah panting as they arrived.

'The Sea Hunters caught Chang's sister on the Skimmer,' the duty officer said. 'With no approval or security clearance, they took her away for questioning. There was a scuffle with a Harvester security officer.'

'Jesse, it's Jonah and Rick. Are you okay?'

'All fine,' she said. 'The docking clamps are locked, and we can't leave.'

'What about Chang? Is he okay?' said Rick.

'He's pretty upset about the whole thing. Chang's sister was threatened. Chang was told to get a copy of Connor's work and give it to her or else.'

'She has it now?' asked Rick.

'Yes,' said Jesse.

'What did you do that for?' said Jonah. 'No one can even get to his sister out there on the Harvester.'

'Well, whatever that security breach is from last time,' said Jesse. 'It has happened again.'

Rick thought carefully about what to say. He didn't want everyone to know exactly what was going on. His people were not ready. They hadn't even reached the point where they were ready for the next stage. He decided to play along.

'The Sea Hunters,' he said. 'She must be giving it them.'

'How would you know that?' said Jonah looking at him fiercely.

She always suspected he was involved in something.

'Just a hunch. Don't panic,' he said. 'It's a logical solution to the situation. Even in a security breach here who would give the technology to the Chinese. It must be for someone else. The only other organisation out there is the Sea Hunters.'

'True,' said Jonah cautiously as she tried to gauge what Rick was up to. 'But what would they do with it apart from keeping it safe for someone else. Like last time ay Rick?'

'Where are they now?' said Rick ignoring the remark. 'The Sea Hunters I mean.'

'They were going to the drone deck to take Ying Yue back to the Hunter vessel for questioning,' said Jesse.

'Did she say anything?' said Rick. 'I mean Chang's sister.'

'She said something odd and then she stared at me intensely,' said Jesse. 'What was it?' she thought out loud. 'That's right.' When they were taking her away, she said *Sometimes things are just meant to be Sue if you know what I mean.*'

'Somethings not right,' said Rick looking at Jonah. 'Sue is a senior officer on the Harvester.'

'I need to speak with Chang's father,' said Jonah. 'Just get those docking clamps off and get out of there and head for your next mining run.'

Rick thought quickly. He needed to get in touch with his contact Max on the Sea Hunter vessel. He hoped they already knew something wasn't right with all this.

'I will talk with the Sea Hunter liaison officer here on campus,' said Rick.

'Okay,' said Jesse. 'We will report in once we are enroute to our mining location.'

With that, her image disappeared.

'Continue to monitor crew vitals,' said Rick to the supervisor and the duty officer.

'Let's talk quickly,' said Jonah. 'I need to get hold of Chang's father. He needs to step in on this before it becomes one big mess for us and for them.'

They walked across to the stairs and up to the enclosed mezzanine overlooking the monitoring stations and main display at the front.

'What's going on with Chang's sister?' said Jonah calmly as they walked up the stairs. 'If anything happens to her and I find out it has something to do with you, there will be hell to pay,' she said as they walked across the mezzanine. 'Their father will be devastated. It could jeopardise everything.'

Rick thought carefully. How much should he say and what were the implications for the various stages of the project to come. What was Jonah's agenda in all this as well?

'That research of Ying Yue's,' said Rick. 'On drones and Skimmers. When combined with what Connor is developing has huge potential. In fact, dangerous potential in the wrong hands.'

'Let me guess,' said Jonah. 'You want access to it and are quite happy to expose everything we have built up here to get to it. That's folly.'

Rick stepped back and tried to say something.

'You're always talking about your people,' said Jonah. 'And what about your agenda with the council and the future of what we have here. You want to spin out a technology company. Why don't you just say it.'

Rick stood for a moment in silence thinking carefully about what to say. It wasn't quite like that.

'You may be right with some of that,' he said. 'But let's deal with this situation before someone gets hurt.'

Jonah glared at him but reluctantly agreed.

'Right,' she said with a sigh. Rick was not going to budge on any of it yet. 'Let's see what Chang's father has to say.'

She swiped her smart watch and sent an urgent request to speak with Chang's father. She tagged it as an emergency call. It wasn't long before her message board activated, and Chang's father's image appeared.

'Jonah,' he said. 'What is it? What's happened?'

'Your daughter is in the custody of the Sea Hunters. As far as we know they are still on the Harvester. She was in breach of the protocols for Skimmers using the moon pools. She is an unauthorised person on a contractor Skimmer. Also, Chang's Skimmer can't leave as the docking clamps are locked.'

'Lee and Sue will have it in hand,' he said. 'I will contact them straight away. But you owe me Jonah, remember last time. It all sounds a bit heavy handed and unnecessary by the Sea Hunters. They are well within their rights to just issue a warning notice, strange.'

'I will deal with it,' said Rick. 'I will contact them now to stand down and just question her on board the Harvester.'

'Sounds good,' said Jonah. 'We are agreed then and time is short. Rick will contact the Sea Hunters and you will contact Lee and Sue. Both parties are to back down.'

With that, his image disappeared. Rick raced off to contact Max and warn him before it was too late that it could all go pear shaped fast. Jonah raced back to her office to think carefully about what her next move would be.

***

On the Harvester drone deck, Max and Alex were standing near their patrol drone with Sue and Lee.

It was a tense situation.

They waited for the two Skimmer inspection officers to arrive. Coming up the set of stairs to one side they approached.

Everyone was watching them.

'Why is Ying Yue with them?' said Max innocently.

'Sir,' said one of Max's Skimmer inspection officers. 'Ying Yue is in violation of Skimmer contractor security protocols. She was found on board during an inspection. We are taking her for questioning.'

'That is not possible,' said Lee. 'You are on a GlobeCorpMining Harvester. The rules don't apply. We can detain Skimmer crews if we suspect Chinese sovereignty is compromised. You can't detain Chinese nationals.'

'Not in the moon pools or accommodation,' said Max. 'That is how it is all set up. It means any contractor Skimmer can come and go offloading nodules without fear of interreference. That's our role to inspect and ensure compliance as a representative agency of all State Sponsors and their contractors. If a Chinese national is in those areas and breaks protocols, we can detain and question them.'

'You can't take a Chinese national off this ship,' said Sue. 'You are welcome to question Ying Yue here.'

'We will return her after due process has been followed,' said Max.

Alex looked around; everyone was on edge. He motioned for the two inspection officers to go and power up the drone ready to leave.

Max looked at him quickly and nodded.

'That is not possible,' said Sue.

Max and Alex were standing with Ying Yue about five metres from the others. Max looked at Sue. She put her hand inside her tunic and rested it there.

'Perhaps you could do the initial questioning here,' said Lee. 'If it warrants it, then take her aboard your vessel to do all the paperwork.' The Sea Hunter drone powered up behind them and the rotors spun up. The humming meant everyone had to talk louder to be heard.

Damn it thought Max to himself. This isn't going to work. It will cause a world of trouble for us. He needed to think fast. He could buy some time by doing the questioning on the Harvester, get the information off her and then they could return in the morning with the excuse of inspecting more Skimmers. That would give him the time to contact Rick.

His smartwatch vibrated and he quickly looked down at it.

Urgent message
Stand down
Mission compromised
Danger

Well, there we have it, he thought to himself. Timing is everything.

'Perhaps you are right,' he said smiling at Lee and Sue. 'Let's go to a meeting room and debrief Ying Yue about her transgression.'

Sue took her hand out of her uniform top.

'That sounds like the right thing to do,' she said smiling at Max and Alex.

Alex signalled the other two inspection officers to power down the drone.

Another Harvester security officer came up behind Lee and Sue. He said something to them. Max couldn't make out what it was.

'Right,' said Lee. 'Our two security officers will escort you to a meeting room to debrief Ying Yue. You and your team are welcome to stay the night and finish your Skimmer inspections tomorrow. Accommodation will be provided.'

Alex looked at Max and nodded. Slowing things down was a good thing at this point until they could sort out what the hell was going on.

'Sounds like a good idea,' said Max.

Everyone relaxed a little.

They followed the two Harvester security officers over to the Hex tower, which was raised again. Entering the foyer, they waited for it to lower to the drone bay below. Everyone then exited and walked across the drone bay. In silence, they followed Harvester security to a lift and down to operations level. They exited the lift and walked through the main concourse to a meeting room; one they had used previously. Max and Alex followed behind with Ying Yue. A Harvester security officer stood outside with the two Sea Hunter Skimmer inspection officers.

Lee and Sue made sure everything was in order and then left to discuss what was going on.

'Sir,' said a moon pool Skimmer offloading officer on duty as they walked past him. 'That Skimmer the Sea Hunters boarded and found Ying Yue on tried to leave. The docking clamps are locked of course. As soon as we were notified of what was going on by security, we secured their moon pool.'

'Good,' said Sue turning to face him. 'Decline any request to leave before they are meant to. In case, we need to question them.'

'Yes, ma'am,' said the duty officer as he walked off and returned to his post.

Lee and Sue carried on walking through the concourse to the restaurant and sat at a table to one side.

'We have to assume that our device was able to access some of the details of Connor's work on that Skimmer,' said Lee.

'What's more important,' said Sue. 'Is what she saw there and talked about with Connor. Alex and Max will have no idea about what she is carrying. We will let them have their little excuse for a debrief.'

'Yes,' said Lee. 'It's just an excuse to try and get hold of Ying Yue.'

'The main thing is to ensure she is not taken off the Harvester,' said Sue. 'Chang's father may have told us to back off and let things happen but there is no way Ying Yue is going anywhere no matter what.'

The conversation continued for a while.

Lee and Sue discussed various options.

Chapter 21

It had been a long day. Alex and Max sat with Ying Yue in the meeting room on the Harvester.

'It was innocent enough,' said Ying Yue. 'Chang just wanted to show me what Connor was up to.'

'Do you have it?' said Max.

'I do,' she said. 'Pass me a cup of water please.'

Alex poured her a glass and handed it to her. She reached for it and passed him the tiny device as their hands crossed. Little did they know the crew had arranged for it to be corrupted. It would not reveal how Connor's technology worked but it would look like it did. The ocean bubble hologram was just the shell of Gilgamesh. He slipped it into a small pocket on his uniform pants and nodded at Max.

'You know it's against protocol to step on board a contractor Skimmer offloading at a Harvester moon pool. It's off limits to anyone except crews and Sea Hunter inspection officers.'

'Well, it's my brother isn't it. Family counts above all else.'

'Even if that gets you into a world of trouble,' said Max leaning back in his chair and folding his arms.

'Oh, I think I am already in a world of trouble,' she said with a hint in her voice that something was not right.

'What do you mean by that?' said Alex.

'Sue me if you want. I mean you could Sue me, but my father would get me out of anything. Except if you SUE me of course.'

Max looked at Alex. They figured out that she was talking about Sue. Something was up with her.

'You realise we have to write you up and submit a report on breaching moon pool protocols though don't you,' said Alex.

'Of course,' she said. 'It's not as if I need to get out of here, IS IT. My work is crucial. I was just interested in what Connor was up to. You can't SUE me for what I just said. My LIFE is SHORT you know.'

Alex and Max were onto it now. 'Sue me' was code for anything she referred to that linked to Sue.

'Well,' said Max. 'We are here overnight. My team will finish inspections in the morning. They were interrupted by all this.'

'Nothing to do with me,' she said. 'Although, I would like to see Chang again. Maybe not on a skimmer,' she said smiling.

'You have got that right,' said Alex. 'I am sure Lee and Sue will allow the crew to come to accommodation and meet you at the restaurant.'

'Yes, and let's not see this happening again,' said Max. 'Right, you can go, we have enough notes to write this up don't we,' he said to Alex.

'Should be fine,' said Alex as he folded his notebook.

They all got up and walked to the door.

Ying Yue was escorted by the Harvester security officer down the concourse to the restaurant to meet with Lee and Sue. She also wanted to go back to her lab before the night was out.

'Let's go,' said Max to his team.

'Accommodation and some down time it is then?' said Alex.

'You lot stay sharp,' said Max. 'Something is going on and it isn't good. I don't think Chang's father is aware of it either.'

'You two can finish the rest of those Skimmer inspections in the morning,' said Alex.

'Yes, sir,' they said turning and walking off to the lift to the accommodation level. A Harvester security officer escorted them away.

Meanwhile, Ying Yue had followed the Security officer to the small private room off to one side of the restaurant that was also on the operations level. Lee and Sue saw them coming and stood up.

'Let's go to the lab complex,' said Lee as they all walked off. They exited the restaurant and walked along the concourse to the lab complex. They entered and walked past the Skimmer suspended over the moonpool below. To one side, Ying Yue's lab still contained the Xtracts she was working on. It was empty as it was late in the day. They walked into the small foyer and the lights activated.

'It's been a rough day,' said Sue putting her hand on Ying Yue's shoulder. She reached under her tunic collar and pulled a small device out and held it in front of her.

Ying Yue tried not to look surprised or worried.

'Interesting,' she said as Sue took it over to a workstation and loaded it.

A string of source code loaded. Embedded were a unique combination of algorithm stacks and a range of schematics of the ocean bubble hologram.

'SAI run this source code,' she said.

'Confirmed, running source code,' said SAI.

They all watched as SAI projected the display that was generated from running the source code and algorithm stack. In the centre of the console, an ocean bubble hologram appeared with an Xtract mining simulation in it.

'Good,' said Sue. 'We have it.'

Ying Yue looked on. They were missing something key. The Red Queen sequence she saw in Connor's lab. She breathed a sigh of relief. They didn't even know. It wouldn't work.

'SAI run the mimic program,' said Sue.

'Confirmed,' said SAI. 'Mimic program running.'

'SAI,' said Sue. 'Initiate search for insertion sequence.'

'Confirmed,' said SAI. 'Running search.'

Ying Yue watched. She knew that all they had was the shell. They didn't know that though. It just made Connor's work fun to look at for now.

'Right,' said Sue. 'Incorporate this ocean bubble hologram thing into our project from now on. Maybe we can overcome the issues you have come across.'

'Of course,' said Ying Yue nodding her head. 'But this is dangerous. Once inserted there is no longer human oversight. The only control will be through a shutdown.'

'Welcome to a new world for mining,' said Sue.

'It could be weaponised,' said Ying Yue.

'Enough!' said Sue. 'That is not your concern.'

'On another note,' said Lee as he quickly looked to calm the situation. 'How did it go with the Sea Hunters?'

'Not as bad as I thought,' said Ying Yue. 'They questioned me about the tour with my brother. They said a report would be written up and submitted. They will let you both know if there will be any further follow-up on the breach of Skimmer protocols.'

'Right then,' said Sue. 'I certainly don't appreciate one of our Harvester security officers being roughed up in the process. I will speak to them at some point as well. Let's go Lee, we have a few things to sort out.'

Lee and Sue walked out of the lab complex leaving Ying Yue to contemplate everything that had happened.

She hoped Chang was okay and the rest of his crew for that matter. She wished her father was here right now.

***

On the Skimmer in the rec area, the crew sat at the main table and discussed unlocking the docking clamps. It could be done manually. It would override the locking mechanism, which was controlled remotely from the operations centre. It could be done without them even knowing the mechanism had been tripped until they left.

While talking, SAI announced that there was an incoming message from the Harvester.

'Incoming message from Harvester security,' said SAI.

'SAI, open message board,' said Jesse.

An image of a Harvester officer appeared.

'Due to the prior incident docking clamps have been locked until the Sea Hunters and Harvester security have finished their inquiries. You are welcome to use the Harvester accommodation overnight. The situation will be reviewed first thing tomorrow morning.'

'What about my sister?' said Chang as the Harvester officer waited for their response. 'I must see her.'

'Request permission for Chang to see his sister Ying Yue in accommodation level restaurant,' said Jesse.

A few minutes of silence followed while the security officer checked with Lee and Sue about their request.

'Approved,' he said. 'Ying Yue will meet you at the accommodation level restaurant. A security officer will meet you at your Skimmer and take you all above.'

The security officer's image disappeared, and the message board closed.

'Well that settles that then,' said Jonny.

'I can talk with Chang's sister about the ocean bubble hologram and my work. It will be great,' said Connor excitedly.

'Is that such a good idea?' said Ngarra. 'Ying Yue is in enough trouble with the Sea Hunters. We didn't get away with showing her around. And if Lee and Sue already knew that was going to happen then something is up.'

'We will all be together,' said Jesse as she looked at Connor. 'Connor will be fine. Let's assume we will all be watched. We'll sleep on board though.'

Everyone agreed and nodded their head. No argument ensued this time about staying on board.

'And Stella you can unlock those clamps when we get back, is that right.'

'Of course,' she said. 'Chang knows just as much about it as me, so that makes two of us.'

'Of course,' he said. 'I can break into lots of things.'

'Let's go then,' said Ngarra. 'Let's play this game and check in on Chang's sister so we know she is okay. After that, we are going to be up half the night sneaking around unlocking those clamps. We need to get out of here sooner rather than later.'

'I see our escort is here,' said Jonny looking out the entrance and down the gangway. They got up and walked towards the entrance. They all walked down the gangway and followed the security officer to the lift and up to the accommodation level.

'Do you think my sister will be okay?' said Chang as they entered the lift. It took them above.

'I don't know,' said Jesse quietly. 'If it was that straight forward, the Sea Hunters would have just let her off with a warning. Somethings up. Besides, Lee and Sue will deal with it internally. Assuming they approved the Skimmer visit that is.'

She looked at Ngarra and moved close to him to whisper. 'I think the whole thing was set up on both sides. A game is being playing and we are caught in the middle.'

Ngarra nudged Jesse and reminded her that a Harvester security officer was with them and might overhear them talking.

The lift stopped and they excited and walked through the common area to the accommodation level restaurant.

'I will leave you here,' said the security officer. 'When you want to return to your Skimmer, come and get me from the administration office over there.

He pointed to an office near the lift and main foyer where someone was working.

'Right, let's get some food and sit down and eat,' said Jonny. 'All this excitement isn't helping. Look at me, I'm fading away.'

'Hardly,' said Stella. 'Looks like you're eating for two.'

'I am,' he said. 'You and me babe.'

The others managed a nervous laugh. It was their way of coping.

'There she is,' said Connor racing off towards Ying Yue.

The others quickly followed.

After greetings all around and checks that Ying Yue was okay everyone got some food from the buffet and sat down.

'So, what happened?' said Jesse.

'No big deal,' said Ying Yue calmly. 'The Sea Hunters wanted to take me to their vessel. Lee and Sue insisted that was not happening. I ended up being interviewed here.'

'What about the device with the information on it?' said Chang.

'The Sea Hunters have it,' she said.

'Ah, so it was them,' said Chang.

'Makes sense,' said Jesse. 'What about Lee and Sue?'

'They were okay,' she said. 'They were very curious about what I saw on your Skimmer though. I didn't say much Connor. It's your work and it's such a great concept.'

'But what about the mimic drones?' said Connor hastily; seeing an opportunity to jump in and talk about his work.

'Connor no,' said Jesse.

'Ah, a very interesting topic. It's okay,' said Ying Yue 'Connor and I have a common interest; truly autonomous mining drones, don't we Connor.'

'To right,' he said. 'Our "Red Queen" is key, still some problems to sort out but looking good. We are onto it.'

'Yes, Red Queen,' said Ying Yue. 'Who's the we in this?'

'Connor,' said Jesse smiling. 'Always the joker. He's just being smart.'

'But it's key to everything, I can explain,' he said excitedly.

'Connor, what about that ocean bubble hologram?' said Ngarra. 'How does the simulation work?'

Jesse nodded at Ngarra. They had managed to distract Connor from saying too much about Red Queen itself.

They watched as Connor launched into a long conversation about how the ocean bubble hologram worked as a simulation-testing platform for his work.

For a short time, everyone else was silent; eating and listening to Connor.

'How is Father?' said Chang interrupting Connor.

Connor paused to eat a little of the untouched food on his plate.

Ying Yue looked across at Chang. She was concerned about their father but cautious about what to say.

'He is fine,' she said. 'He wishes you would talk to him though.'

'Sure, he does,' said Chang gruffly. 'Just like he talks to our mother all the time.'

The sarcasm in his voice cut across the table like a knife.

'It was never his fault,' she said calmly. 'What happened I mean. At least, you're not stuck on this Harvester carrying on a project Mother was involved in all those years ago.'

'No,' said Chang. 'Instead, I'm stuck on a tin can submerged in a giant bathtub for weeks on end.'

The others all laughed. Even Connor smiled at that one. Chang managed a chuckle as well.

'Good one, Chang,' said Jonny. 'You're stealing my thunder here.'

'That was a good one wasn't it,' said Chang.

'Well, we are glad you are okay,' said Stella.

Ying Yue smiled at them. Little did they know how tense the situation was on the Harvester. Connor was onto something with all that work of his but there was no way she was letting Sue get hold of it. She hated her; something was not right about her. She was PLA Navy. She worried about her father to. Something was not right. She had to be careful. If her plan worked, she would expose Sue and get rid of her.

'So, you will be leaving for your mining run in the morning I take it,' she said.

'Yes, they locked the docking clamps,' said Ngarra. 'It was because of what happened. I guess until things are sorted out with the Sea Hunters and all. We have to wait until morning.'

'Yeah, we will unlock them ourselves if we have to,' said Stella.

Jesse glared at Stella. She shrugged her shoulders as if to say what.

'We will get underway first thing in the morning hopefully,' said Jesse.

'Probably a good thing,' said Ying Yue. 'Get on with mining and keep Connor away from here. Too much interest in that project of yours Connor.'

Connor looked at her with a mouth full of food. He hadn't been listening. In his excitement, he tried to say something and dropped a mouthful of food onto his lap. Jonny was in the middle of gulping his drink. He sprayed it over himself and choked, laughing at Connor.

Everyone laughed at Jonny. The mood lightened and for a while the conversation shifted to personal interests.

***

The evening was getting on and the conversation had quietened down. For a moment, everyone had forgotten the situation they were in.

'Time we were going,' said Jesse looking around at everyone. It was getting late.

Ngarra nodded and got up. He went to get the security officer to ask them to escort the crew back to their Skimmer.

The others said goodbye to Ying Yue and walked back towards the common area foyer and the lift. Chang had a brief talk with his sister.

'We need to get you out of here Connor,' said Jesse while they were waiting.

'Yeah,' said Jonny. 'It's what Chang's sister is not saying that I am worried about. She seemed way too relaxed about everything.'

'You're right about that,' said Jesse. 'Too relaxed.'

They quietened down as Chang walked over to them.

The security officer came over and escorted them into the lift and down to the moon pools.

At the moon pools, they exited and walked along the boardwalk next to the conveyor and robotic arms. A few other Skimmers were docked overnight. Their crews were taking advantage of Harvester accommodation. They had seen some of them in the restaurant, but they kept to themselves.

'Here you go,' said the security officer at the bottom of the gangway to their Skimmer. He waited while they walked across and boarded their Skimmer. He disappeared back along the gangway next to the dimly lit moon pools.

'Can we disengage the docking clamps without the cameras detecting us?' said Ngarra as they boarded the Skimmer and stood in the rec area.

'Sure,' said Stella. 'If you all stand at this end of the gangway in front of me, I can get underneath and crawl along it. There is a raised rim around each moon pool. I can circle it to reach docking clamp. I just have to bypass the automated system, so I don't trip the alarm when I switch them to manual and disengage them.'

'Can you do that?' asked Jesse.

'Sure,' said Stella. 'I know these Harvester moon pool and offloading systems inside out. So does Chang.'

Stella went and grabbed a small tool bag from the maintenance bay below. On her way back up, she strapped it to her waist.

The others waited at the start of the gangway and pretended to have a causal conversation pointing out features of the moon pools around them. They discussed the offloading of nodules. While they were chatting, Stella crept behind them and hoped over the gangway.

'Done,' she said whispering up at them. 'I will whistle when I am back.'

The others went back inside.

'Jonny,' said Jesse. 'Wait here until she gets back. Come and get us so we can cover her getting back on the gangway and inside.'

'Sure,' he said getting himself some food and grabbing a chair to sit near the entrance.

The others went off to their cabins to get some rest for a short time. It would be a long night and an interrupted sleep.

Meanwhile Stella crawled along the space under the gangway to the side of the moon pool. She dropped down into the recess unnoticed. Squatting down she crept along to the first docking clamp. She opened the control panel and got busy bypassing the automated system. Once that was set up, she pressed the manual bypass icon. She then used the lever and moved the docking clamp to manual. She then unlocked it.

Stella moved on, she had to get halfway around the moon pool to the other docking clamp. She heard footsteps and froze, melting into the shadows. A security officer approached. In the dimly lit shadows of the recess, she hoped to go un-noticed. The security officer paused not far from her and shone his torch around the moon pool. Given what had happened earlier they must be concerned, she thought. She waited and watched the torch light moving around the sides of the moon pool. If it shone directly on her she would be made, and it would be over. Then they really would be in trouble.

'Hey,' said Jonny from the top of the gangway. 'I thought I saw movement before. Over in one of the other moon pools when we were walking back. I heard a splash as well.'

The security officer nodded and walked off quickly shining his torch along the edges of another moon pool.

Stella breathed a sigh of relief. She could see Jonny trying to make her out in the dimly lit moon pool recess. He walked back into the entrance of the Skimmer.

Stella carried on and made it to the second docking clamp. She repeated the process. She was nervous and shaking. She paused, calmed herself, wiped the sweat from her face and hands and carried on.

Having disengaged the lock from the second one she slowly made her way back to the gangway. She gave a whistle and climbed under the gangway, crawling along it to the Skimmer entrance. The others had come out one at a time so as not to raise suspicion. While they were chatting, she popped back over the gangway and inside.

Chapter 22

Everyone was tired but up early, nonetheless. The plan was to slip away before anyone realised.

Jesse was in the SAI console. She was talking to Jonah and Rick at Xed Academy to discuss her growing concern about Connor's safety and the situation between Ying Yue, Chang and the Sea Hunters.

'We know Ying Yue violated Skimmer contractor protocols,' she said to Jonah. 'And that the Sea Hunters questioned her here on the Harvester and stayed overnight. We had a meal with Ying Yue last night. She seems worried about her own safety although she won't admit it.'

'Is she okay?' said Rick.

'Yes, as far as we know the plan worked, she was here to help Chang. We corrupted the copy of the technology that Chang gave her. Only Ying Yue will be able to work that out. Someone would have to stand and watch the ocean bubble hologram for a while before realising it was just stuck in a simulation loop.'

'Damn it,' thought Rick out loud to himself. They could have said something yesterday. Those kids always muck things up. Best intentions for sure but they don't realise what's going on.

'Damn what,' said Jonah hearing him.

Jesse heard it as well and wondered what was going on.

'Nothing,' he said. 'Best to leave as soon as you can and return to your mining run.'

'We unlocked the docking clamps manually,' said Jesse as she looked at Jonny and Ngarra. 'We are getting ready to leave now.'

In the background, Rick and Jonah could see the others preparing to leave. Jonny had his interface lenses on. Ngarra was looking over the navigation hologram.

'Connor needs to run those trials for longer out there,' said Jonah.

'Just a minute Jonah,' said Ngarra. 'SAI prepare to exit moon pool and proceed to next mining location,' said Ngarra.

'Confirmed,' said SAI. 'Preparing Skimmer for departure to next mining location.'

Sensing movement outside Ngarra looked up and out. The outer hull shields were still retracted. Running up the gangway appeared Ying Yue.

'Take me with you,' she yelled out. Of course, no one could hear her shout, but they could see from the SAI console that she was trying to say something and in a panic.

'What's going on?' said Jonah seeing the commotion around the SAI console.

'Chang's sister is here, she wants to come with us,' said Jesse.

'No,' said Jonah it will cause us a world of trouble, kidnapping a Chinese national from the Harvester.

'Chang is on the gangway!' yelled Jesse. 'My crew are now trying to stop him grabbing her.'

'If we have her, we have their technology and ours,' said Rick 'We can stop all this here and now.'

'Are you kidding me,' Jesse heard Jonah say to Rick. 'The key to all this is their father. If we have him, we continue to have a stake in all this into the future.'

'No time for debate,' said Jesse. 'We can see her from here. Shit, security officers are coming with Lee and Sue. There are two Sea Hunter Skimmer inspection officers not far behind them.'

'Damn it,' said Ngarra as he raced off to help stop Chang grabbing his sister and brining her aboard.

'Do not take her with you!' demanded Jonah. She saw Ngarra leave the SAI console.

'If she doesn't get off the gangway, she is going in the water with us and will get sucked down as we descend,' said Jesse.

***

Prior to the situation unfolding at the moon pool Sue and Lee had been at a breakfast meeting with Alex and Max. They were discussing the incident from the day before.

'To wrap up this report,' said Alex. 'Did you know of or allow Ying Yue to go down to the moon pools and board a contractor Skimmer.'

Sue looked at him and smiled innocently.

'Of course,' she said. 'It was necessary. She was concerned about her family and knew Chang wanted to see her. Rather than have her continuously distracted from her work we allowed her to go.'

'But it's against Skimmer protocols,' said Max. 'In addition, why would you knowingly breach the conditions set up that allow contractor Skimmers to come and go from the moon pools without any interference whatsoever from the Harvester?'

'It's hardly interference,' said Lee. 'It's Chang's sister.'

'The policy applies to everyone,' said Alex. 'Irrespective of intent.'

'We acknowledge that,' said Sue calmly. 'It won't happened again.'

'I will note that in my report,' said Alex.

'I am sure you will,' said Sue smiling.

The smiling assassin, Max thought to himself looking at her expression with growing concern.

'We will finish up our inspections this morning,' said Alex. 'Then be on our way. We have a few Skimmers to inspect on location.'

'I'm sure you do,' said Lee. 'We have no intention to compromise the conditions of GlobeCorpMining tenures in "the Area". The whole reason "the Area" works is because all signatories signed and agreed to how it would be run. I mean using contractor Skimmers and coming and going from here. The Sea Hunters were a big part of getting everyone to agree on that. From environmental monitoring to contractor compliance with mining protocols to running and use of the GlobeCorpMining Harvester.'

'Exactly,' said Sue. 'No one would want to compromise their right to be in "the Area" and operate under "the Authority" regulations and International Maritime Law.'

A security officer came over to their table and whispered in Lee's ear. His expression changed to one of alarm and concern.

'We have to go,' said Lee getting up quickly and nodding at Sue to follow.

'Anything we can help with?' said Alex.

'No,' said Sue. 'Please feel free to complete your inspections and be on your way.'

Lee and Sue left and followed the security officer.

Using his smartwatch Alex contacted their two inspection officers.

'Stay close to Ngarra's Skimmer. Something is going down.'

'Yes, sir,' was the reply.

'What do you think it is?' said Alex.

'Somethings up that's for sure,' said Max. 'Let's go to the drone deck and power up our patrol drone on the pretence we are doing some flight checks.'

'I'll check in with the Sea Hunter unit and give them a heads up to be ready to make haste and exit the security perimeter,' said Alex.

'We need to get this copy of Connor's technology out of here as well,' said Max. 'Second time we have attempted this and now we have it. Ricks contact came through.'

'Looks like a family affair,' said Alex smiling.

'A dangerous one at that,' said Max as they moved off quickly. 'I wish I had a handle on the big picture and what in the hell this is all about. This technology everyone wants I mean.'

They left quickly. A security officer met them in the common area and escorted them to the lift and up to the drone bay.

They exited the lift and crossed the drone bay to the hex tower which had been lowered.

They waited as it rose up to the drone deck. Some flight operations were underway so it would be raised for most of the day now. They thanked the security officer and walked over to their patrol drone, glistening in the morning sun.

***

Meanwhile, Sue and Lee had followed the security officer to Ying Yue's lab. She had asked them to come and look at the simulation. They walked into the hanger and past the Skimmer suspended over the moon pool. Technicians were working on it but there was no sign of Ying Yue. They entered her lab and walked past the Xtract drones. In one section, they could see the ocean bubble hologram.

Fascinated they watched a mining simulation. A scenario started that interrupted it. They watched the Xtracts respond initially and then the simulation fell apart. After a while, they figured out it was 'stuck' in a loop.

'Damn it,' said Sue. 'This isn't it; something is missing.'

Another security officer turned up and said they had not found her.

'Ying Yue said to come and get you. She had something to show you regarding the technology,' said the security officer.

'Get onto moon pool operations,' said Sue harshly. 'See what those damn kids are up to, if I can call them that. Smart little shits.'

Lee looked at her. She was very uptight about the whole situation. There were other ways to get hold of this technology she so desperately wanted for this mimic drone program.

'Let's go,' she said angrily. 'To the moon pool. And get a security detail to the drone deck as well to monitor what those damn Sea Hunters are up to.'

Sue was fuming. Someone had out manoeuvred her. They took off with security through the lab and past the Skimmer hanger. They raced to the nearest lift that went from the lab complex to the moon pool below.

Coming out of the lift in the distance they could make out some figures standing in the entrance to one of the Skimmers. It was dimly lit and hard to see. They raced along the boardwalk next to the conveyor and robotic arms. A skimmer was offloading, another getting ready to leave. A few crewmembers saw them. They passed the two Sea Hunter Skimmer inspection officers that were also heading quickly towards Ngarra's Skimmer to see what was going on.

As they all got closer, they could see and hear Ying Yue pleading with the crew to take her with them. The Skimmer had powered up and Ngarra, Stella and Jonny were holding Chang back. He was trying to grab Ying Yue.

'Stop,' yelled Sue as they arrived at the start of the gangway. 'Ying Yue get back here now.'

'They said if I didn't come, they would hurt Chang,' she yelled.

'Rubbish,' said Jonny. He was now holding Chang back. *It's the other way around*, he thought to himself. This is all about to go pear-shaped.

'Don't hurt him please,' she said. 'Look Sue please do something.'

'Get off that gangway Ying Yue,' said one of the Sea Hunter inspection officers as they raced up behind everyone.

Ying Yue knew Sue would do anything to keep her from going. Sue walked further along the gangway.

'Where is Connor,' she said to Ngarra.

'On board of course,' he said as they tried to pull Chang and Ying Yue apart.

At the other end of the gangway, Sue reached into her tunic with her hand and rested it there.

'We can't let you go Ying Yue. No matter what,' she said calmly and stepped forward again.

The two Sea Hunter officers looked at each other. The situation was delicate.

Lee looked over at them and put his hand out to tell them to back off.

In the SAI console, the message board was still open. Jesse was still talking with Jonah and Rick. She kept them informed of what was happening.

'Jesse,' said Rick. 'There is a solution. Let her go with you. We can then inform GlobeCorpMining that protocols for moon pool offloading and a whole bunch of other maritime regs have been breached. The Sea Hunters will then pursue you, will board, detain your crew and return Chang's sister to the Harvester. In the meantime, we get their father to fly out there as well.'

'For once, I agree,' said Jonah. 'Do it.'

'Okay,' said Jesse. 'Signing off. We must get out of here. Talk soon.'

The message board went blank. She ran down to the entrance and raced up to Ngarra. She whispered quickly in is ear about what was going on. Ngarra then whispered in Chang's ear. Jonny and Stella heard what was said and nodded their heads.

'If you don't let her come with us, we will toss Chang over,' said Ngarra as he looked at Ying Yue and motioned for her to come with them.

'No,' said Ying Yue moving towards them. She had picked up on what was going on now.

'Stop,' said Sue stepping forward again.

'Let it go, Sue,' said Lee moving forward and behind her. 'The Sea Hunters will deal with them and return Ying Yue to us.'

The two Harvester security officers moved around the sides of the moon pool. They got the lifesaving rings ready.

Jonny and Stella lifted Chang up and over the gangway.

'No!' said Ying Yue yelling and running forward.

'Stop now!' yelled Sue. 'You must stop, she screamed again and pulled a pistol from beneath her tunic.'

'Stop, now Ying Yue!' she demanded, aiming at her.

'No,' said Lee yelling.

Behind them and along the walkway a Sea Hunter officer felt his smartwatch buzz. He looked at the message.

Watch and let it happen
Declare your pursuit and apprehension of the crew
Then return to patrol drone immediately

Ying Yue was almost within reach of Chang.

'I will come she said,' pleading with them.

'Get everyone in now, we're out of here,' said Jesse as she ran inside and up to the SAI console.

Just as Lee got to Sue, she yelled, 'Ying Yue I said no!'

'No!' said Lee as Sue took aim.

Ying Yue turned to look at Sue.

Sue squeezed the trigger and the world seemed to slow.

The bullet hit her in the shoulder as Lee pushed into Sues arm, grabbing it.

The others turned and ran up the gangway.

Jonny and Ngarra pulled Chang back over the rail.

'What have you done?' said Lee.

The Harvester security officers raced around and onto the gangway.

'Get her inside,' yelled Ngarra.

They lifted and dragged Ying Yue into the entrance. It closed behind them. Jonny raced up the stairs and to the SAI console. He put his interface lenses on.

'SAI exit moon pool for next mining destination,' said Jesse.

'Confirmed,' said SAI. 'Exit moonpool and proceed to next mining location.'

The Skimmer had been in standby mode and was ready to go.

Outside Lee and Sue backed off the gangway as the Skimmer started to submerge.

'She's been shot,' yelled Jonny as the Skimmer started to submerge.

'Shit, shit' said Jesse at the SAI console hearing him yell.

She looked out as the outer hull shields close and the camera system activated.

Around the moon pool everyone watched from the end of the gangway. They were arguing with each other and talking with the two Sea Hunter officers. They all took off to the nearest lift.

Then they were underwater, descending through the moonpool and out underneath the Harvester. The Skimmer paused, orientated itself in the direction of the next mining location and moved off.

Chapter 23

Ngarra, Stella and Chang were sitting next to Ying Yue on the deck of the rec area. She was lying face down and not moving.

'Shit, shit,' said Chang.

He was beside himself and bashing his fist on the deck next to her.

'Ying Yue, Ying Yue,' he sobbed and yelled at the same time. Shaking her.

Stella went and grabbed a trauma kit and came racing back.

'Help me roll her over,' she said.

They grabbed Ying Yue and gently rolled her on onto her back.

Stella checked her vitals.

'She's still breathing. Quick, get these clothes open so I can see the wound. No blood. The bullet didn't come out the other side either.'

'Why did she do that, shoot her I mean,' sobbed Chang. 'What is so important it's worth her life. This is all my father's damn fault! Damn him and what he has done to this family,' he said punching the deck again.

He grazed the skin off his knuckles. They were bleeding.

Ying Yue moaned and opened her eyes. Chang stopped sobbing. Stunned, he looked intensely at her.

'That hurt,' she said groaning again and not moving.

Stella removed her clothing and started laughing.

'Crazy bitch,' said Chang yelling at Stella. 'She's been shot, what's so funny. It's my sister,' he said shoving her in the arm.

'Look, you fool,' said Stella pushing him back. She grabbed the back of his head and pointed.

'It's a vest! A bullet proof vest.'

Ying Yue moaned again and tried to sit up.

Chang helped her.

The others helped her get the vest off.

'One giant bruise is what you are going to have,' said Stella.

'Holy smoke. Geeze, I mean wow, I thought you were gone,' said Chang whipping his eyes and gathering himself together.

Then he got a little angry again.

'Why the hell did you do that!' he yelled. 'That's the dumbest thing I have ever seen. Just to get on here.'

'No, not on here,' she said and winced at the pain. 'To expose Sue. She's a witch and was undermining everything our father is trying to do.'

'But she shot you!' yelled Chang.

'Exactly,' said Ying Yue.

'Yeah, well what if it was in the head,' said Chang.

'Ah,' said Ying Yue. 'When you hang around people in the military long enough, you learn a lot. They aren't trained to go for the head. They go for the largest body part, the torso.'

'The military,' questioned Chang.

'Yeah, the PLA, she's military.'

'Still,' said Chang. 'You took massive risk and now what?'

'We are meeting the Sea Hunters at our next mining location,' said Jesse. 'They will take Ying Yue back to the Harvester. Your father will be there as well to sort this mess out. It's being arranged.'

'I had to take a risk you know,' said Ying Yue as she nursed her shoulder. 'I had to bank on your organisation contacting my father and using the Sea Hunters to pursue and get me.'

'I'm going up to the SAI console,' said Ngarra. 'You guys look after Ying Yue and get her settled.'

He took off and bounded up the stairs and through the watertight bulkhead into the rear of the SAI console.

'How's Connor?' said Ngarra as Jesse came down the stairs.

'None the wiser,' said Jesse. 'Just as we planned. He was absorbed in his work for the whole thing.'

She looked over at Ying Yue.

'Bullet proof vest, well played Ying Yue. Are you okay?'

'Considering what has happened, I guess so,' she replied wincing at the pain.

'Good,' said Ngarra pausing on the stairs. 'Let's contact Xed Academy crew monitoring and talk to Jonah and Rick again. They will be waiting to hear back. Our vitals will be all over the place on their monitoring displays.'

Ngarra and Jesse entered the SAI console.

'SAI, message to Xed Academy crew monitoring and communications. Request to speak with Jonah and Rick. Priority urgent.'

'Confirmed,' said SAI. 'Grid buoy and Eel drone proximity nominal, live feed available.'

There was a pause and then Jonah and Rick's images appeared on the message board. The Sea Hunter liaison officer was there as well as the Australian defence attaché to New Caledonia.

'Jesse, Ngarra,' said Rick. 'What's the situation? We have everyone here. Your vitals have been all over the place.'

'Chang's sister was shot by Sue. She's okay. She had a vest on. We have her with us now.'

'Damn it!' said Jonah.

'She was shot on the gangway,' said Jesse. 'She said the whole point was to expose Sue and her intentions. She's PLA. The two Sea Hunter inspection officers saw everything as did Lee and the Harvester security detail.'

'Right,' said Rick. 'Proceed to your next mining location and carry on with your nodule extraction schedule. As discussed, the Sea Hunters will meet you there on location. They will use a breaching pod and board. They will follow procedure and detain Ying Yue and return her to the Harvester. Her father will be there to sort all this out.'

'Is Connor okay?' said Jonah.

'Yes, he is fine,' said Jesse. 'He didn't see any of it. He was in the information hub the whole time.'

Rick looked at the defence attaché and nodded.

'What about the technology?' he asked Jesse. 'Is it compromised.'

'No but Ying Yue knows a lot more about it now,' said Jesse.

'Just sit tight and carry on with your mining run,' said Jonah. 'We will be in touch.'

With that, their images disappeared. Jesse went to check on Connor.

***

On the Harvester, the situation at the moon pool was tense. Sue and Lee were arguing over shooting Ying Yue. The two Harvester security officers were watching them both and keeping an eye on the Sea Hunter inspection officers.

'That wasn't called for,' said Lee angrily.

'We can't have our technology leave this Harvester,' said Sue fiercely. 'She knows too much.'

'You're wrong,' said Lee. 'Your ambitions with the PLA are clouding your vision.'

'This is a breach of Skimmer contractor protocols,' said one of the Sea Hunter inspection officers. 'We will track them down, detain Ying Yue and write up the crew for their involvement in all this.'

'Go,' said Sue as glaring at them. 'In fact, let's all go to the drone deck. I want to speak with Max and Alex now.'

Everyone backed down. Following the Harvester security officers, they walked back along the boardwalk next to the conveyor and robotic arms to the nearest lift. A few other Skimmer crews looked on, wondering what on earth had just happened.

In the lift, there was total silence.

Once in the drone bay no one said anything either.

They walked over to the hex which had been lowered.

On entering the foyer, it rose to the drone deck above. They walked out of the foyer onto the drone deck. The hex tower remained raised.

A short distance away stood Max and Alex, waiting by their patrol drone.

'So,' said Max casually as they approached. 'What's the situation?'

'That Skimmer crew has abducted Ying Yue,' said Sue sternly. 'She also has a bullet wound in her shoulder.'

'Really,' said Max remaining calm. 'They can't deal with that on a skimmer.'

Alex looked at him. Max nodded and pointed to the patrol drone. Alex got the two inspection officers to board the patrol drone ready to go.

'She refused to stay,' said Sue. 'It's a matter of national security.'

Lee looked at Max and shook his head.

Sue didn't notice.

'We will deal with this,' said Max turning and entering the drone as it powered up. 'Our team will intercept them. We will deal with the gunshot wound and get her back here for treatment. Then I will have a mountain of paperwork to write up on this so don't go anywhere. A lot of questions will be asked.'

'Of course not,' said Sue smiling as the personnel ramp closed and Max disappeared behind it.

Lee and Sue watched as the docking clamp heaved upwards and released the patrol drone. It hovered, tilted forward and headed out over the water. Banking steeply, it headed straight towards the Sea Hunter unit that had been lingering with intent inside the perimeter.

'What did you see?' Max asked the two officers that had been at the moonpools.

'Somethings going on,' they said. 'Lee tried to stop Sue from shooting Ying Yue. Lee was adamant that her father would not want any of this to happen and to just let Ying Yue go for now.'

'Okay, let's meet up with this Skimmer at their mining location and deal with Ying Yue. Her shoulder will need seeing to on our vessel before we get her back to the Harvester. I also need to write all this up and report it. A bunch of mining regulations and maritime law has been breached here. I don't know how our contact is going to make all this go away. We need to be prepared for the worst.'

In no time at all, the patrol drone flew up alongside the Sea Hunter vessel. The Hunter unit was still within the security perimeter.

The patrol drone moved sideways across the drone deck and into position. The docking clamp grabbed them, and the drone powered down as it was lowered into position. It moved the patrol drone inside the drone bay.

'Let's go,' said Max as they quickly exited the drone.

A couple of technicians boarded the drone to run some system checks.

As they left the drone bay heading for operations and the SAI console Cam met them.

'Get that breaching pod and boarding team of yours ready, Cam,' said Max stopping to talk quickly. 'We are intercepting Ngarra's Skimmer. Chang's sister has been shot, take a medic with you. Make sure she is stable and get her back here. Their crew will be mining. We can't interfere with a mining operation. Get details from the Skimmer crew about what happened.'

'Got it,' he said looking concerned. He hastily walked off. He hopped down the stairs to the well deck below to arrange a boarding party, interceptor drone and breaching pod.

'To the SAI console,' said Max. 'Let's go.'

They took the stairs up to operations and walked through the main passage forward.

'We need to contact the Skimmer,' said Alex.

'Yep, and tell them what's happening,' said Max.

They walked into the SAI console. The outer hull shields were retracted. It was a calm day.

'Break off from our perimeter patrol,' he said to the duty watch keeping officer. 'Head for these coordinates and send the drone vessels ahead.'

Max pulled up the navigation hologram and using his hand drew a line to where the Skimmer would be.

The duty officer got SAI to change course and head for the location. He then got SAI to send the drone vessels ahead of them.

'SAI,' said Alex. 'Communication request with Skimmer heading to location coordinates.'

'Confirmed,' said SAI. 'Grid buoy and eel drone proximity nominal, live feed available.'

The Skimmer signature was identified by SAI and confirmed by the duty watch keeping officer.

Alex and Max nodded at him and waited for the message board to activate.

Jesse's image appeared.

'This is Max, officer in charge of "the Area" Sea Hunter unit. What is Ying Yue's condition?'

'She's okay,' said Jesse. 'Had a vest on just bad bruising.'

'We are closing you. Once you are in position for mining, we will board you and take Ying Yue with us. She must return to the Harvester. Her father will be there.'

'Okay,' said Jesse. 'But Chang may be a little resistant to that.'

'My team will interview your crew and take details on everything that happened for our report,' said Max.

Max closed the message board.

'I hope this technology is worth it,' said Alex. 'What a mess.'

'As do I,' said Max folding his arms, turning and looking out at the ocean. 'As do I.'

Max and Alex left the SAI console and made their way to the well deck to talk with Cam about boarding the Skimmer. It would be a few hours before they reached the mining location.

***

The Skimmer had arrived at their next mining location. It had been a long and eventful day. Ngarra watched the view through the camera system as the Skimmer moved into position.

Everyone was at their stations.

'I have never been on a skimmer underway,' said Ying Yue as she watched what was going on through the external camera system.

'Quite a view, isn't it? The void out there I mean,' said Ngarra.

'Ying Yue,' said Connor over comms. 'You must come and look over our technology. We still have so much to talk about.'

Ying Yue was sore and had been resting in the rec area.

'I don't think we will have time Connor,' she said in reply. 'Once we are in position Jesse informs me that the Sea Hunters will board us. I must go back to the Harvester. My father will be there to sort all this out.'

She didn't want to appear keen to understand more about the technology. Like her father she always played the long game. Another time.

'Oh, okay then,' said Connor in a glum voice.

Probably a good thing, Jesse thought to herself as she looked at Ying Yue. This situation was not meant to happen. A danger existed that Ying Yue new too much. As it was, she already had a fair idea about how the technology might work.

'That's right, there isn't time, Connor,' said Jesse over comms. 'We'll arrange another time.'

Connor had been hiding away over the previous day, somewhat oblivious to what had unfolded around him. *Perhaps that was a good thing* Jesse thought to herself.

The Skimmer turned in a wide arc, circling the location it would stop at. Ngarra, Ying Yue and Jesse watched as the Skimmer straightened up and slowed. Jonny had his interface lenses on and was monitoring SAI's approach in first person view.

'On final approach,' he said.

Ngarra turned back to the SAI console and zoomed in the navigation hologram to fine scale.

The Skimmer came to a halt.

'In position,' said Jonny. 'Sensor scans all clear.'

'Communication streamer being deployed,' said Stella over comms from the Xtract bay. 'Xtracts powering up, monitoring systems check underway, preparing to deploy.'

'An endless expanse. It's like looking into infinity,' said Ying Yue.

'Wait a day or so,' said Jonny. 'Then all this marine life will gather around us.'

'Haven't you been out on that Skimmer you have in your hanger?' said Ngarra.

'Not outside the moon pool,' said Ying Yue. 'I'm usually stuck in the lab.'

'Xtracts being deployed,' said Stella over comms.

They watched as each Xtract detached from their docking clamp along the recess on each side of the Skimmer. They moved out over the mineral trays and paused. Each one in turn started its descent to the depths below.

'Communication from Sea Hunters,' said SAI. 'Grid buoy and eel drone proximity nominal, live feed available.'

'Open message board,' said Jesse.

'Jesse,' said Alex. 'We are closing your location. Interceptor drone and breaching pod will be deployed. Prepare for boarding. Make sure Ying Yue is ready. Assemble your crew in the rec area for a debrief.'

'Got it,' said Jesse.

The image of Alex disappeared.

'Jonny,' said Jesse. 'Stay here and wait for the breaching pod to attach and the boarding team to arrive through the top side air lock. Get Connor to come down to the rec area while you are at it.'

'Got it,' said Jonny taking his interface lenses off.

He walked out of the SAI console and down the passage to the information hub.

'Stella, Chang,' said Jesse over comms. 'Come to the rec area as soon as the streamer is fully deployed. Sea Hunters boarding soon and will debrief us.'

'On our way shortly,' said Stella.

It took about an hour to deploy the streamer. Chang monitored its descent. The Xtracts followed it down.

Jonny stayed at the SAI console and waited for the Sea Hunter inspection officers to board them.

Jesse, Ying Yue and Ngarra exited the SAI console and walked down the stairs to the rec area.

They got something to eat and sat down.

Shortly after Chang raced up the stairs from the Xtract bay, eager to see his sister again before she left for the Harvester.

'I wish you didn't have to go back there,' he said getting something to eat and sitting down. 'Sue will chain you up and you'll never be able to leave.'

'Father will sort it all out,' she said to Chang wincing as she moved her shoulder the wrong way. It hurt a lot.

'I'm sure this will all be sorted out,' said Jesse.

'You still haven't seen Red Queen,' said Connor with a mouth full of food.

'Red Queen,' said Ying Yue. 'Oh yes, that.'

'Evolution of learning,' said Connor. 'In our ocean bubble hologram. Gilgamesh.'

'Not now, Connor,' said Jesse sternly. 'Let Chang catch up with his sister before she goes.'

Keeping these two apart was a headache, thought Jesse. The sooner she is off here the better. At least, what happened to Ying Yue had distracted her from the technology.

It seemed Ying Yue was onto something though. This mimic drone stuff Connor kept going on about. It sounded sinister though.

There was a slight shudder, and everyone looked up. The breaching pod had docked with the Skimmer.

'Sea Hunters are here,' said Jonny over comms.

'How are you feeling Ying Yue,' said Jesse.

'Better but very sore,' she said holding her badly bruised shoulder.

'If it weren't for our father, you would not be in this situation,' said Chang.

'I choose to do this,' said Ying Yue. 'It's not his fault. I'm good at it, better than most. It's not forever. Our father will deal with Sue.'

'It's still all his fault,' said Chang. 'Our mother, now you. Working on all this; all it has done is give my family misery and grief. Now people are running around threatening my friends, my family and me.'

'Do you have friends?' said Stella smiling.

'Not now,' said Ngarra frowning at her.

Chang ignored the comment.

A short time later Jonny came down the stairs from the SAI console with two Sea Hunter boarding officers.

One of the inspection officers was a medic and checked over Ying Yue.

The other set about debriefing the crew before they took Ying Yue with them on the breaching pod back to the Sea Hunter vessel.

Chapter 24

It was late when the interceptor drone was recovered at the well deck of the Sea Hunter vessel. They surfaced and the docking clamp attached and lifted it up and out of the water. It moved across to the deck and locked into place. The breaching pod detached and lowered onto its cradle. The crew got out with Ying Yue.

'How are you?' said Alex walking over to them.

'Okay considering,' said Ying Yue.

'I have debriefed the Skimmer crew,' said one of the boarding officers. 'I will have the report to you tomorrow.'

'Good I can read it before we get Ying Yue back to the Harvester,' said Max.

'You must be exhausted,' said Alex. 'It's late so let's get you checked out and then to a cabin. You can get freshened up and rest.'

The medic spoke briefly with Max and then headed off with her.

'Right let's get this show on the road,' said Max.

He contacted the duty watch keeping officer at the SAI console and told them to take the Sea Hunter unit back to the Harvester.

'Let's head up to the SAI console,' said Max after he finished talking with the duty officer. 'I want to speak with our contact at Xed Academy. Tomorrow will be another long day then hopefully, and I mean hopefully we can get back to some sense of normality in "the Area". I'm over all this.'

Alex chuckled and agreed.

They headed off, through operations, along the main passageway and to the SAI console.

'What about the technology Ying Yue gave us?' said Alex as they were walking.

'He said to keep it safe for now,' said Max. 'I think the idea was to create a copy.'

They talked about the implications of what had happened at the Harvester.

'Hunter unit is heading towards the Harvester,' said the duty officer as they walked into the SAI console.

'Good,' said Alex. 'Make sure we arrive around the time Ying Yue's father arrives.'

'Yes, sir,' he replied.

'Right,' said Max stretching out his arms and shaking himself. 'SAI open secure link to Xed Academy contact.'

'Confirmed,' said SAI. 'Secure link open.'

A pause followed and then Rick's image appeared on the message board.

'We've been on alert here at Academy Skimmer monitoring and communications. It's been a long day. What's the situation?'

'Ying Yue is on board and getting checked out. She is getting some rest. She will be fine. Just some bad bruising. We are returning to the Harvester.'

'Good,' said Rick. 'The situation on the Harvester will be tense. Her father will arrive not long before you.'

'Don't interfere in their affairs,' said the Sea Hunter liaison officer. 'Just hand Ying Yue over and carry on with your duties.'

'Yes, sir,' said Max. 'Ngarra's crew were a bit shaken up. My team debriefed them on board their Skimmer at their mining location. They are okay though. I will have a full report to file.'

'A full report,' questioned Jonah.

'All information directly relevant to "the Area" regulations and maritime law will be addressed,' said Alex. 'That's it.'

'Some normality will be good for Ngarra's crew,' said Jonah.

'We have them on location mining and crew vitals look good,' said the duty officer.

'Can you contact us once you have returned Ying Yue to the Harvester,' said Rick.

'Will do,' said Max. 'Signing off.'

The message board closed.

'It's late,' said Max yawning.

'That it is. What a day,' said Alex as they walked out of the SAI console and headed to their cabins.

'See you soon,' said Max smiling.

'Another day in "the Area",' said Alex chuckling.

'Yes, interesting times,' said Max.

They parted ways and went to their cabins to get some rest. The Hunter unit made slow passage through the calm seas and moon lit night.

In her quarters, Ying Yue thought about how things had gone. She had exposed Sue and now her father would deal with her. Lee would be important in times to come, she needed him onside. Connor and Chang were another story. How to approach that situation weighed on her mind. She drifted off to sleep.

***

The next morning on the Harvester Sue and Lee were up early. Ying Yue's father was due to arrive. Lee was nervous but Sue looked indifferent. They stood on the observation deck of the hex.

'Are you worried,' said Lee.

'Why should I be,' she said. 'Security was compromised. It could have been anyone.'

'But it was his daughter,' said Lee.

'The technology she is working on is too important to the PLA. The CCP subcommittee will see it my way. It doesn't matter who it is.'

'I think you underestimate the importance of relationships Sue,' said Lee turning to face her.

'I have got this program to where it is,' she said sternly. 'The research is stalled at present. Connor knows something. The two of them cannot be together unless it is on here. The project could carry on without her if needed.'

'I?' questioned Lee. 'Don't you think that such an isolationist approach is why the project has stalled.'

Lee stopped talking and they both looked out over the water. A humming could be heard. Ying Yue's father's drone was approaching. In the distance, they could just make it out. The morning sun reflected off it as it crossed low over the water.

'Sir,' said a duty officer coming out onto the observation deck. 'The Sea Hunters have just cleared perimeter security. They have Ying Yue with them.'

'Good,' said Sue as the duty officer disappeared back into the hex.

'I want a security detail at the base of the hex now,' said Lee turning to the officer standing behind them.

'Yes, sir,' he said moving off to organise it.

Lee and Sue walked down the stairs to the drone deck. They walked out onto the deck heading towards the docking clamp the drone would land on.

The security detail exited the hex following behind them.

They all watched as the drone came in low over the deck and at speed. It tilted up and back, levelling off. Sleek and black it hovered while the docking clamp engaged. The arm retracted and lowered the drone to the deck. The drone powered down.

A pause followed, a deathly silence.

A moment of silence before the reactions of each person present to the situation at hand would determine the way forward.

The ramp at the rear of the drone lowered, and a security detail walked out. With complete calm, they placed themselves either side of Lee, Sue and their security detail.

Ying Yue's father emerged with his assistant and a high-ranking security officer just behind him. Within arm's reach, he could push Ying Yue's father back and behind if something went wrong.

'Good morning, sir,' said Lee.

'Hmm,' he said. 'Is it? Where's my daughter.'

'The Sea Hunters have cleared perimeter security,' said Sue. 'She will be here shortly. The technology is secure; the project is not compromised.'

Ying Yue's father walked up to Sue and stood in front of her. Sue stood staunch and unflinching.

'Do you have any idea how far this goes?' he said to Sue.

'What goes, sir?' she replied.

'Sir, the Sea Hunters,' said his senior security officer pointing towards the approaching drone.

They turned and looked out towards the Hunter unit that had arrived and was now stationed not far from the Harvester. A patrol drone had taken off from it.

They watched as it approached.

Flying low over the drone deck, it slowed and hovered above a docking clamp. It was secured by the docking arm and lowered to the deck.

The drone powered down.

The rear ramp lowered, and Max and Lee walked out of the drone followed by Cam and Ying Yue. They walked over to the group.

'Father,' said Ying Yue coming forward and embracing him. She winced. Her shoulder hurt.

'Are you okay,' he said stepping back and looking at her.

'Very sore,' she said. 'But otherwise good.'

She looked at Sue and smiled briefly.

'We intercepted the Skimmer,' said Max. 'We boarded it and took Ying Yue. Our medic checked her over. Just bad bruising. She had a vest on.'

Her father turned back towards Sue.

It was hard to tell what he was thinking.

'A vest. That implies that my daughter felt threatened enough to plan to wear a vest. Why would she be in the moon pool area. Why would she feel the need to leave the Harvester on a skimmer? Why would she breach a longlist of protocols, regulations, codes and standards?'

'She was going to leave the project and compromise national security,' said Sue. 'I did what had to be done for the PLA.'

'You did what you thought needed to be done,' he said. 'Not what had to be done. Ultimately, what must be done is up to me. In fact, it's up to the CCP subcommittee I report to. Your selfish attitude towards all this and singled minded pursuit of controlling what you have no control over has caused all this,' he said waving his hand around.

'I have a mess to clean up, and that is on you,' he said calmly. 'The PLA has been told to defer to me on this so I can clean this mess up and ensure our relationships and ability to operate in "the Area" are not compromised.'

Ying Yue's father was an imposing man but so calm and collected. Behind this imposing persona was what and who he represented, and that was not to be messed with.

'I am protecting our interests out here,' said Sue angrily. 'You're not out here so you don't know what's going on.'

'Enough!' he said sternly. It was unusual for him to raise his voice, but this was his family they were talking about. 'I know more than you think. Lee, get over here.'

'Yes, sir,' he said and walked across to stand in front of him.

'You are now in charge of all this. What's more Ying Yue is your second now.'

Ying Yue looked at Sue and smiled. It was more of a smirk than a smile.

'You can't do that,' said Sue angrily.

Sue reached inside her tunic and rested her hand there.

Cam was standing to one side and noticed the movement. The others didn't. They were focussed on Ying Yue's father.

Lee looked at Sue, noticing where her hand was as well. He shook his head. Sue looked blankly at him and back at Ying Yue.

'Ambition is a great thing,' Ying Yue's father said stepping forward and directly in front of Sue.

His personal security officer stepped close, worried about proximity and the look on Sues face and where her arm was positioned. He was about to step between them and grab Sue.

'But ambition without direction is something I will not tolerate,' he said and calmly put his hand on Sue's forearm tucked into her tunic. 'However, I would like you beside me, to work with me and help push this project forward.'

Sue took her hand out of her tunic. The others stepped back. Everyone breathed a sigh of relief.

Sue relaxed and managed a smile.

'Yes, sir,' she said calmly.

'Right, that's settled then,' he said. 'Lee, I want a full report on all this. Ying Yue, continue with your program and assist Lee as required. Sea Hunters, thank you for ensuring the integrity of "the Area" was maintained. As for the Harvester. We will take it from here.'

Max, Alex and Cam left on their patrol drone. They returned to their Hunter unit to continue operations in "the Area".

Ying Yue took her father to the restaurant to catch up.

Lee returned to operations and resumed his duties coordinating Harvester operations.

Sue stood on the deck by herself for a moment, watching everyone disappear. *We will see where all this goes*, she thought to herself smiling. Her people in the PLA had more ambitious plans.

***

On the Skimmer, Connor was in the information hub absorbed in his work. He was focussing on the ocean bubble hologram, Gilgamesh and Red Queen and lost in his own thoughts. Speaking out load, SAI was recording everything he said and searching databases and script libraries for information. Displays streamed data and code. On a main display, Connor had got SAI to display a header that read 'What is Red Queen'.

Inserting "Red Queen" into Gilgamesh meant the simulated Xtracts were now learning to respond to disruption to mining operations.

Behaviours evolve after being selected for over multiple generations, he thought to himself. As in individuals that survived and passed on those traits at the population level.

It was different to his thought about a colony of ants, chemical signalling, or schooling fish and their reactions to an intrusion. Even his thoughts about radial nerve and regeneration in tissues of starfish that was localised and not centrally controlled.

Autonomous group behaviour wasn't something that could be represented by a piece of code. It required algorithms that allowed it to evolve innately.

Ingram Content Group UK Ltd.
Milton Keynes UK
UKHW022032120323
418425UK00007B/117